Lost Shores of Thonis

by

E. L. Tenenbaum

Cover Art by *Teddi Black*

The Wild Rose Press, Inc.
PO Box 708
Adams Basin, NY 14410-0708
Visit us at www.thewildrosepress.com

Publishing History
First Edition, 2025
Trade Paperback Print ISBN
Digital ISBN

Published in the United States of America

Dedication

B"H

Acknowledgments

A mighty river of thanks to the team at The Wild Rose Press, specifically my editor Nan Swanson, for guiding this manuscript to completed book. I am ever grateful that you took this story on. Waves of gratitude to Teddi Black for the eye-catching cover.

The current of thanks flows on to family and friends who've graciously championed my books over the years.

A massive flooding of the riverbanks of thanks to the members of a most wonderfully talented former critique group, whose advice, feedback, and encouragement significantly contributed to the shaping of this story: Jodi Rizzotto, Chris Jelbert, Lisa Gold, and our admirably patient leader Tim Burke, who never fed us to his trolls and whose emails always make me laugh. Please all, remember to wave at the rest of us when you're fantastically famous!

The final thanks always goes to you, the reader, without whom a story is no gateway but mere words on a page.

Historical Note

During an author visit for ninth graders several years ago, I explained to the students how a simple "What if?" can be a key to unlocking untold worlds for writers.

"Try it, it could work for you too," I encouraged. "For example, what was your most recent writing assignment?"

Subject: History. Topic: Something to do with ancient Egypt.

"Well," declared I, "what if X, what if Y, what if the servant doesn't drink the poison?" And just like that, the key unlocked a whole new world.

It took a few years to turn that key again. Once I started to research, I learned many new things about ancient Egypt, which shaped and reshaped the world I'd unwittingly unlocked. Foremost, the real, but lost-for-centuries-beneath-the-Mediterranean, port city and gateway to Egypt Thonis-Heracleion. Plus, after the first drafts of this story were already complete, news broke about a newly discovered mummy of a pregnant woman.

As the Egyptian empire lasted centuries, much changed over the course of those years, including borders, origin of rulers, and other notable aspects impactful to a society. Thus, although much of this writing is based in history, fiction always overtook fact, so much has been jumbled to tell this story. However, much like Thonis itself, this story can well serve as a gateway to learning more about the past.

Once you start exploring, you never know what keys you may find.

Chapter One

Day 1

"Don't drink the poison."

Bakari's deep rumble startles me even though I've been waiting for him.

"All right?" he asks carefully, the light from his lamp inching along the painted stones toward mine.

"All right," I say quickly, turning to face him.

That isn't entirely true. Since Meryt's death, I haven't been able to keep my mind in place, to form thoughts or images or words that aren't gut-wrenching flashes from the past.

"Azizi?" The concern in his voice says he doesn't believe me.

"I'm fine," I insist.

As Meryt's most esteemed maidservant, I'm expected to lead the select group of three in serving our lady in the afterlife, faithful in death as we were in life. We are honored to be chosen. We are honored to offer this sacrifice of our very selves.

I should fear death, but do not because so much of life has been taken from me already. Little holds me here, sunken as I am in a dark sea of grief for the girl we grew up with and called Meryt. Our pasts were stolen after her marriage to the king, and now my future has been pilfered with her passing. The death of the king's second

1

wife marks the end of what was and what could one day be as well. Yet, through this sacrifice, I will finally be reunited with the many I have struggled to live without. Abrupt and terrible as Meryt's passing is, perhaps there's good in it too.

Bakari steps beside me, the light of his lamp eagerly joining mine. He raises a doubtful eyebrow at my illuminated expression, the flickering lights casting shadows which deepen his lines of worry. He doesn't say anything, but I hear him pressing for the truth in the way he watches me.

I meet his dark eyes and don't either speak. Why repeat what I've already said?

He shakes his head at my stubborn silence, disbelieving yet realizing he won't get any more from me.

In the combined light, I make out a thin layer of dust coating his almond-colored skin. The dark kohl protecting his eyes from blinding sunrays is slightly smudged. His shaved head is a shade lighter from the white dust of limestones he must have been unloading from the boats ferrying them from the quarries. His torso hints at muscular anatomy; his strength built from muscles well used.

From the look of him, Bakari has come straight from construction without pausing to properly rinse off first. Caught unprepared for a death that shouldn't have occurred for decades, King Pa-Ankh-Entef has brought in hundreds more workers, including soldiers and guards, to finish building his pyramid. Specifically, the chamber for his late wife, his Lady Tadinanefer-Hatshepsut, our Meryt.

Subverting the tradition of centuries must be

important enough for Bakari to forgo his usual meticulous appearance. He didn't even change his battered short white linen kilt.

"Promise, Azizi," he says, his tone more urgent.

Let me die, my mind screams back.

"Promise you won't drink the poison next week," he adamantly repeats.

"Eight days," I correct.

"Whenever, don't."

"How can I *not*?" My voice belies my roiling emotions as it echoes loudly against the walls of the empty room. "My lady is dead and it is my duty to serve her in the afterlife."

"I'll explain all of it," Bakari replies in a way that's meant to be soothing but only puts me more on edge. "But you must agree to listen well and consider what I have to say."

I fold my arms over my chest. Bakari lifts his free hand as if to undo my crossed-arm resistance, but stops himself. I can't tell what's caused his hesitancy in the shadowed light, especially with a mind flickering from thought to thought in agitation.

"You may yet do her a greater service in this life."

I openly study him, squinting to see past his uncharacteristic tone. Bakari usually speaks in smiles and mischief and teasing, not weight and solemnity and seriousness. It makes it harder to process his words.

"How can you say such things?" I demand, body trembling with ill-contained anger at him, at this palace, at a life of subverted choices. "How dare you send her into the afterlife alone? Hear me clearly, I do not offer my life for Lady Tadinanefer-Hatshepsut, I do this for Meryt, *our* Meryt."

3

I emphasize my cousin's old name, the one given to the girl we grew up with on our little islet of Thonis. The carefree girl raised amidst laughter and friends and clear waters sparkling like sapphires, gulls calling jubilantly as they swooped through sea breezes. The same winds brought ships to our port and life to our city. They also brought the sailing king to our shore in time to see a beautiful girl ankle deep in surf in a moment stolen from a painting.

A scene so far removed from this cool subterranean room with no windows to catch the sun or overhear the gurgling of the great river beyond. Far from days warm and safe and bright, days from well before the king noticed the kind girl we'd loved as a sister and renamed for her unmatched beauty. From days before I traded freedom for servitude, before Thonis and her thriving city silently sank to the depths of the sea, taking with the joy and brightness of thousands of lives. Before the people stopped speaking our beloved city's name for fear of inviting upon themselves the same curse that sank her.

But not before Bakari signed up for the royal army, making a name as Bomani-Bakari, a charioteer and warrior who exemplifies the best of the king's service. Joining Meryt in the afterlife, I will show exemplary service too.

"Zizi," Bakari tries.

"*Don't* call me that!" I snap.

Bakari is mistaken if he thought my use of Meryt's name from the past allowed him such permissions as well. He does not get to call me by the nickname given to me by my mother and sisters. He does not get to drag it out of the mouths of my family now filled with the water of the sea. If they can no longer call me by it, no one can.

I'm also surprised he knew that name. Bakari is four years older than my seventeen years, older even than my sister Unika is. Was. Our fathers were close friends, who shared many celebrations, but Bakari and I didn't spend too much time together before I came to the palace.

"Azizi," Bakari tries again, hands raised in half surrender, his body blocking the way out, "just listen."

I sigh, resigned to not being let go until he's said his piece. All I want is to get away from here, away from the memory of Thonis and Meryt and everything else that no longer is.

"We need you alive to help us," he presses.

"Have you been stricken by madness?"

"No, Azizi, it was Lady Tadinanefer-Hatshepsut who was stricken. Meryt's death wasn't 'untimely,' that's just the official word to keep order."

"What are you saying, Bakari?"

Bakari's black eyes lance into mine. "Meryt was murdered."

Chapter Two

Day 2

My mind is a traitor.

I fled before Bakari could say more. He called after me to *just* listen, but I didn't even look back. Barely a day later, I'm trying to keep busy and forget we ever spoke, forget the last words still chasing after me and all the frightening things they could mean. My heart yearns for the next life, but my mind remains stubborn. Worse, in the shadows of grief he's ignited a spark of curiosity.

A low crunch makes me jump in disgust, thinking I've stepped on a beetle with bare feet. Instead, I find a small square of papyrus paper was pushed under the door leading from my room to Meryt's at some point before I woke. There's no doubt who it's from.

Please talk to me.

But I refuse to speak one more word to Bakari after what he said last night, after what he asked me to do. I intend to avoid him the next seven days, and once I'm gone the questions he provoked will still.

Murdered.

The word ricochets through my thoughts, shoving all others away. I fiercely crumble the note and toss it into the fire where such nonsense belongs.

Let me die, I silently beg the burning note. *Let me see my family again.*

I was never meant to live in a palace. I was raised by a father who came from across the sea. He educated his daughters, determined to open the world for us even if we never left Egypt. My older sister Unika stayed in Thonis after she married, as it was likely she'd eventually inherit our father's shipping trade. We were so pleased she chose to stay close. But as she'd married, Meryt couldn't make her a maidservant at the palace, and so she asked me to accompany her. My ability to write undoubtedly influenced Meryt's decision, an additional skill to rely upon in the one person she knew she could trust so far from home.

Yet she was murdered under your care.

I never wanted to be a servant, or to draw the limits of my life around my family, despite how much I love—loved—will always love them. I wanted to climb a ship's mast just as I climbed the forking narrow doum palms of our islet to see where ships disappeared beyond the line of the sky. An endless horizon of discovery; a world vast and beautiful and filled with so much to know. I never dreamed I'd end up stranded between the soaring painted columns of the king's palace, to cast eyes thirsty for the vastness of sky and sea down in subservience. Meryt couldn't have known what she was asking of me, or I'd like to think she never would have. Will it even matter once I'm also gone?

I gave up so much for Meryt, and it will be wasted if I don't fulfill my duty to her now. Bakari never knew her as I did, so he surely has no place to speak for her, to keep me from going to her.

Murdered.

The word blares its meaning clearly, but doesn't fit in thinking of Meryt or Lady Tadinanefer-Hatshepsut or whatever name she was called. In death as in life, she is more than her name, more than what a single description can say. Her *ka* was so bright, her essence so pure, not one of us wondered that she'd caught the king's eye and didn't let it go. There is no logic in thinking someone wanted her dead, then took steps to make it so. How could anyone even want to harm Meryt?

I rub my temples as I watch the fire eat the note, then turn away from it, turning my back on the words and all they imply.

Considering all we've had to bury in our past, how much was taken from us after we escaped an untimely death once, it doesn't seem possible that Meryt's life was still cut short. Intentionally. Meryt, Bakari, and I are supposed to be the blessed ones, the lone survivors of a city that disappeared beneath a bejeweled sea, blessed in our survival as the city was cursed in its end. It makes no sense that fate caught up to her now.

Chapter Three

Day 3

My mind is better focused after I avoid Bakari a full day and redirect it toward my duty of ensuring everything is set before my journey into death. Over the next few days, I must oversee the organization and packing of Meryt's personal possessions, sift through her most cherished items and decide what will be transferred to the storage chambers in the pyramid for her to use in the afterlife. The first few crates were the easiest, filled as they are with her newest, and least memory-weighted, items. The basics are the next easiest to pack, even items like her wigs, which I'm sure she'll want with her.

The wigs were one of Meryt's favorite parts of life in the palace, impractical as they are for a family of sailors living on an islet in the sea. Meryt loved her wigs, loved having new hair each day of the week to twist and pull and brush in a way she could hardly do with her hair. She was rather adept at it too. Once she came to court, many noblewomen immediately sought to imitate her, but Meryt changed styles so frequently it was almost impossible to keep up.

I tuck away her wigs and look for other generic items. I'm avoiding her more personal possessions, the ones containing pieces of her life.

In the week since Meryt died, no part of this is any

easier. Each time I see her bed, I imagine her lying somewhere else, imagine the embalmers mummifying her body, removing every organ to preserve in canopic jars. Only her heart will remain inside to be weighed by Osiris when she reaches the afterlife. Or so the many believe.

I unwittingly wince in pain thinking of each one they've taken from her. Then I can't continue as shivers rack my body, knowing salt was poured all over to dry out her soft skin and once lovely features. Dry, dry, dry, until it's ready to be stuffed and wrapped and wrapped and wrapped in layers of wards and incantations and linen strips.

When I finally still, I force myself to sort her personal possessions, each touch igniting a memory or scent or image which brings her back to life in brief sparks and flashes. Her absence grows even heavier as each one fades away.

The headpiece she wore to the banquet celebrating her first year of marriage to the king. The way she held her head high under the soft clinks of bright blue and yellow beads and glittering jewels framing her face. How regal she looked embracing her role as the king's wife. Everyone was certain the king would soon make her his new queen.

My hands brush the beautiful leopard shoulder cloak King Pa-Ankh-Entef gave Meryt that fateful day in Thonis, when he declared his intention to make her his wife hours after seeing her for the first time. Even in a city of merchants, who handled and shipped goods of all qualities and sizes, that cloak was admired for its bold spots and vivid colors. A cloak of royalty given to Meryt, who wore it like a gift from another world.

That day is so clear in my memory. I climbed my favorite doum palm tree on our islet, high above the seven other homes of our friends and neighbors to see all the islands of Thonis laid out before me. I wanted to catch sight of the royal ship above the cheering, flower-tossing crowds. As I waited, smaller skiffs rowed through canals from island to islet to island again. Great ships unfurled their sails as they readied to carry trade across the sparkling waters of the Mediterranean. I first started to watch when I learned how to spot father's ships, but soon began to watch all ships that came and went, the wind whipping my black hair as I pointed my chin toward sea and imagined myself finally reaching the horizon they sailed into.

Below, kids old and young ran barefoot through the grass surrounding our homes, carefree, joyous, and safe from the waves that would one day swallow them. Near the shore, older boys and girls toed the waters as they teasingly kicked up the surf and dared each other to dive first. Bakari was already in service to the king and had taken advantage of the trip for a quick visit home. As most of the officialness took place earlier in the morning, he was back on our islet by mid-afternoon, waist deep in the sea as he splashed his ecstatic younger siblings and their friends.

Unika clasped her hands to send long sprays of water at her future husband Hamadi. Meryt was laughing and playing and embracing the day as much as the rest, infused with the full delight of youth and innocence.

And from above I watched as the royal ship glided past at that perfect, idyllic moment.

King Pa-Ankh-Entef had come to oversee the installation of a new stela, an engraved dark stone slab detailing the laws and taxes of Thonis. We all came out for the ceremony that morning, giving honor and praise to its maker, even though it was just a formality. We all knew well who we paid our taxes to.

After, our governing nomarch invited the king on a leisurely cruise around the finest of his majesty's coastal cities. Weaving through Thonis, the king would have seen joy and prosperity and contentment. The day and mood were perfect for a stroke of good fortune. And we were caught in its fateful strike.

The king was already ten years married to Queen Sekhmet, who is beautiful and proud and kind and loved but has yet to bear an heir. The king, it seems, wasn't about to let his illustrious line end. So, when his wandering eye found Meryt framed by family and friends and happiness and crystal droplets, it barely moved from her face thereafter. From the moment he stopped his boat to ask her name, it became plain to any who looked that the king's hope for the future rested upon her.

When she came to the palace just weeks later, Meryt became Lady Tadinanefer-Hatshepsut.

Queen Sekhmet was unexpectedly kind to Meryt when she arrived, proclaiming her love for the king and people of the Nile dictated that she open her heart to its possible future. Perhaps the queen never thought as we all did that she might very well lose her position should Meryt bear the king's heir, but I doubt it. Queen Sekhmet is too smart and quick to overlook what every servant assumed at first sight.

"Anything you need, anything at all, simply ask," the queen told Meryt more than once in those first few months. "Be it etiquette, be it information. This is your home now too."

Meryt had been deeply grateful, so I know little of what the queen intended in her kindness toward her. Maybe she truly thought she would never lose her crown, even as her husband frequented her rooms less and less and gave more and more attention to the new Lady Tadinanefer-Hatshepsut.

After all, the queen is from our southern neighbor Nubia, and her marriage to the king is the foundation for the current peace between our two oft-warring countries. That alone is enough to assure her that an heir from an Egyptian woman could never be a true threat to her place beside the most powerful man in Egypt. Besides, although we'd come from relatively rich merchant families, we both appeared dirt-poor farmers within the vast halls of the opulent palace of Thebes. Meryt was innocent and pure and beautiful, but she could hardly compare to the grace and experience and poise of a woman raised from birth to be a queen. That was how I saw it, at least.

All the more reason murder is impossible.

"Why is the queen so nice to you?" I questioned more than once, but only very softly, and only in Meryt's ear.

"Because the king wishes it so," Meryt would reply, her words careful and tinged with rebuke. "You've inherited your father's skepticism and turned it into suspicion against any who don't share your blood."

"That doesn't make me wrong!"

"No more, Zizi. We cannot speak this way about the queen."

Without evidence to counter with, I couldn't pursue the argument on gut feeling alone. The queen really was gracious to Meryt, and relentless protestations would only appear like jealousy on my part. So I sealed my lips and pushed the matter aside.

Though Meryt asked me to join her at the palace, I long suspected it was Unika's idea. Possibly to keep me out of the trees Mother always feared I'd tumble from. It wasn't as though I had my own Hamadi tying me to Thonis.

"I need someone I can trust with me," Meryt had said in making her request, rounding her large, innocent eyes which so often brimmed with joy. "Someone from home so I won't feel so far from home."

"Bakari is in Thebes," I'd pointed out. "You can trust him."

"Bakari is a king's soldier," Meryt had countered. "I'd like a friend and family beside me, to see and hear and watch for what I might miss."

I didn't fully understand her request until I also packed up my life and sailed with her up the Nile to Thebes. Despite years of watching ships begin and end journeys across the Mediterranean from our shores, despite my father's stories of the lands north and east and west, Thebes is the farthest I've ever been from home. Only then did I truly understand how small and sheltered our islet had been.

Even so, I hadn't exactly jumped at the chance to be a servant in the palace, curious as I was to see it. Which is not the same as settling for good. But through Meryt's request it was decreed that I wouldn't be seeing much of the world after all.

"Meryt asked but I don't want to go," was how I'd bluntly told my parents.

"You should be very proud to be chosen," was

Mother's pleased response, which wasn't very helpful in releasing me from my feeling of obligation.

"But—"

"Who can refuse serving the wife of a king?"

Mother beamed at me over the collar she was beading for Unika to wear at her upcoming wedding. She probably thought palace servitude would finally bring order to her second daughter, who scratched her arms and cheeks on bark and mussed her hair in the wind instead of keeping her skin clear and feet firmly on land.

"It doesn't have to be forever," Father had whispered, understanding better why I didn't want to go inland when my eyes had always been cast out to sea. "It is the greatest honor to serve a friend and wife of the king," he'd added aloud for mother's benefit.

I suspect my parents knew how much Meryt would need someone from home to rely upon and keep her grounded, somehow, although Father's willingness to let me go surprised me. Despite all the years he'd lived in Thonis, he'd never taken well to Egyptian culture. He quietly mocked their manifold "animal-brained deities," an attitude I embraced, granting me the skepticism and critical eye Meryt chastised me for. After all, these were not doubts to voice in the palace, where the king was deemed the greatest living deity of all.

Father would never dare speak such words, but he never saw his king, or any other, in such light.

"How can we worship that which we can tame?" he'd question. "The Divine Force of this world is much greater than man. Even the much admired pyramids are but the work of mortals."

"The pyramids will last centuries," I remarked.

Father shrugged. "Decades. Centuries. How long is

any of it to the Creator of all time?"

"No one thinks that way, Father."

Father grinned and gently tugged my ear. "Since when have you thought like everyone else, Kyky?"

Does this mean I shouldn't drink the poison? Stand down, you traitorous mind.

Many of his thoughts and beliefs were affected by his Phoenician origins, not their many gods but his travels to lands and peoples with other practices and worship, including a land to the northeast which seemed oddest for believing in a single, invisible deity. Growing up in Egypt with its dozens and dozens of gods, I couldn't understand his focus on a singular, unseeable being, but something about the unknown of a great Divine Force spoke to Father. And he spoke it to us in turn.

I think it was the sailor in him whose mind was filled with the vastness of an open sea, a life where, as he'd say, idols and images are useless as men against the might of a towering wave or raging of a torrential storm. He scoffed at the idea of multiple gods each ruling their own domain.

"If one is such a powerful god, then why does he share with others? Must he ask permission before he crosses from his domain to another? The Divine Force is big enough to own the entirety of land and sky and sea."

I sometimes wondered why Father would live in Egypt with so much distrust of it. Though it's only now I realize he spoke much more of where he'd been than of where he was actually from. In many ways, he didn't live in Egypt but in Thonis. He trusted our islet and the close circle of families and friends who lived on it with us.

He obeyed the king and would say no ill against the

royal family, but he didn't believe in Egypt and her laws and customs in the same manner as a true citizen. He called the practices of the upper classes immoral, called priests and priestesses charlatans. He condemned kings who married their sisters to preserve royal blood, and women who had multiple firstborns even though they only had one husband. He wouldn't say most of this in front of Mother, but his tongue was free before his brother and friends, and certainly within hearing of his children. And I listened when he spoke.

So I wondered that he would allow me to attend Meryt at the palace, the symbol of a land he didn't believe in and a way of life he didn't trust. I suppose he realized there was nothing to do about Meryt's leaving. Perhaps he encouraged me to go with so we could look after each other, so we could remind each other of the life we'd been raised in.

The only thing those thoughts and beliefs and philosophies mean now is that the last remaining person who knew Meryt best can pack her belongings for the afterlife. My father's words that my life in the palace would not be forever once comforted me, but I would give anything to undo their need to be said. I would gladly be a servant all my life if it would keep Meryt alive. In less than a week, with one little drink, I will remain in her service forever. Especially if I can continue to avoid Bakari.

I sigh as I pull my mind away from the past, refocusing on the packing I'm supposed to be supervising because I only have one chance to get this right. I may have been hesitant at first, but once I agreed to accompany Meryt, I was committed to serving her completely. Once in the pyramid, once I too am gone, I cannot come back for anything I may overlook from distraction.

I only pray that in the afterlife we can return to that sparkling moment in time. Meryt and Unika and Hamadi and everyone from our islet will rejoice in the warmth of a sea still at bay. Once more, I will watch from above as I climb the highest tree I can find.

It's all just six days away.

Chapter Four

Day 4

I should've known Bakari wouldn't just let me die if there was trouble to brew.

He intercepts me as I make my way back to Meryt's rooms after a quick midday meal. It feels foolish to eat when I'll be gone in five days, but I can't starve before I finish everything here first.

"Zizi!"

The name stops me, even though I should ignore him. I turn just enough to show that I've heard him, but only so he won't call out again. Then I harden my scowl.

"Zizi," he repeats anyway as he closes the distance between us.

"I have work to do." I try to move around him, but he neatly steps into my path. "Packing."

His hand is extended to stay me, but it drops at my last word. Noticing his wrist guards, I assume he's been pulled from the building rotation and sent back to training at the barracks adjacent to the palace. He'll probably race in the funeral games before the burial. His torso is absent the dust from a few days before and he looks his usual neat self. I try not to think about how that means the pyramid must almost be ready for Meryt.

Bakari sighs and passes a hand over his shaved scalp, shaking his head at my obstinance. "Why are you making this difficult?"

I stare at him in astonishment. *I'm* making this difficult?

He smiles off my look, his familiar mischievous grin peeking through. "Let me rephrase." He pauses. "This is already difficult enough. Please let me tell you everything. Then you can decide."

"There is no *everything*," I say fiercely. "She's gone, and I must serve her there as I served her here. I *must* go. *You* must let me go."

Bakari bites back his reply as a group of noblemen passes us. He nudges me toward the closest wall, ignoring the open looks from the small group of servants trailing their masters. Without Lady Tadinanefer-Hatshepsut to raise me above them, and slated to die soon, I may as well be a faceless servant without status or currency in the palace of Thebes. Bomani-Bakari, however, well, that's a name even visiting servants learn quickly enough. Usually, Bakari can't ignore their fawning admiration. Now, he doesn't even acknowledge them.

"I won't keep you from your duties," he says slowly, "but agree to meet me later tonight. Please?"

I want to refuse again, but there's a softness to his request that makes me hesitate. There's something beside the sadness too, something I can't identify turning his simple question into a worried plea. It's so foreign to Bakari's boisterousness and teasing, it throws me off balance so I can't refuse.

"All right."

His broad shoulders loosen in relief. "Thank you," he says sincerely, his cheeky smile widening again.

"I have to get back to my duties." I repeat, and hurry

away.

****

We meet later that night in the same place we have for over a year now, a cool subterranean room forgotten among the passageways under the great palace. I first discovered the room when I took a wrong turn on an errand for Meryt, made worse by a sudden, crushing fear of being stuck underground. I would have been lost a long while had I not inexplicably heard singing from down the passageway. Faint and gentle, the song didn't gesture but pull, a firm tug insisting I follow. It wasn't the voice or the singing as much as the song itself that called to me. I knew even before I heard the words it was a song of Thonis.

It was mere months after we'd lost everyone, and my heart was still drowning in the same waters that had taken the rest of our city. Hearing that tune was the first time the pressure of the watery depths eased some. No matter that I was choosing to remain deep underground, I went after the song willingly.

And found a soldier painting the glittering majesty of the sea.

His back was to me, but the scuff of my feet must have alerted him to someone else in the room. He hesitated when I entered but didn't turn around. He finished the last few strokes of a cresting wave in shades of lapis and pearl, softly singing his unintentionally haunting refrain.

Only then did he turn to me, but my eyes were no longer on him but the home he'd brought back to life on the walls of that forgotten subterranean room.

Even though I usually shrank from small, enclosed places, and really any place that could not glimpse the sky, I eagerly stepped inside, mouth unabashedly open as I followed the images of Thonis unfurling along the walls like the bright, promising sails of ships taking to sea. I walked with couples strolling on the main island streets, frolicked with children in the surf from the sea beneath my feet, loaded cargo with sailors on the docks, and bartered with merchants for goods in trade houses. The scenes, the people, the moments were all so vividly reimagined I could smell the salty breeze lacing through my black hair.

I could hear it all too. Sailors calling to each other as they prepared their ships to sail, captains shouting orders and berating clumsy movements, merchants haggling over prices with traders, children splashing and laughing in the sea that was our life even more than the Nile revered by the rest of Egypt, because the great river ended its journey through land in the sea. Our sea was everything. And it took everything too.

I'd stopped in front of the soldier about two thirds of the way around the room because there were no images left. I'd looked up and he'd looked down. Dark eyes meeting dark eyes, each taking in a face darkened by the same seaside sun. His mouth quirked into an amused, yet sad, grin.

"Hello, Zizi."

It took me a moment to recognize who he was, a moment to remember that we were no longer children in Thonis but elevated servants in his majesty's great palace.

"Bakari, you brought us home."

He'd nodded silently, then lifted his chin toward the lives memorialized in paint.

"I wanted to see it again. I wanted to give life to the

city they will no longer name."

"I say her name. Often."

He'd nodded toward the walls. "I miss them."

"I do too."

He'd gestured toward the last empty space on the wall. "For our islet. A section apart, as it well deserves."

A thick lump in my throat prevented any more words from coming out.

"And a doum palm here," he'd added, pointing to a smooth section of wall. "For you to climb."

I didn't know he knew anything about how much I loved to climb, mainly because he'd always seemed too much older to notice what anyone younger was about. Although I didn't exactly speak much with anyone high up in my trees to find out what they did or didn't know.

Bakari had motioned upward, and I craned my head back to find the night sky painted on the ceiling, even though bright sunlight glinted off the sea he'd frozen in time.

"Do you remember?" he'd asked. "Do you remember the stars of Thonis?"

The constellations overhead jumped out at me. All at once I was returned to the night sky draped over our islet, the rise and fall of the sea the music to which the shimmering stars danced in the dark.

"How could I forget?"

"You can watch them dance from the roof of the palace, especially away from the sentries' torches. But the music isn't the same, for the Nile sings a different tune from the sea."

I was surprised he'd thought to look for the stars in Thebes, surprised he could use such poetry to describe something I wouldn't have thought he'd have cared to look for. I was also impressed that he'd noticed the difference, that he'd used the words of our fathers to describe what a sleeping sun revealed in the night sky. I had thought such details lost once Thonis vanished and her name became a curse on people's tongues. I hadn't thought beyond my weighty grief and the jagged chasm of absence yawning in the wake of their disappearance. As he'd reminded me then, there were still three of us left to keep Thonis blessed and her stories alive.

Standing in that room the first time, I wanted to ask if he still heard the quiet that fell after the entire city sank with all her inhabitants. If he also remembered how deafening it was, the memory of a world cut short so much louder than the empty sea left behind. Not even driftwood marked where a prosperous city was once the gateway to Egypt.

I'd looked back at the wall awaiting our islet and instead asked, "May I help?"

Bakari's smile had widened enough to chase away the lingering sadness. "Of course. We will ensure they will not be forgotten."

I went often to that little storage room. Sometimes Bakari was there, sometimes not, but no matter, once it was painted, I would sit against the wall with our little islet and live in the image of the city that was. Often, I would look up and watch the stars dance in the night sky, my breath even, despite my surroundings. It was here that Bakari and I began to spend more time together, where we began to rebuild the friendship our families once had. From then, whenever we passed him in the corridors he would nod or slip me a gleeful wink after he greeted Meryt. He even stopped at Meryt's rooms a few times after training, but only long enough to ground ourselves again in the reminder that we three together were home.

Each of our encounters seemed to say the same thing. We of Thonis would not forget. We would not let her memory sink in silence.

But as I sit now waiting for Bakari in that little room with fresh grief over Meryt's passing washing over me, all I can think is maybe it's time to let go. When the many becomes three, and the three become two, the two near dwindling to one, what are we still holding onto? How much did Bakari really need my help and how much was he merely trying to grasp at the last remnants of the past? The thing with no one speaking about Thonis is that no one would know if we finally let go. Once we're all gone, no one would care that Thonis was. Perhaps it's finally time to leave the burden of remembrance in the past.

The thought is interrupted when a muscled torso steps into view. I glance up and Bakari looks back at me. Dark eyes meeting dark eyes, taking in faces darkened by the same seaside sun. His mouth quirks into an amused, yet sad, grin.

"Hello, Zizi."

Then he's crossing his legs and sitting on the painted floor across from me, back rigid as a long oar, posture soldier-perfect. There's a quietness to him that's obvious to me now that I know how to find it, now that he's away from his duties and the name he's created for himself. I wonder if the other servants see it, the pretty girls who compete for the coveted attention of Bomani-Bakari. Many favors came my way once they found out I was on friendly terms with him.

Bakari watches me, holding my sight so I can't look away. He holds it one second, two, stalwart and steady, as if death had not followed us to the palace.

His measured calm helps me focus, at least enough to push away that ever-present feeling that my lungs are trapped beneath the sparkling waters of an emerald sea as a city drowns. We are not blessed to have survived the sinking of Thonis, but cursed. Cursed to never be free of the haunting, horrible reality of her absolute, silent destruction.

I wait for Bakari to speak.

"Azizi," he says seriously, for once using my full name without prompting. "Please listen to what I have to say. No running off before I'm done, agree?"

I want to shake my head no, but my mouth opens and says, "Agree."

Gaze never wavering, dark eyes solemn and resolute, Bakari begins, "Meryt was murdered, and we know she was murdered because the embalmer found poison in the *metr* carrying blood through her body. It was cleverly done, slowly, over a few months, and it would have gone unnoticed had we not been looking for it."

"Who's we?" I interrupt.

Bakari shakes his head. "No names yet."

"Why?"

"Not yet. But know that we are not alone in this."

I nod, resistant. Embraced by the painted arms of the past, I almost feel like he's telling me a story of another time. Stories like the ones our fathers used to tell of people and places beyond our glittering turquoise shoreline.

"Whoever it was has to be someone at the palace."

"Why are you so certain?" I question. "Why were you even looking for poison?"

Bakari hesitates. "You know she was with child?" he asks gently.

"Yes."

She was still early in her carrying, so I was one of very few to know, and only then because there was no way to hide it from me. Not when I was the one to hold back her hair when sickness overtook her body in the morning so she threw up what little she had inside. Not when she was so thrilled to finally be carrying the king's heir she couldn't resist sharing her joy with someone she could trust. Not when I had been there to see how the king's face lit up, how he'd swept her up and spun her because his joy was as great and magnificent as the midday sun. The royal physician and the royal priestess were the only others who knew. The plan had been to announce the good news as soon as they were sure Meryt had carried safely into her fifth month. And then it would only have been a matter of time before King Pa-Ankh-Entef made her queen.

The boxes I can't bring myself to look at contain things for the baby Meryt had quietly begun to collect.

A new thought startles me back into the present. When Meryt's sickness continued past the physician's reassurances, was it the poison racking her *metr*? Or the child growing in her, as we'd all assumed? Could the evidence have been right before our eyes but we failed to see it?

Some of my thoughts must be written in my expression, because Bakari offers a sympathetic look. "There's no way to know."

"Why are you telling me this?"

"Because we need your help."

I shake my head at the soldier. "There's nothing

more to be done. Only to pack her things and ease her way into the afterlife."

"Stop talking about death and start focusing on now," Bakari cuts in.

That certainly focuses my attention. Bakari notices my look and sighs.

"I didn't mean to be harsh," he apologizes, "but we're running out of time."

"Time for what?"

"To find the murderer."

"What does *that* have to do with me?"

"We need someone who knows the palace, someone who knew Meryt best, someone we can trust to do what needs to be done," Bakari explains. He pauses, then adds, "Someone assumed gone."

"A spirit," I conclude.

"Someone no one would look for," Bakari amends.

"For what?" I press, though I'm sure I don't want to hear the answer, especially if it needs my cooperation, especially if it means I cannot also die.

"Foremost, you need to stay alive," he says, then holds up a hand before I can protest again. "When you and the other maidservants are given the poison to drink, don't."

"They'll notice if they return to mummify us and I'm still alive."

"Not if we have certain arrangements with those who come for you," Bakari asserts. "We'll keep you hidden and out of sight until the burial, an ideal time to poke about the palace unnoticed."

"And if I'm caught?"

"Don't be."

"Easy for you to say."

"Worst, you'll die. Which is what you want anyway."

"But not after endless hours of torture. Not with a body left to dry in the wind without burial or path to the afterlife."

"Zizi, stop worrying so much and start thinking about how we're going to find Meryt's murderer."

I throw my hands up in frustration. "Why are you so sure we'll find anything? Why are you so sure I can be of any help?"

Bakari grins. "Have you already forgotten? Because we are of the Blessed."

"I doubt it."

"I don't."

"Little help that's been."

"Azizi, please."

I let out a long breath, uninterested in any of this poking about, but also unwilling to spend my last days hiding from the only person who will know when I'm gone.

"Fine. I'll think about it."

"That's not a yes."

"Okay, yes, happy?"

"Look, Zizi, if you find something over the next few days, you can still die. Happy?"

"No."

"Then we're getting somewhere."

Chapter Five

Day 5

Bakari's words ring in my ears through night and into morning no matter how much I wish them unsaid. I may have agreed to his request, but only to get him to stop asking. A part of me, a part right alongside that traitorous curiosity, insists that once a word is given it must be honored. After all, that side argues, I can't claim to love Thonis and my family and my cousin yet also be unwilling to bring them peace. Perhaps I'm selfish for wanting to join them in the afterlife, to escape the unrelenting pain of their absence.

I focus my energies into sorting and packing the rest of Meryt's rooms, including the items I've been avoiding. If I don't allow myself to think past the task at hand, then maybe I won't have to answer any of the burning questions of *Why murder? Why Meryt? Why us?*

Two other maidservants have also been chosen to serve the great Lady Tadinanefer-Hatshepsut in death. Benerib and Madu were selected for their beauty and youth and loyalty. Both have lives of promise that slip away like grains of sand in an open palm. So, as we sort and fold and wrap, we focus on anything but what will no longer be.

"Should I include the senet board in the box with perfumes or tuck it between these sandals?" Benerib asks, as if we're merely preparing for a trip up the Nile.

I take the beautiful jade senet board Meryt's father carved as a gift for what turned out to be her last birthday he would celebrate. The one before the king whisked her off to Thebes. I knew when she was most homesick because, though she hid it from everyone else behind beauty and smiles and laughter, she would take out the senet and we would play into sunrise. We played to take our minds away from Thebes, enough so we could pretend the rustle and sighs and whispers of people in the palace were the familiar sounds of our friends and pets and lapping waves of Thonis.

My fingers count down the three rows of ten squares on the board then trace the patterns on the side of the narrow rectangular box below it. I slide out the drawer that rests in its hollow and thumb the set of four throwing sticks, one side rounded, one side flat. I count through both sets of matching green pawns, confirming the five spindles and five cones are there. I see them moving across the board like the *ka* to the afterlife. Just like Meryt's. *Just like mine.*

I close the drawer swiftly, flinching as if it slammed, and quickly hand it back to Benerib.

"It'll hold better if you wrap it in something first," Madu answers, offering a piece of an old fur cloak.

"Have you asked after goblets and dishes for Lady Tadinanefer-Hatshepsut from the kitchens?" I ask.

"What about these?"

Madu holds up a series of sketches Bakari drew of Meryt, captured about the palace. The backgrounds are unfinished, as they were meant to be filled in later, whenever he had a few moments to spare. Another thing cut short.

"Wrap them with the senet," I reply, and Madu hands them to Benerib, who must now unwrap and rewrap the cloak.

We're precise in our words and careful in our movements, feeling that Meryt watches us as we move through her rooms and sort her possessions. We don't say it out loud because it would sound ridiculous, but there's an unspoken question of whether things can spill or break or be a burden in the next world, if each object will have weight as it does in this one. So we keep our speech simple and mundane, directed to the task at hand and away from anything beyond the immediate present. After all, we have nothing but the present left.

Yet I wonder what the others think about when they're alone in their beds at night with death just days away. I haven't been able to bring myself to ask, as now is definitely not the time to start growing closer to them. Especially if I'm to betray them and stay in this world when they leave it. *Can such betrayal be worse than murder?*

As for myself, I certainly *don't* think about my parents. I certainly don't imagine what Mother would say to me now, imagine how she would remind me of the honor I have of serving Meryt once more. She may even remind me that I'll finally see my family again, finally come home to the Thonis I was so reluctant to leave.

And what about Father? Would he encourage me to follow Meryt as I should, or stay as Bakari asked? No longer is there a vague promise that I may yet sail the seas as he once did, that I will nurture and cultivate his same wonder for the world and its peoples. No longer is there hope that another life awaits me should my time at the palace ever end. There is no way he can assure me that following Meryt this time will not be forever.

Chapter Six

Day 6

Three days.

In three days, I will have mandrake poison in hand. If I drink, I finally reunite with my family in the afterlife. Bakari won't be there to stop me. The choice is still mine.

I worry that breaking my word means my heart's measure will be found wanting, that it will not measure true. But I also hope Father was right in maintaining there's no such thing as a green-headed god who will weigh my heart after this life. If I drink the poison instead of staying, I can't be certain of what the scale will show.

It's odd to be given the chance to bid farewell to life, knowing exactly when death will come. That is one advantage Madu, Benerib, and I share. My family had no chance to say goodbye. Meryt had no chance to say goodbye. Then again, who do I have left to say goodbye to, except perhaps Bakari?

In the quiet of night, in the space between breaths, I think long and hard about the charioteer's adamance that I not die. I think about exchanging the finality of death for the uncertainty of what other pain or mystery or secrets life may yet hold. I think of how someone who doesn't know his own death can demand that someone who does should remain alive.

And then I wonder how a girl of only seventeen years could be so resigned to death when she finally has a way to hold onto life.

When did I become like this?

Why do I not vow eternal vengeance upon the one who made me so?

Chapter Seven

Day 7

I jump as a shadow crosses over me, then laugh at myself when I realize I've walked through the shade of a column. The surety of murder surrounds me with such a dense fog, I'm skittish as I walk through familiar palace hallways toward the training grounds. A weight presses into my shoulders, convincing me someone watches, waiting for a chance to strike me down. The world will not mourn one less of the Blessed.

Murdered.

I manage to only suck in my breath at the next large shadow, wishing there was another path, as there are so many columns patterning the outer walkways. The heat is not remarkable, yet a cool sheen of sweat breaks out over my body. I am certain Meryt's murderer is closing in on me. I know too much.

I finally reach the training grounds, and quickly press myself against the wall. My eyes scan the hallway in both directions, clearing the way I came and the last several paces to the exit.

There is no one around. The hallway is empty save me.

The *clangs* and *shouts* and *thumps* from outside float toward me, and I heave a deep sigh of relief. I close my eyes and remain that way for almost an hour before I hear the first of the men leaving.

I keep flat against the wall, careful not to make eye contact, as if any of these men could possibly mean me harm. I watch patiently, stoically, until I see the one I'm here for.

Sweat trickles from his forehead, into his wrist guards, and rivulets through dirt across his barren chest. For a moment I muse that while I've heard so much about Bomani-Bakari, not just in giggles from other servant girls, but also in praise from noblemen, I've never actually seen him train. I have no image of his skills or abilities.

Well, the time for that has certainly passed.

Bakari raises an eyebrow as I intercept him, not caring who might see as I and my reputation will be gone in a few days anyway. Guards and soldiers eye us, the celebrated soldier and once high-ranking maidservant, survivors and the Blessed. Then they quietly step around us. If I weren't days from death, I'm sure they wouldn't allow such an approach to occur without a fair share of snickering and not-so-subtle asides. Instead, their expressions only show a mix of sympathy and sadness. Soldiers are not unaccustomed to sudden death, but that doesn't mean it sits easy with them.

I speak before Bakari can. "If this is to be, then you must be absolutely certain it will work. If any tiny part goes wrong, then you have to let me go."

I step away before he can reply, before he can catch my wrist and reassure me that leaving Meryt alone in the afterlife is truly the right decision. I don't either want to hear about everyone I'll be serving well by staying alive. Honestly, if there was a way to avoid my conscience and newly ignited suspicion, I wouldn't think about it at all.

Message relayed, I hurry from Bakari and leave him to figure out the details, though not before I glimpse a pleased expression sweep across his face.

I wish he wouldn't be so assured, and silently chastise him for believing in me so much. What if I stay only to discover there's nothing to find? What if I stay only to uncover an answer we'd rather not know? What if I stay and find something only I can tell?

There's no guarantee that what would happen next wouldn't be worse than death.

Chapter Eight

Day 8

The night before I'm supposed to die, my mood is somber. I should be gladdened that I've been given a way to cheat death, but I'm too conflicted and leaden with sadness to feel much else. I've agreed to stay in this world, but can't help thinking how easy it would be to cross over. Or for something to go wrong and prove we never should've tampered with tradition. Whatever will be, sleep seems pointless on such a night.

I climb to the palace roof to watch the stars dance to the music of the Nile. Even choosing to stay alive, I doubt I'll get a chance to sneak onto the roof just to look at the sky anytime soon.

I find a spot away from the torchlight of the sentries and lie on my back to drink in the Heavens. I wonder if staring long enough will grant me a glimpse of the path before me. I wonder if Father is in the sky above, as he believed he would be, rather than in the afterlife the rest of Egypt believes in. Father may have dressed like an Egyptian, married an Egyptian, and raised three Egyptian daughters, but he was never truly an Egyptian.

I try to call to Father and Mother and Unika and Kebi across whatever veil divides us. I know Mother would celebrate the honor I've once more been chosen for. I think Unika and Kebi will be happy to see me again. But I want to ask Father if his Divine Force would want me to live or die. I want to ask if my responsibility lies in eternal service or in this burden of finding the truth. Is my death truly the way to honor my cousin's life?

Murdered.

Bakari's planted a seed in my mind that's growing at an alarming rate. If I really want truth, then the truth is I want to know who did this. I want to know who stole our homes and lives and favored daughter. I want to bring assurances of justice and peace when I finally do reach the afterlife.

I'm not sure how much time passes before soft footsteps approach and a figure stretches out beside me on the roof. Not too close, but close enough to sense the warmth and aliveness of his *ka*.

I glance long enough to confirm it's Bakari, but for the first time since I've known the soldier, he doesn't say anything. He merely nods in greeting, then turns his face to the sky to watch the stars with me.

It may well be that he is also trying to steal a few moments of peace from the intensity of life, from the clamor of being one of the king's most celebrated charioteers, not only one of the Blessed but also the Favored. Or maybe he's thinking of the stars of Thonis, of the way they twinkled and danced in the sky above as we twirled through our lives on land below. Or perhaps he's only thinking of his chariot and horses.

We stay like that a long while, silent yet strengthened in the reassurance of the other's presence.

Sometime later, Bakari stands and leaves behind a rustle of papyrus paper. I'm about to call after him, but stop when I see what's on the page, knowing without doubt he left it for me.

A black and white sketch of a doum palm with a girl in it. Me.

The image lingers in my vision as I return to my room and the absence of Meryt. Unlike the mural in the underground room, I sense Bakari's not offering a memory but a message.

He's urging me to return to what I once loved most, not a place or a time but a reaching.

Urging me not to cross over.

Urging me to climb again.

Chapter Nine

Day 9

The time to die has come. Benerib, Madu, and I wait quietly in Meryt's room for our escort to the embalmers' room, leaving each other to final private thoughts.

I stand in the doorframe between my room and Meryt's, debating if I should take some sort of lead with a prayer or farewell gesture, and certainly *not* thinking about how Bakari may have left me to die after all.

Then I feel a warm presence behind me and a tug at my hand. I barely glance over my shoulder.

"Cutting it close," I hiss at the soldier.

Even without turning my head all the way, I can see his smile as he presses a square of sea sponge into my open palm.

"See you soon," he whispers in my ear.

He's gone just as suddenly as he appeared, the item I grip the only proof he was here.

Moments later our escort arrives and we're brought to a neat room with three long stone slabs. A physician stands ready with the draughts that will take us to the afterlife to serve Lady Tadinanefer-Hatshepsut forever. Despite the new sense of duty I feel toward her in this life, I can't help thinking that I can finally rid myself of the ever-widening chasm of loss, of all deep and gutting pain, if I just drink. It's no easy thing to squeeze the sponge to my palm, knowing it will keep me in this life, subject to all the ways it can drown me and make me wish I'd chosen differently this day.

Benerib and Madu enter the room behind me, maintaining brave faces though their hands tremble and their eyes water in their struggle to force back tears. After me, they were most highly regarded among Meryt's servants, their exalted life among the palace staff now granting them the honor of entering the afterlife earlier than natural death. We are all grateful to be chosen. Blessed, as we're told. Still, we are too young to die. Guilt quiets the thought as soon as it forms, not just because I'm selfish to begrudge Meryt her servants in the afterlife but also because I know not joining them is not only a break from centuries of tradition but a betrayal that can never be undone.

Benerib is the older of the two. In the brief time I've known her, she's spoken often of how much her mother prayed for her to reach such a lofty position. I suppose her mother also emphasized what an honor it would be to serve the king's wife, though, like mine, she couldn't have expected it would all end so soon. And there's no knowing what her father said to encourage her service in the palace, though he would surely point out the benefit of such an opportunity for someone from so simple a family. Benerib has two younger sisters whom I've met in the few times they were allowed to bring her parcels from home. They both adore her and treat her as if she was the one married to the king.

"She's...young," was the first thing Meryt had said when Madu was introduced as her newest maidservant.

"Only a year younger than Kebi," I pointed out. "If you don't accept her graciously, she'll think you are displeased."

Meryt stopped herself short of shaking her head and bestowed a warm smile upon Madu, who'd flushed becomingly under the assumed praise. She'd been chosen to serve Meryt when soldiers riding through Thebes had spotted her and immediately reported their finding to the king. Her undeniable beauty was seen as a fitting tribute to the lady she served.

"That Madu of yours is a rather popular face among the palace guard," Bakari had once remarked not long after she'd joined Meryt's entourage.

"She pauses every guard and soldier at practice just by appearing at the overlook," Benerib muttered.

I'd never seen it for myself, but her wide brown eyes lined with deep green kohl, her softly bronzed skin, and her black as night hair was enough to convince me it was true. Her once enviable beauty is much the reason why she's in this room instead of turning heads as she ought. I doubt other servants envy her now, though none would dare say so out loud.

There's something so innocent about Madu which makes my heart ache, knowing she'll be gone soon. Then again, I also know she's not as innocent as she seems, not only because of Father's warnings of the ways at the palace but also because of what I've seen for myself.

Benerib is more sweet than beautiful, and her *ka* relays a promise of a good life led. There's something about the willing sacrifice of so much potential that makes me want to drop the sponge and reject the escape Bakari's given me. I am ashamed to know such youth will die alone while I elude death a second time. Do all those marked for life over death carry so much guilt within them?

I force myself to offer each girl a warm, comforting smile, a reassurance that we truly are blessed to have been chosen. Beneath it all, I wonder if I will see them in the afterlife once this life no longer finds reasons to make me stay. I wonder if I will be made to answer for my choice today.

"We will soon be reunited with Lady Tadinanefer-Hatshepsut," I say with forced conviction, as if it's the only thing left to be desired in the world.

The girls nod respectfully as they must, outwardly peaceful despite their shuddering breaths. We wait in silence upon the stiff beds that will be used to embalm us, each held in the unbreachable pocket of the last minutes of our lives.

My mind turns to dying, to crossing over into the other realm even if that means I remain a servant the rest of my days. A small voice reminds me there's nothing Bakari can do to stop me once I have the poison in my hands. It's my duty to die, after all.

The strip of papyrus I slipped between my right foot and sandal flashes to mind. The girl sketched onto the page propels me to reject any further thought of death so I can return to what I loved. Climbing. Reaching. Upward.

I don't remember if the first time I climbed so high was on a tree or the mast of a ship, or if one compelled the other, but I do know that I always loved squinting into the uncapturable stretch of horizon visible from the top. That girl with the sea in her hair and eyes searching for life against the glare of the sun is not yet ready to be entombed for eternity. Even as a royal servant. Even as a citizen of Thonis.

A priestess begins to chant, signaling the time has

come. I block out the funeral dirge by imagining the faces my father would make with the rise and fall of her wailing. I choke on a laugh and slap my hands over my mouth in a gesture of prayer. Thoughts of my father and his disdain for a religion that mandates our deaths ignites a new defiance within me and I quickly slip the sponge under my tongue. I pray intensely to father's Divine Force that it will work, that I will not be caught, that the poison will not do half a job should any seep out.

The sponge is a grave risk, and not just because we may be found out. Bakari warned that I couldn't keep the sponge in my mouth longer than it would take to soak up the poison because the longer it's there the more time the poison has of leaking into my *metr*. If enough of the poison gets into my bloodstream, well, I'll never know what happens next.

I'm given the honor of drinking from the cup first. In so small a setting, with the few eyes watching intently, I have no chance of removing the sponge before the other two drink. So I say another prayer that they will move quickly.

I raise the cup to my lips, but a gasp pauses my hand. I peek over the rim and see King Pa-Ankh-Entef has entered the room. I gladly lower the poison to dip my head in obeisance to him, relieved even though this only delays the inevitable.

The king is tall and striking, with an angular face, but thinner than expected for such a wealthy man. His dark eyes are red-rimmed and his usually deep brown skin appears ashen. I know it's because he's slept little since Meryt's passing. More than once, I've caught sight of him in her rooms, sitting on her empty bed and staring into silence or fingering the items we were sorting for packing. I've even caught sight of him raising her beloved leopard cloak to his eyes—

I left when he buried his face in it and wept. I had no desire to intrude on his broken heart when I was still tripping over the pieces of my own.

"Bless you, children," the king says to me, Benerib, and Madu, coming close to touch his fingers to each of our foreheads. "May you have safe passage to the afterlife. May your hearts' measure be good and true."

"Thank you, Illustrious Highness," we humbly respond.

The king comes back to me and lifts my chin so I'm forced to look at him. The way his eyes flit to mine to the cup then back to mine again make it look like he's ready to take a sip himself.

The king reaches for the hand not holding the cup and a lightning bolt of panic courses through me. Will I be required to say or do anything that will reveal what lies beneath my tongue? Half formed thoughts skitter through my mind as I frantically consider what to do.

A knocking of ceramic bowls, echoing louder in the descending tension, breaks the moment.

The king glances over his shoulder to see an embalmer straightening the table he's clumsily bumped into. The king turns back to me and forgets about taking my hand, reaching for my shoulder and giving it a comforting squeeze instead.

"Send Tadi my love," he whispers, his voice breaking. "Kiss our child for me."

"Yes, Illustrious Highness," I choke out thickly, sniffing for good measure as though my voice is muffled from emotion.

The assembled watch as we each drink and climb to

our slabs, then the room is cleared so we may die in peace. As Madu and Benerib watch the door click shut, sealing the reality of our fate, I turn my head and lift a hand to slip the sponge out, praying none of the poison has leaked into my *metr*. The girls reluctantly lie back and the room becomes eerily quiet.

An off-beat thumping soon tells me convulsions have begun and I prop myself onto my side, unwilling but determined to see the fate of the two girls I've sent on without me. In the bed beside me, I see Madu's body slowly succumb to the poison, her limbs twitching as the draught takes hold.

I glance at the next bed over, expecting much of the same. Benerib stares back at me.

I startle guiltily as her eyes meet mine and there's no doubt she knows I am not going to die today. *She knows.*

Will she call out? Will anyone come? Will she give me away?

A low rumble of unintelligible sound escapes her, a warning to the guard or a plea to me, it's not clear enough to decipher. I watch her unable to decide, guilt surely written across my features as bright as limestone in the desert sun. Her lips move as she struggles to form words, and I'm nearly off my bed, afraid enough to consider suffocating her ahead of the poison taking too long to shut down her system.

Her next moan has me flying from my bed, my feet bringing me halfway toward hers, my mind only thinking to pause when I see how large her eyes grow in response. I cannot tell if it's fear or hope that widens them, if she thinks she also may not die today. I only know that she cannot remain alive, watching and knowing what I have done.

Then my feet freeze as I flash back to a moment when I was almost suffocated in my father's warehouse. I relive the enclosing walls of the room and the resulting surety that I would die.

I look for a way to hasten the poison's work so Benerib's suffering will not be prolonged.

A moment passes which feels a lifetime, and indeed its passing ends it.

Her head falls back and her organs shut down. Madu is gone. Benerib is gone. I am here.

I loose a heavy breath, glad I will not have to finish her, embarrassed at the recent course of my thoughts.

The room turns deafeningly silent.

I stumble back to my slab and haul myself up, telling myself I need more than one try for the guilt weighing me down. Once on, I turn my head away from the others, not only from the shame and death, but also from the accusation of their *ka*-less bodies angrily condemning the lie that said I would die beside them. There's a bitter taste in my mouth from the sudden surge of bile I have to force back down. My muscles weaken, and I think for the first time that maybe some of the poison did leak through. Perhaps after everything, I will die anyway.

Where's Bakari now? What is he waiting for?

I close my eyes and flee to Thonis, seeking comfort and a chance to catch my breath in the wide openness of our island. All I really want, so deep it nearly burns, is a tree to climb, to settle on an outstretched limb and turn my face to a sea ruffled by a salty breeze. I want to throw my head back and drink in the blue of sky so vast and deep it overwhelms the waters beneath, so much so all they can do is reflect its color back. Above, below, beyond, the world around me speaks of possibility. It speaks of life and exuberance, joy and largess, a place where anything can happen to any life which embraces all it has to offer.

My thoughts drift through Thonis, which some may say is a bad omen at such a time, but I can see no other way. I recall to mind every wave and every grain of sand until I can imagine living in the life we left behind instead of the one that led to the palace with Meryt. If she hadn't been on the shore that day, her feet in the jewel-like water, the wind playfully tossing her hair behind her pretty face so the moment painted an enticing picture even a king passing by on a twelve-oar ship couldn't miss, this would never have come to pass. No murder, no poison, no betrayal, no lies. Then again, if I hadn't come here, I would probably be under the sea with the rest of our families, truly drowned instead of this imagined weight of water-clogged lungs.

My thoughts still underwater, I hear a faint sound I'm certain is in the room. Have we been here so long the rats have come for us? I haven't heard a door open, but I'm feeling muddled enough to have missed it. Exhaustion, high emotions, and possibly poison are a potent, immobilizing mix. Perhaps Benerib or Madu aren't truly dead, but I forcefully dismiss the thought. I know what I saw.

Ever so slightly, with enormous effort, I turn my head and peek through my eyelids to the other beds. The angle is awkward and I can barely make them out, even straining with such singular focus. Both girls are still there and neither appears to be moving.

I can't open my eyes to look around now. Not only are they heavy as boulders, but if someone is in the room, and not someone who knows what we're about, then he'll make sure to finish the job I didn't. If he doesn't torture me for answers first. I lie still and listen deeply for several moments, then decide that I must have imagined the noise. I allow myself to exhale again, but fear keeps my breaths shallow.

I jolt at the sudden, unmistakable sound of stone scraping stone. My heart flutters in panic, unsure if it's safe to look or breathe or make any sound or movement. How much time has passed since we were left to die? Who slips in so quietly now?

Bakari had assured me I'd be taken out of here somehow, but it seems the others are returning before that can happen. What will be if they catch me still alive? Will they force the poison into me? Will they embalm me or feed me to a crocodile?

Without answers, I force my breathing still and keep my eyelids firmly shut. I don't expect to last long like this, but it need only be long enough for whomever it is to think me gone.

There's a pause in movement, then, unmistakably, someone steps into the room. Sandaled feet slap lightly against the floor as they approach the embalming tables. A set of bare feet follow, so light a scuff and so soft an occasional shuffle marking their path.

"Gone," says a deep voice not close enough to be over me, so I assume he's referring to Benerib.

The voice is gratingly familiar, but in the haze of my nerves and panic, I can't place it. A quiet slap of sandals against stone. A pause.

"Gone," the same voice repeats, probably about Madu.

A presence leans over me, and I pray my body

doesn't betray me, even as I wish to stiffen and sink deeper into the table. A hand fumbles for the heartbeat at my wrist.

"Gone?"

The word's a question, a challenge to the certainty of the other two.

A soft touch travels down my cheek.

"Azizi," a familiar voice whispers and my eyes fly open, instant relief flowing through me upon seeing Bakari.

"Alive," he confirms.

From my place on the table, from the way he's standing, I can't see who he's talking to. I suppose it's one of the nameless few that are supposed to assure me we're not in this alone. If I could only see him to know.

"Good," the deep voice replies. "Let's get out of here."

"Time to go." Bakari offers his hand to help me.

I ignore him as I push myself up, but immediately regret it as a powerful wave of dizziness washes over me. I want to lie back down and close my eyes to the overwhelming fatigue, to yield wholly to this new force pulling me back to the table. Bakari's relief vanishes.

"Are you all right?" he asks.

"All right."

Was that not the very question that brought me here?

There's a pounding near my temples, but I hear a slight slur in my voice over it. Black spots crowd my vision and Bakari's face blurs. Why does he look so concerned? Should he not be glad his plan will continue?

"Did you ingest any poison?"

"The sponge!" I protest, except the words are slow

and muffled as they leave my mouth.

"Did it hold?" Bakari presses.

"You gave it!" I manage to push out, almost clearly.

"You'll be all right," he says quickly.

I know I'll be all right! I did as you asked, didn't I?
But words have suddenly become too difficult for my heavy, swelling tongue.

"—go!" I vaguely hear the other man command, his voice urgent.

Bakari says something about me being unable to walk, but I shake my head at him to chase the words away. I'm still alive, of course I can walk. As soon as the room stops spinning and I can clearly see which stones are the floor, which are the walls, and which are the ceiling.

Suddenly, strong arms hold me against a chest with a racing heart. Unless it's my own pulse racing. The haziness makes it difficult to discern between one sound and the next, between one person and the next.

Then we're moving quickly through cool passages, still in the royal palace of Thebes, I presume, though to my eyes all looks like a mess of spilled and mixed-up pearl and lapis paint.

I expect the walls will close in any second. I suspect the shore will no longer hold the waves. I squint ahead and search for Meryt, but grow confused when I cannot see her. I want to ask Bakari to help me find her, but a swift force is carrying me farther and farther from him. Has my father and his Divine Force come for me?

I don't understand why it won't just let me walk.

Chapter Ten

Day 15

When I finally manage to pry open my eyes, the first
face I see is Bakari's.

"Didn't this happen already?" I scratch out past a
throat parched as the desert sands.

"She's awake!" he cries jubilantly.

I'm confused at the excess of joy and relief in his
tone and expression. Didn't he just arrive to get me from
the embalmers? He must be teasing with such an
exaggerated reaction.

"How do you feel?"

"Seeing you?"

"Your usual sunny outlook hasn't suffered a bit."

"Living hurts," I grunt.

Bakari nods. "Much harder than dying."

I shift my gaze to confirm my surroundings. Instead
of the embalmers' room, I'm surprised to find we're in a
new room, sparse but elegantly appointed. I'm fairly
certain we're still in the palace, but it's not anywhere I
recognize. Then again, there are dozens of rooms I never
had a chance to see.

"Where..?" I trail off weakly.

"Safe," Bakari assures.

I try to sit, but my body doesn't want to hold itself
up. I frown at my condition. Bakari presses a hand

against my shoulder.

"You're barely done fighting the poison that slipped into your system."

My frown deepens. "How long?"

"About a week."

"Long enough lying around."

"Fine."

Bakari props pillows behind me and I wriggle into a sitting position. I begin to smile in thanks, but it falls away when I see who else is in the room. A woman, tall and regal, in a simple white dress and enough bracelets on each arm to form a cuff stacked together. Her skin hasn't spent much time in the sun and her black hair drapes past her shoulders. My eyes spot the amulet around her neck and I recoil in horror.

"What is *she* doing here?" I hiss.

Bakari squares his jaw. "*She* kept you alive."

"*Still*," I insist.

I glower at the "medicine" woman. Let others fool themselves with fake titles, I know she practices the dark arts, and I don't take well to her being part of this at all.

Bakari is much more courteous than I. "Thank you, Rasidi. We'll see you later."

Unfazed, the proud woman bows her head in acknowledgement. She may be used to eliciting either scorn or reverence, which is less about her as an individual and more about someone's views of the dark arts in general. Rasidi might have a heart of good measure, but I cannot believe it endures untainted. Not when I know what dark arts can do.

Rasidi's bracelets jingle as she sets a small bowl on the bedside table. I clumsily scoot back from her, though she makes no move toward me.

"Steep in hot water and drink at least three times a day," she tells me kindly, as if my opinion of her hasn't been made plain.

"I won't touch it," I warn Bakari.

Bakari frowns at me. "Rasidi *saved* you. And she's important to what we're doing."

The "medicine" woman speaks before I can respond, her smile so deep, the blue kohl framing each eye almost meets in a single swirl.

"A mix of herbs for healing and a toss of spices for taste," she assures me. "Your *ka* is safe."

I don't say anything, and again Bakari thanks her for me. After she leaves, I turn on him.

"Our fathers would never have dealt with a woman like her!"

"You were *dying*!" he shoots back. "And they're not here."

"But how could you forget?"

Bakari grows quiet. "I didn't," he says softly. "I couldn't."

He inhales a ragged breath, and it's like we're back in that warehouse years ago.

Our fathers held a decidedly grim outlook on the dark arts, and their distaste for it wasn't just theoretical. Bakari and I experienced why because of Chisisi, a woman whose name we never dared say. Not that we were ever supposed to know about her. We were just in the wrong place at the wrong time.

It had been a quiet afternoon. The main warehouse of my father's shipping company was relatively calm. Unika must have been taking stock elsewhere, or she would have been sitting next to Father with brow furrowed as she worked through long columns of numbers.

Mother had sent me with bunches of fresh, crisp grapes, a small treat to bolster Father's afternoon. I searched for Father when I arrived and finally found him in an underground storeroom. Father had brightened upon seeing what Mother had sent.

Bakari was also there with his father, who hadn't yet given up hope of training him to be a merchant. Bakari had three younger brothers, but he looked so much like his father they were oft confused as he grew older. They were similarly tall and broad-shouldered, with angular features and the same lines around their eyes. His father's were a mark of his profession, Bakari's were a mark of his nature.

Bakari grabbed a handful of grapes from the plate I'd brought and popped some in his mouth, mischief sparking in his eyes. Before he could begin his usual teasing, a woman entered, muttering strange phrases and interrupting herself with waving hands trailing bright obsidian sparks. She was dressed like a priestess from the temple; she raved about a recent shipment that had spoiled some mystery ingredients.

I glanced at Bakari in confusion, and he shrugged in reply.

"Can I help you?" Father asked.

Her mutterings grew louder; the obsidian sparks glowed brighter.

"Please come upstairs where we can speak properly," Father pressed.

Suddenly, there was no air in the room. Suddenly, the walls were closing in, intending to trap us forever as they collapsed with our lungs.

The plate dropped from my hands, the carefully

selected fruit tumbling to the dirt. As we scrambled for breath, the woman's skin glowed darkly from the sparks of her anger and her curses. Immobilized, helpless, there was no doubt we would die.

Bakari was the one to break us out. He pelted the woman with the rest of the grapes he held, just enough to crack her focus. The momentary pause was all our fathers needed to tackle the woman and hold her down. Bakari's father placed some sort of bracelet on her arm, even as she writhed and screamed and cursed to the skies. Within seconds, the obsidian sparks disappeared and the woman's crackling rage was replaced with gasps and ragged breathing.

Bakari helped his father take her away. I stared at my father when they left, eyes round, heart pounding.

"Who was that?"

"A 'medicine' woman."

"That wasn't medicinal."

Father's lips formed a straight line. "Dark arts," he explained, disdain thick in his voice. "She uses it in the temple to play tricks on worshippers so they'll believe in the gods she claims to speak for."

My head spun. Despite Father's beliefs, I'd been to the temples, but had never experienced anything quite like the suffocation she'd brought upon us.

"What did Bakari's father do? *How* did he know what to do?"

"A device to cut the flow of power. We each carry one, as a precaution."

I stared at my father, a whole new view of life bursting open before me.

"How do you know all this? How did you know what she was doing?"

"She used to be a good woman," Father said with a sigh. "She's not much older than your mother, and their houses were near each other growing up. She originally became a priestess to help others."

"Was Mother friends with her?"

Father shook his head. "She knew the home she was raised in and the woman she grew up to be. Before she became a priestess."

Something wasn't making sense. Father had claimed the woman wanted to help people, yet, even before she'd tried to kill us, she'd appeared overcome with madness. The woman from my mother's childhood didn't align with the one I'd seen at all.

"How does a priestess become a practitioner of dark arts?"

"Serve long enough in a temple, and you'll see a fair share of the world's suffering," Father replied, one of the only times he spoke of Egyptian worship without mockery. "Some prefer to focus on prayer and service, others share the burdens of hardship. Chisisi was one of the latter."

"But why dark arts?" I pressed.

"She must have learned from some of the priests and priestesses in the temple. It's not uncommon among their kind. Another blight against their forsaken religion."

"And Chisisi?"

"Couldn't bear the suffering anymore," he continued. "She turned to the dark arts to override nature, and it overtook her. It started with healing a sick boy bound for the next life, and descended from there."

"Yet healing is noble."

Father fixed me with a stern look. "Was there nobility in her actions now? Any sense to what she did?

One cannot immerse in the dark arts and think it will not affect a heart's true measure. Whatever her beginnings or reasons, there is only one path for such choices."

"Maybe she didn't know."

"She *knew*," Father said with unexpected force, enough to pierce my heart with his unequivocal rejection of such practices. "They all do, and yet they embrace it anyway. Each one thinks they will be different, untouched. They tell themselves lies of how the purity of their intentions will protect from the inevitable outcome of calling upon darkness. The dark arts give generously to their host, then take just as greedily."

"Why has no one stopped her? Why is she allowed in the streets?"

"The temples are glad for their priests and priestesses to be feared and revered for their powers. They want it. Besides, there is no undoing what has already been done."

I turned his words over, wondering what to make of it all. Wondering if I too should be so quick to condemn a woman who'd been overtaken by a force beyond her control, albeit a force she knew could harm her and had still welcomed inside.

"Does the Divine Force you believe in have no control over the dark arts then?"

"What dark arts exist must be within His province, and He allows them to exist so we can choose. The allure of power is much more enticing than goodness for those who can't see beyond this world."

"Your path does not appear well trodden, Father."

"Plain truth is a harder sell than sparkle and spectacle."

But I bought what Father sold, for he knew his trade

well. Since that day, whenever I think of the dark arts, I think of small places and the desperate inability to draw breath.

Bakari claims to remember yet doesn't seem wary of Rasidi at all. Then again, he's always been more ready to forgive than I. Perhaps his frequent asking of it from others made him generous in dispensing it as well.

"Rasidi is not like that woman," Bakari insists.

"How can you be sure?"

"Stop being difficult, Zizi," he chastises me. "You see how she was in control."

I massage the sides of my head, my mind aching. Rasidi seems nice enough, her bearing noble enough, and Bakari plainly trusts her, yet my father's warning about delving too long into darkness cannot be ignored. She will not avoid an end like Chisisi forever. And I do not want to be there when she can no longer fight what she did to herself.

"You can be grateful to Rasidi without becoming a champion of dark arts," Bakari adds.

I eye him, wondering how he's so clearly read my thoughts. His understanding softens my anger somewhat.

"Thank you," I tell him sincerely.

He smiles. "I told you once, and will repeat as many times as I must, you're not alone."

I don't counter that I feel I am. Not only since Meryt and Thonis, but also because I left Benerib and Madu to travel to the afterlife without me. I'm certainly alone in my deception, alone in being the only one alive but dead, so now I feel an intruder in the world of the living.

"What will be done about my missing body?" I ask to take my mind away from the confusion of working with Rasidi.

"The embalmer will make sure no one is suspicious of your sarcophagus," he answers.

I nod. Whatever Bakari's dragged me into, I should have suspected there would be a carefully crafted system of people involved. Almost no man in a palace survives without spinning a tight web of allies, and there's no reason why this deception should be any different than the hundreds of others at play.

"What?" I ask, catching Bakari studying me.

"Whatever happens," he says somberly, "there will be no thanks nor honor nor favor. No one can ever know what we've done. No one but the very few of us can ever know you're alive. You may have to leave Egypt entirely."

Leaving Egypt is all I ever wanted to do, but it's no option now when it's most convenient. If anything, agreeing to help investigate this murder has bound me tighter to the palace I never wanted to live in to begin with. So much of my life hasn't fulfilled the dreams I used to hold tight, dreams woven from starlight when night blackened the horizon beyond my line of sight.

"What now?" I ask, pushing such heavy thoughts aside.

"Now, *chibale*," Bakari replies, the corners of his lips lifting into a smile, "you quickly recover so you can become a very inquisitive spirit."

Chapter Eleven

Day 16

It takes almost a full day to get myself out of bed and standing without support. I'm alone for most of that time, so I work at my own pace and don't worry about being embarrassed each time my knees wobble like a newborn foal. I'm exhausted when afternoon rolls around, but at least I've walked to a chair on the other side of the room without toppling over.

If this is what a healthy girl is like after a week in bed fighting mere drops of poison, I can't imagine what Meryt must've struggled with over months of slow poisoning. Being with child for the first time, she could've easily confused her symptoms. And, knowing how long the king has waited for a child, she probably didn't want to worry him over what she mistook for trivial ailments. If we truly are looking for a murderer, it's someone very clever. Which doesn't help inspire me any.

Despite my reservations, I drink the herbal mix from Rasidi. I avoid it all morning at first, but as just trying to stand drains me, and it sits so innocently on the table where she left it, I reluctantly decide to trust in Bakari's faith in her. Besides, Rasidi wouldn't try to kill me right after she saved my life, as she could've made excuses for letting me die to begin with. Or so I tell myself.

From what I can taste, the blend is an innocent mix of herbs, though there's something to it that swiftly restores my *ka*. I've never heard of dark arts having a taste, so she could have done anything to the herbs while growing them and I wouldn't know how to spot it.

How quickly my life has been upended, how willingly I've defied centuries-old tradition and now sidestep my father in trusting Rasidi, even begrudgingly. Though I would be losing my mother even more if I fail to show her gratitude and respect. The confliction of each part makes my head ache.

Antsy from my thoughts, I make my way back to the bed but freeze in middle of the room from a different kind of breathlessness. Namely, a slamming realization about newly gained freedom and the inability of anyone to stop me from slipping out of the palace, finagling my way onto a ship, and finally sailing for the uncatchable horizon I've so long cast my sights toward. With everyone believing I'm dead, no one can raise a cry over my absence without a lot of unwanted questions being asked. The image comes with a deluge of all the wishes and desires and even fleeting musings of all I had to give up in becoming a servant to Meryt. Climbing. Sailing. A home and family of my own.

For the first time since coming to the palace, I don't feel resigned or even stifled. Instead, I listen again for the call of the sea, for the familiar creak of great ships riding the waves, for the snap of sails in the wind. Much as I want to be on the water again, a much heavier anchor of obligation tethers me to land. So, adept as I've become with packing life away, I carefully tuck away each hope and dream and urge, and refocus on the present. Which is all I really have anymore.

Bakari returns once night falls. I'm bored enough by then to be glad to see him again. I'm back in the chair, which is set against a table, another chair opposite. Bakari places a plate of warm food before me.

"Whatever you can manage," he says.

"Shouldn't you be in the barracks?" I ask, reaching for a piece of plain bread.

"My fellow soldiers agreed to cover for me in the belief that I seek a quiet corner to write flowery poetry to the woman of my desires," he announces as he adds quill, ink, and roll of papyrus to the table with a flourish.

"Only one?"

"Only one is needed."

"Unlucky girl."

"Jest not unto my love, my rare desert *zahur* flower—"

"Please, I've only just recovered!" I feign a retching sound.

"Whose lips like petals in boldest hues—"

I clutch at my heart and slump against the chair, head lolling as if I've died after all.

"And eyes of starlight—"

He yelps as I sit up and spill ink across his fingers.

"You'll ruin the papyrus!"

"And you've ruined your love heart's poem!"

"In truth, what need have I for ink when it's forever written upon my heart?" Bakari declares as he takes the seat across from me. He glances at the thick lines of ink dripping across his fingers. "Well," he reasons, "may as well get some use out of this."

He punctuates his comment with jabbing his hand quick as lightning over the table and imprinting his fingertips on the top of my hand. I won't give him the satisfaction of a response, and it's all I can do not to retaliate. I deliberately ignore the dark spots and fix my focus on his face instead. Not that it helps, his goofy smirk is annoyingly infectious. I eat more bread and force myself to remember why we're here.

"How can you still laugh so freely?" The words tumble out before I can regret how they'll sober the moment.

I've thought of this over and over and over since Thonis, since our families were ripped away and we were left shaken and without a body or grave or ruin to mourn over. The guilt of laughter has burdened me since the day everyone disappeared; it's hung over every moment and festival and even over Meryt's news that she was carrying the king's heir. Yet, with Bakari, not only does his laugh sound genuine, but he also does not give up trying to elicit the same from me.

My question quiets the mood, and I'm not sure he'll answer, unsure if he'll hear it as an accusation even though it wasn't intended to be. I watch him consider what I've asked, and that's how I see the honesty in his eyes, in his whole expression as he forms his answer.

"So I can still live," he says.

Meryt lived through the building of a new life, Bakari chose humor, and I? I've numbed myself with grief.

"Breathe and you live," I counter.

Bakari shakes his head. "Breathing is being alive, laughter is *living*."

I stare at him and he meets my gaze openly. My lips work to form words, but I don't know what to say.

"But our families—"

"Loved each other, loved laughter, and loved living.

Not only tears honor and remember them."

Bakari's response unexpectedly eases the guilt pressing upon me, granting permission I wouldn't have accepted from anyone else. His choice let him keep living, mine robbed my life even as I lived it. I'd like to think his answer will one day allow me to rediscover life beyond grief and sorrow, beyond regret and reckoning.

I glance to the papyrus and clear my throat. "What's this for?"

"Maps," he answers. "Very detailed maps."

We spend the next several days drawing multiple maps of the palace. Every quarter of every floor gets its own sheet of papyrus, so we accumulate a tidy stack. As it turns out, some of the diagrams are already complete, including kitchen, physicians' quarters, barracks, and numerous storage rooms. The nameless others Bakari's hinted at have been at work, though I still only know of Rasidi and that mysterious voice in the embalmers' room.

"What are we looking for?" I press.

"Anything amiss, really."

"That isn't very specific, or helpful."

"Whoever did this is so far ahead, we're struggling to figure out where to begin."

"And that isn't very reassuring."

"It's what we have until we find a definitive clue, perhaps catching those lower on the power pyramid so we can know where to aim to catch those who are higher." He shuffles through the pages and hands me a few. "I'll take the barracks, stables, and royal docks. Places soldiers are commonplace. You take guest chambers, rooms of royal officials, and kitchen. Make sure no one sees you."

"Of course."

Bakari studies me and I shift self-consciously.

"What now?"

He frowns. "Too many people might recognize you as the maidservant of the most esteemed woman in the land."

I know what he means. Most servants are usually overlooked, but important servants are not always as fortunate, as we're seen as a path toward gaining higher favor.

"A disguise then," I suggest.

So my hair is cropped from shoulders to ears and the beautiful thick green kohl under my eyes is replaced with thinner lines from Bakari's less noticeable black.

"You'll have to switch your clothes," he says, pointing toward a pile of folded white clothing in a corner of the room. "And your *kyphi,* so no one has a chance of remembering you through your scent."

I search for a dress and immediately scrunch my face as I hold it up. The simplicity of the design doesn't bother me, but rather, "It's so rough."

"Lowborn servants don't wear fine materials. Or jewelry, for that matter."

I stare at him and he stares back expectantly. Finally, I discard my earrings, my jangle of bracelets, and my exquisitely beaded collar.

"You must learn how to walk like a lowborn," Bakari adds.

"What does that even mean?"

"Well, for one, listening without questioning."

My glare speaks well enough for me.

Bakari laughs. "That too. A lowborn keeps her eyes down, a lowborn is not curious, a lowborn shrinks from notice."

"Our fathers would never allow this."

"Well, they aren't here and this is what must be done."

"How can I hold on to them and squash their memories at the same time?"

"Life is a balance, is it not? It just depends on the day. Now, try to hunch your shoulders more."

I let out a low breath. "For Meryt," I remind myself.

****

Almost three years a servant at the palace, I know enough about guard rotations and the back passageways servants use to easily get in and out of most areas I'm familiar with. I begin to steadily comb through the rooms on the maps, reasserting what I've learned in my short time here; the eyes of a servant can see so much below the surface.

Quiet conversations tucked into hallway nooks as noblemen spin their webs beneath everyday workings of the palace. High-pitched giggles rising from risky moments and quietly locked doors. Individuals who wear one face before servants and another before faces at court.

Sneaking about a palace is so different from climbing, as I must slink around corners and stay close to the ground instead of rising toward an expansive sky. Unlike the safety afforded by trees or walls, I'm within most lines of sight, and there is no height advantage to keep me out of their reach.

I sneak into offices late at night, close the door, block the cracks and work by the light of a solitary lamp to sift through pages and pages of correspondence. I steal into rooms in daylight, during mealtimes, or when some grand visitor has come to court and everyone hurries to catch a first glimpse in the throne room. Some rooms take a few days because of the little time I manage to snatch for each one. Some could use a better look with more light, which isn't always possible.

Getting caught in the act is obviously dangerous. Even more, getting caught as an exceedingly rare and unlikely servant who knows how to read, never mind one that should be dead, brings enough terror with it that I choose care and caution over speed.

Most of what I find among the regular noblemen is of little use to us. Missives about taxes. Missives about crop yields. Missives about property disputes and other legalities that have nothing to do with Meryt.

In truth, I still don't really know what I'm searching for, and Bakari isn't much more help as the days pass.

"If it was poison," I point out after a few days scouring the kitchen during its few quiet hours in the depths of night, "wouldn't the murderer have disposed of the vial and any other evidence immediately? Someone so smart wouldn't be foolish enough to leave a recipe lying about."

"It probably won't be as easy as that," Bakari agrees, "but we can be sure that anyone who takes measures to remove the king's favored wife is planning something bigger. Hidden correspondence, secretly exchanged coin, suspicious alliances, anything to suggest the schemes go beyond gaining favor at court."

"And you expect me to find this in the kitchen?"

Bakari shrugs. "Even unlikely places must be checked, because whoever we're up against might be relying on us to overlook them. People pass through the kitchen all the time, so just watch for anyone with dark intentions."

I stare at him. "Almost the entire court qualifies."

Bakari rubs his hands together. "Then we're about to become some of the most knowledgeable and powerful people in Thebes."

"And what is a dead servant and a simple soldier supposed to do with such power?" I rejoin. "What good is knowing if no one else may know?"

He shrugs in reply. "One step at a time. Until then, we seek every secret and every hideaway. No corner, no stone, no grain of sand unexamined."

I'm pretty certain the king had no intention of murdering the woman carrying his long-awaited heir and even more sure that whoever regularly works the kitchen is far removed from these sorts of plots. Still, I will search them all. Even Meryt's rooms, which I know so well. Even as my throat thickens at seeing the neatly arranged crates, full of items containing Meryt's life, awaiting her burial with the completion of the tomb.

After I eliminate most of the least likely rooms, I turn my attention to the higher-ranking individuals, the vizier, the revered royal officers and scribes, well-respected nomarchs and their personal attendants and servants, dreading yet hoping to unearth some clue, any clue at all.

Chapter Twelve

Day 17

My hands are red, my back aches. Being a spirit in the palace is more draining than anticipated. I've been learning that even unoccupied rooms are their own kind of mystery. Secret chambers and hidden passageways wait to be found by those with the patience to seek them section by section. Thus, I was on hands and knees, feeling out the corner of an empty room this morning, when I was caught.

"What are you doing there, girl?" a harsh voice demanded.

I jumped, my mind frightened out of coherence. "A mouse!" I squeaked.

"So kill it and get over here. This bed won't set itself."

The words carried enough snap to get me moving, even though I wasn't trained to respond to them. The quiet rooms of just seconds before were suddenly bustling with activity, so much so I was swept along without anyone realizing I shouldn't have been there. Everything happened so quickly my heart barely had a chance to skip a beat.

Thus I spent the afternoon washing linens with slave girls. After, I was ordered to help prepare the rooms where I'd been found for a very important guest. I ducked my head and did as told, well, because I couldn't *not* do so. But I also kept my ears open.

"What happened to your hands?" Bakari asks the moment he sees me in our underground room later that night.

Of course, he laughs when I tell him, which I suppose is better than anger.

"At least it means I'm a convincing lowborn," I huff, defiance coloring my embarrassment at being caught.

"Only a fool would mistake you for a lowborn," Bakari mutters.

I glare at him. "Then what are we even playing at here?" I demand, gesturing at my altered appearance.

Bakari raises his hands in placating fashion. "You're right. Now, did the other girls speak to you? Did you learn anything from them?"

"Most stay focused on their work to avoid punishment. If you're asking after their gossip, no one is suspicious of Meryt's death."

"Nothing?"

I purse my lips. "They did not know her as we did."

Bakari nods. "What else?"

"Several court ladies are missing small pieces of jewelry which have already become unrecoverable."

Bakari chuckles. "Not much to report to my superiors."

I shrug, leaving him to decide what to do with the knowledge of palace servants and sticky fingers. "Exploration is limited when knee deep in water, scrubbing linens."

"Who was the room prepared for?"

I pause. "I—I didn't get a name. Every indication was toward someone important."

"Too early for the funeral celebrations, but a guest at the palace isn't unusual," Bakari muses to the painted stars. "Is it suspicious, or does timing create suspicion?"

"I'll find out what I can."

Bakari nods. "Without arousing suspicion yourself, of course."

"How do you relay what I find out? How do you claim to know it?"

Bakari gives me a look. "From a rare desert *zahur*."

I wave my hand at him. "No poetry, please!"

"It's the poetry of my heart!" Bakari protests.

"Sound it to the crocodiles! They won't interrupt."

Bakari laughs again. He moves toward the door, but stops at the threshold and looks back, expression serious. "You're certain no one recognized you?"

I nod. "The most likely to look twice would be servants of other officials or the others who served under Meryt, and they're—" My voice breaks as I think of Benerib and Madu in the embalming room.

That broken realization that I would not be joining them, the betrayal... Did Madu wonder why I hadn't appeared with them in the next life? Does Benerib see what I am about and understand what I had to do?

"Still, don't grow careless. The more eyes that see you, the greater the chance someone eventually recognizes you."

I don't even argue the point, not least because I'm certainly not interested in rubbing my hands raw again.

Chapter Thirteen

Day 18

I bolt upright early the next morning with a single distinct image of splayed tree limbs and rays of sun blinking between swaying leaves. Once it's appeared, I can see nothing but the path up a rough tree trunk and a view of the rustling Nile from above. My fingers itch to grasp and pull and even get scratched. I quickly clamber from my mat, knowing sleep will not return, barely pausing long enough to wrap my dress around me and cinch it closed with a simple belt. My toes curl in anticipation of pushing against crackling bark, and I have to command them to walk so I can make it to a tree at all. I don't bother with sandals.

I can't believe it took me so long to remember I can finally climb again, specifically without having to worry about provoking disapproving glances from others because "such behaviors are not for the palace." I very clearly remember the look Meryt gave me the first time we walked through one of the extensive palace gardens, that warning when she caught me wistfully glancing toward the upper boughs of a tamarisk bedecked with pink flowers.

"Not here, Zizi," Meryt whispered sharply. "Here both feet stay on the ground."

So it was that not only the open sea was taken from

me, but the soaring sky as well. Not anymore.

I attempt to excuse my oversight because I've been so mired in grief, then recovering from poison, then crawling through rooms, and yet... Climbing! I've missed it so.

I slip out of the palace and move away from the main grounds, keeping a sharp eye out for something close, densely covered, but not enough to block my view. I finally choose a lush acacia closer to the river but within sight of the palace. My body immediately remembers the motions, the roughness, the pulling, the balance, the reach. I quickly clamber up to a thick branch high enough to hide my feet. My arms ache from the neglected effort, but it feels good.

I settle onto the limb and cast my gaze across the ribbon of blue Nile, momentarily forgetting that I won't find unfurling sails set for the sea but only for the opposite shore. The shore which is home to the Valley of the Kings and the tombs encased in the mountainside beyond the docks. There, reaching higher than the tallest palm and spreading out farther than the widest sail, King Pa-Ankh-Entef's pyramid is being hastily completed for Meryt. I can already spot the movement of small dark forms along its sloped surface, no doubt a push to make significant progress before the midday sun heats the stones to a burn.

The docks are also awake, and long boats powered by oars unload the large white limestones dug from downriver quarries near the Nile delta. From there, they will be pushed and pulled and tugged up the ramps of the pyramid's triangular sides. The limestone will brighten the façade and the peak capped in gold to sparkle in the sunlight.

There's a great hurry to complete the tomb before the seventy days of Meryt's mummification are through. After which will be the Opening of the Mouth ceremony, with its festive parade, the crates we've packed, and so much more, all moving from Thebes to the Valley, from life unto death. Three sarcophagi for maidservants will be included in this bustle, but only two will be occupied.

A large boat suddenly cuts into view as it pulls alongside the royal docks, refocusing my attention. A flurry of activity ties the boat down, and as servants and oarsmen run about, a tall, princely-looking individual materializes from the hustle. He may have been on deck all along, but once I notice him, I barely see anything else.

The guest the palace is expecting?

He wears the same short white linen kilt as most other men, yet it shows differently against his skin, skin unmistakably darkened by long hours under the very sun which makes the sea glisten. His head is shaved, making visible a row of gold earrings on each ear glinting sharply in the light of the rising sun. He casts his dark eyes around him as if to say he sees all but is bothered by none, standing with command, assurance, and certainty. There is no mistaking this is a man who stands apart.

"A *kyky*!"

The short exclamation disrupts my attention again, and I glare down at the source.

Bakari smiles pleasantly and gestures for me to join him on the ground. I want to refuse, but he's holding up a slice of bread surely hot from the oven, as it's dribbling streaks of yellow honey. Plus, I'm curious about the new arrival and figure joining Bakari is the fastest way to find out more. A soldier at the palace surely has some knowledge of individuals who look like this one.

"How did you find me?" I ask at the bottom of the tree.

"I didn't," Bakari replies. "We were at morning exercises when a fellow soldier claimed he spotted a monkey."

"What did you say when he called you that?"

"That you're being reckless if you're once more so easily found. Besides, don't you have something to be investigating?"

"I'm watching the water," I reply, then gesture in the direction of the docks. "Which is how I spotted the new arrival."

Bakari follows my gaze to the boat that's presently being unloaded. I watch as someone approaches the regal man on deck and offers him some stick I can't make out clearly. The man shakes his head and the person backs away. He takes a step toward the railing, and even from this distance I can tell it's uneven. A limp. I know when Bakari spots the man, because something shifts in his expression.

"Commander Kemnebi," he whispers.

"Who?"

Bakari shifts his gaze to me. "The black panther of the king's navy, recently wounded in service and possibly coming to the palace for recovery."

"Hasn't he anywhere else to go?"

Bakari gives me a strange expression, as if wondering how I could be so ignorant of what every soldier knows. "He's a cousin of Queen Sekhmet through their mothers. The queen must have invited him to recuperate here."

"He's part Nubian?" I blurt out.

Perhaps I shouldn't be so surprised, considering the connections and exceptions being related to the queen must provide. And yet, our muddled past with our southern neighbor is enough to cause most citizens to think twice before eagerly embracing anyone from Nubia, even if they are the source for much of our gold and the methods used to train our archers.

"You don't like Nubians?" he asks. "We aren't at war with them."

"Not today anyway."

If anything, growing up in a port city means being around all types of people from all types of places. Even sheltered as we may have been on our little islet, it was impossible not to meet the many faces of the world. Still, almost every Egyptian holds an inherent distrust of Nubia, and we only embrace our queen because part of her is still Egyptian. We hope the other part will help keep trade open and war at bay. King Pa-Ankh-Entef has so far proven to be a peaceful monarch, but that doesn't mean we freely trust Nubia's king.

"I just didn't expect he'd reach so high a position in *our army*."

Bakari doesn't disagree. "Kemnebi is very skilled and much loved by many."

I tilt my head at the tone of his voice. "Not by you?"

Bakari shrugs. "We're different types," he says vaguely.

I look from one soldier to the other, noting the same wide-shouldered stance, the same grace and strength of movement, the same confident manner. I doubt it. More likely Bakari harbors an inherent distrust of Nubia too, which doesn't help to distill mine.

"The 'injury' may not be suspicious, but the timing

could be. Seems like someone we should keep an eye on," I remark.

"You and everyone else," Bakari mutters.

I shake my head at him. "You don't want me to spy on people anymore?" I ask innocently.

That stops him, and for the first time I see him hesitate to respond. I offer a triumphant grin, take my breakfast, and turn to sneak back into the palace.

Chapter Fourteen

Day 19

I aim to finish the last of the guestrooms set aside for visiting noblemen today, because, despite some sense in Bakari's logic, I think unoccupied rooms a waste of time. I've discovered a few back passageways from here to there, useful to know, but not of particular note.

I make quick work of three empty guestrooms, moving with little caution because the lack of occupancy means there's no one else about in this area of the palace. I enter the fourth room, expecting the same décor, the same furnishings, the same emptiness and quiet as the others.

Then I hear the low murmur of voices. There are no personal items about, but this room is certainly not empty. I press against the wall and slither toward the sound.

"—found out?" the first voice asks.

"All will resolve in time," a calmer voice replies.

I can barely make out what the first voice says next, so I tiptoe even closer to the door.

"—without a doubt, and the king will listen," the second voice says with conviction.

I frown. The voice sounds familiar, a lost echo from a room with silenced occupants and a hazy mind. Even the faint memory of it encourages secrecy, and I struggle to recall the details of something I'm sure was recent.

I shake my head at myself, clearing the haze. The voice is similar, but different.

Before I can puzzle out any more, the door bursts open, leaving me without option to hide. I'm nearly frightened to the death I've only just escaped. I stare at the chest of the man who caught me.

"A spy!" the second voice cries.

I glance up and take a step back in shock. I know this man! Bakenranef, nomarch of Egypt's seventh nome, which includes some very important trading ports. Ports like Thonis.

His eyes blaze in anger. He roughly grabs my arm and drags me into the room he'd been exiting. He throws me to the ground and I barely manage to keep from breaking my face against the stone floor with quickly outstretched hands. My shoulders jolt painfully and air *whooshes* from my lungs as my wrists catch the brunt of the fall.

"What do you say to that?" Bakenranef accuses. "You still assert no one suspects us?"

Instead of replying, someone, presumably the owner of the first voice, kneels in front of me. I stare at his knees but don't look at him until he drops his head into view.

"Hello, Zizi." Bakari grins.

The crashing of emotions threatens to topple me, and I grab his shoulders to steady myself, so hard I almost knock him back. As usual, he laughs.

As usual, I recover enough to glare at him in return. "You could have told me!"

Bakari shrugs. "I'm only permitted to reveal names when instructed."

"You know her?" Bakenranef cuts in.

"You know her too," the soldier replies.

Bakenranef's head dips into my line of sight and he searches my face for familiarity.

"You dined in my home on a few occasions, your honor," I tell him.

His face lights up, then quickly falls into confusion. "The Phoenician's daughter?"

I nod.

"You had a sister?"

"Two."

Quiet. "The king's wife was your cousin."

"She was."

He turns to Bakari. "*Chibale*, when you promised to find someone we could trust, I didn't mean...I didn't think...What has been done?"

"Is there anyone better?" Bakari questions. "We three were of the Blessed, after all."

Bakenranef doesn't react to the slight sarcasm undercutting his comment, doesn't contradict that being a survivor of Thonis is a dubious blessing because of the burden we carry.

The nomarch looks back to me. "So you did not follow Lady Tadinanefer-Hatshepsut to the afterlife."

"Bakari persuaded me to believe I could better serve her here."

Our nomarch sighs deeply. "I should be furious with you. This—this is too much."

"Yet you are not as angry as you should be," Bakari interjects evenly, "because you understand why it needed to be done."

Bakenranef doesn't reply at first, and the heaviness of whatever it is he's gotten us all into is apparent in the new droop of his shoulders. Finally, he nods sadly. "The lady's death is neither the beginning nor end of whatever dark storm approaches."

"*Approaches*?" I sputter.

"The murder of the king's wife is only one piece of a larger picture," Bakenranef explains. "We suspect her death is connected to the disappearance of Thonis itself."

I furrow my brow. "We felt the ground shake, we saw the rise of a giant wave, even far out as we were!"

Bakenranef nods grimly. "An earthquake took Thonis from us, that is sure, but where did it come from? Was it truly the will of a vengeful deity? Or, perhaps, did someone create it?"

"How can any man cause the very earth to quake?" I question.

"We've been working to solve that for over a year now," Bakenranef says. "The disappearance of Thonis was too neat. No force of nature destroys so thoroughly, without leaving any evidence behind."

I stare at my nomarch, struggling to understand, even plain as his words are.

"And Meryt?"

"All tied together. Perhaps whoever it was knew about her visit to Thonis and hoped to strike her there."

"We left a day early," I say dumbly. "The entire city was taken and we survived."

"Which could be why the assassin only now completed what was started over a year ago," Bakari remarks.

I shake my head. It's too much. Just too much.

A hand at my elbow brings me to my feet and leads me to a chair. I sink in and bring my head to my hands, memory reeling with images and sounds and bits of a lost and shattered city.

Our last visit to Thonis, Bakari had joined us, taking advantage of our trip to use a few days' leave. The visit had been a good one. The people had turned out in full to celebrate the daughter of Thonis who'd become so beloved of the king.

In her role of the king's wife, Meryt went with our families to the grand temple for Amun and Khonsov and paid tribute at the statue of Hapy. Unlike our more skeptical fathers, Meryt had made a real effort to learn the names and domains of each Egyptian deity, convinced it was part of her position to do so.

"Fish have no need of precious metals," Father muttered beside me as Meryt cast a sacrifice of gold bracelets into the sea. "Unless to choke."

I barely managed to hide my laugh in a cough, which only made the confused sound louder amidst all the formality.

"Zizi!" Meryt hissed in warning.

Chastised, I quickly sobered up, but a glance at Father revealed no attempt to hide his mischievous smirk. I couldn't help but grin back.

On the second night, Meryt suggested we sneak out to see our families.

"It will bring less attention than if we sailed over on an official visit," she explained, although sneaking out for Meryt meant something entirely different now that she was the king's favored wife.

"Lady Tadinanefer-Hatshepsut, you cannot go alone," the captain of the guard cautioned, respectfully blocking her way.

Meryt laughed, disbelieving. "I'm only going home. Where else is safer?"

The captain shook his head. "You cannot go alone."

"My maid Azizi accompanies me," she said, "as does the celebrated Bomani-Bakari. Both know Thonis and her people well."

At that, the captain agreed to let us pass. We climbed aboard a small papyrus skiff to cross the canals to home, giggling as we imitated the captain's seriousness. With both feet ashore on our islet, Meryt elbowed me and nodded to the water behind us, where another small skiff bobbed in the water. I didn't need to look hard to see four more soldiers inside, evidence the captain was not to be deterred from his task of protecting the king's wife.

We landed at home in time for a grand dinner, the tight-knit group of our eight islet families sharing a meal outdoors in the sea-swept air. They greeted us jovially and welcomed us to a feast of roasted lamb and leek and onion and fine beer.

"Meet your nephew!" was the first thing Unika said to me, thrusting her two-month-old baby into my arms.

Pudgy fists reached out and startled me.

"He doesn't bite." Hamadi laughed. "Yet."

"I know!" I protested.

As my sister Kebi was only two years younger than me, it had been quite a while since we'd had a baby in the house, so I only knew so much. Kebi was nearly old enough then to be teased about suitors and having children of her own.

"Let me see him!" Meryt exclaimed when she saw the baby.

She whisked him out my arms and there was no mistaking the look on her face as she cradled him close, the desire and prayer clear that it wouldn't be long before she too had a child.

We stayed out late that night, eating, drinking,

trading stories with family and friends as the dark sea reassuringly lapped against our islet shore. And, when the fires had died low and most others had gone to bed, we lay on our backs to behold the dancing stars, seeing the promise of our future in their merrily winking lights.

It was an exceptional night, seared so finely into memory it could not be overwritten by what came after.

We embraced our families and said our farewells without sadness, rejuvenated by our visit, certain we would see each other again, and soon. I'd like to think they drowned with lingering joy in their hearts, at the very least. Whatever that may be worth.

I don't remember now why we left Thonis earlier than planned, as we'd been in no rush to return to the palace. It could have been a royal summons or more likely some whimsy of Meryt's, prone as she'd been to such things. I don't know that it even matters anymore, because whatever it was saved us. No matter the cause, none of us left with any sense of regret in our hearts. That would come later.

Nothing had seemed amiss as the king's wife and her entourage sailed away from the islets, flowers tossed by locals bobbing in the sea beside us on our way toward the Nile. There was a lingering moment when Meryt, Bakari, and I stood near the railing and watched our home grow smaller, but we quickly fell back into our royal roles, Bakari with the other guards, me a step behind Meryt, and Meryt to wherever her fancy took her.

We sailed back up the Nile, following its path south to Thebes. Father had once told me that in other countries "upriver" usually meant traveling north, which, being opposite, was a bit difficult to envision and something I'd always wanted to see. I remember thinking of that then, of wanting to sail down the Nile and back into the sea, to see the places Father had always spoken of. To find the heritage he'd held onto and given to us.

We'd barely sailed out of the delta, still a day at least from the dock at Memphis, when we felt it.

A low rumbling which rocked the boat and grew more worrisome as it persisted.

Then increased.

A sound unlike any heard before upon the earth screeched through the air, the tearing open of an abyss in the moments before it's sealed and silenced forever.

A great shadow reached out of the sky, and we turned as one to catch sight of a giant wave arching into the air from the sea well behind us. It crashed down out of sight, and though we did not see it land, we knew it had been uncomfortably close to Thonis. A great growl raced from the sea up the Nile River, reverberating deep through our *metr* and down to our toes. The royal boat rocked unevenly over the jerky waves rippling from its wake.

Then, suddenly, all was still.

We stared at each other, unable to grasp what we'd just experienced. Then Bakari was shouting orders to the oarsmen and guards, ordering them to get the king's wife to safety. I caught his arm when he already had one foot over the side of the boat.

"Where are you going?" I demanded.

"Back."

"I'm coming."

The words came without thought, but there was no other way. The moment that wave disappeared from view, I'd felt a terrible weight crashing down on my heart, breath becoming harder to catch. If he was going to Thonis, so was I.

"We don't know what's there," Bakari tried to protest. "Stay with Meryt."

"Two row faster than one."

"Your duty is with Meryt."

"So is yours!"

He didn't like it, but he didn't argue more. There was no time and no further logic that would not implicate him as well.

"At least tell her," he said, turning to lower a small, swift papyrus boat into the water.

I ran to Meryt's side. "Bakari is going to Thonis," I told her in a rush. "So am I."

Meryt shook her head, wishing me to stay with her.

"I have to see," I insisted. "I have to help."

She pursed her lips and nodded, though, really, everything had happened too quickly. The wave, the crashing, the rush to leave the boat. And the sudden pressing need to get the king's wife far away from whatever assault had just launched from the sea.

Bakari and I slipped away just as all men took up their oars to row as fast as possible to Memphis, even straight to Thebes.

I don't know how long it took us. I don't even remember if my muscles burned or my hands blistered. I only know that a lot of time passed swiftly in our fear for what we might find. For the fright and the fears and the possibly broken and wounded.

Except we found nothing.

Nothing at all.

Every port, every ship, every home, every soul had disappeared.

There weren't even bones or skeletons, amphoras or

crates, flotsam or driftwood, severed masts or lonely lumps of land to mark what had stood there. Not a broken wall, not a palm, not a waterlogged sail to prove something had been there at all.

The sea was empty where Thonis once stood. Silent and vast and glittering. As if our islands had never been.

Bakari dropped his oar and dove into the water. I followed right after him, scrambling for the seabed, only to find unhelpful pieces of broken stone and bits of clay pots. The bottom half of a wall. Partial steps leading to a building that had disappeared.

Just as we'd rowed, we dove, unaware of all reason and time as we frantically searched the waves for any hint of the life that had once thrived above it. Even the nightmare of drowned and bloated bodies would have been better than the absence we found instead. Like this, there was nothing to mourn, nothing to hold onto, nothing to acknowledge what had been taken so suddenly and completely.

It was only after the sun fell beneath the horizon that we collapsed back into the boat and somehow aimed for the mouth of the Nile. We didn't make it very far. We lost the last bits of light bobbing in silence before clumsily rowing for any shore, and stumbling in exhaustion once we'd reached what was now the end of the Mediterranean. The new gateway to Egypt.

Other boats had drifted out of the Nile, other men and women searching the empty sea for survivors.

"How can there be nothing?" I asked Bakari.

"I don't know."

The very notion was too big to grasp, and the lack of any remains made it even harder. More than anger or sadness or grief, which would all come in their time, was the shock, the numbness, the inability to form full thought because there was nothing to wrap the mind around.

Thonis was gone.

An entire city and way of life, a past, present, and future, just gone.

It felt unreal in its absoluteness. It rang loudly in our heads despite its silence.

We slept fitfully on the shore that night, then spent the next morning in fruitless search once more. There wasn't even a where or a what to search for anymore, but we dove anyway. We were convinced we merely needed more time to find something, a clue as to what had occurred, even as we saw without doubt there was nothing there.

Finally, by afternoon, we painfully began to make our way back to Meryt. It took us longer than it should have because of how hard we'd driven our bodies and, even more, because of the new weight we bore. Unwilling to leave, unwilling to stay, knowing we had to tell of what no longer was.

When we finally caught up to Meryt at Memphis, we told her what we could. For some time, we leaned on each other and cried for what we'd lost. Then Meryt tucked away her grief and gathered herself together.

"No more tears," she ordered. "A king's wife gives strength through showing it."

So I dutifully dried my tears, before her at least.

King Pa-Ankh-Entef was beside himself by the time we returned. Unable to act, unable to save so many of his people, and left without clue or kingdom to blame. And, aside from all the trade disrupted when such a busy port city disappeared, his beloved wife had almost been swallowed up as well. In time, Meryt's calm helped him find his, but this was one part of her that he would never know the full truth of. Meryt had chosen fortitude forged by grief because she couldn't live otherwise.

Some claimed the disappearance of Thonis was the act of a vengeful deity, while others shied away from such harsh expressions. Either way, our great king had been powerless to stop it and there wasn't even a strip of bark left to investigate what had been. Priests across temples declared that her name should be forgotten, that the name of Thonis should remain unspoken so the gods would not recall her curse and revisit it upon another. Whispers would soon emerge that we three had been blessed, protected by powerful deities of the palace to survive the curse of Thonis. As the months passed, most were relieved to move on and forget the tragedy of the once proud gateway to Egypt, but we did not.

From that day, whenever we would pass Bakari in the corridors of the palace, a shared look passed between us. An agreement, that, whatever anyone else said, we would sound the names of Thonis and give shape to their memories. We would tell of what once had been.

Who else would if we did not?

There was no one left to speak.

Chapter Fifteen

Day 22

The next three days pass in a blur. I can only retrace steps, unable to think beyond the possibility that all the sorrow inflicted upon our short lives may have been caused by someone we've been living with in this very palace. Someone we laughed with, shared drink with, danced with. Someone who watches now, satisfied a life has been taken, a job complete. And it's not just Meryt and the child she carried who've been stolen, but also the years yet ahead of Benerib and Madu. They shouldn't have had to die.

Their lives were also taken by someone I've walked past or greeted or know by face. The connection to Thonis means we were all doomed for early death, and the narrow escapes coupled with the helplessness makes it ever harder to bear. I cannot fathom that one, or even a few, are responsible for the end of so many. The thought is as ungraspable as the vast emptiness Thonis left behind.

I watch other servants blankly from behind columns and in the shadowed safety of forgotten corners, the rhythmic workings of the kitchens, the silent scurrying of noble staff, the rigidity of the guards in the hallways. I suppose I should feel a tug of something significant watching a part of my former life continue without me, the purposefulness of each task speaking to something I no longer have. Even the cattle are more certain of themselves than I as they low from pasture and stalls.

In our rooms, I was always first to rise and last to sleep, the one to wake Meryt, the one to help her dress, the one to open her chosen jar of *kyphi* and fan the scent into the air so she could walk through and perfume herself. Without that, my days are mere ramblings. I've become a boat adrift without a new course to avoid being lost at sea.

I wind aimlessly around the painted palace pillars, absently itching as I adjust to the feel of my lowborn dress, seeking answers from the brightly colored hieroglyphs, even of the deities my father never believed in. I'd take direction from almost anyone now, even Rasidi. Well, almost.

I spend most of the second day in a cluster of reeds along the Nile, staring morosely across the shore toward the pyramid reaching into the sky. I think of the room they're preparing for Meryt there and shiver in the warm sun.

When I catch myself, I admit to acting somewhat ridiculous. Yet I can't tear myself away or force myself back into a palace that should've been a home to me. This new information, the thread tying the sinking of Thonis to the murder of Meryt, should light a fire within me, a vengeful burning to tear apart every inch of palace until we discover who's responsible for this. Instead, it's a weight dragging me to the depths, another way to fill my lungs so I can hardly gasp for breath.

I'm in Meryt's rooms for most of the third day, grappling with the truth of our situation. The space is bare aside from the crates of clothing and keepsakes and furniture ready to join her once the pyramid is complete. Everything seems just as I left it, and, knowing how careful we were, I'm sure I'd spot anything out of order. Whatever we didn't choose to keep has already been whisked away, taking stray moments and snatches of memories with.

I sit for hours on the cold stone floor, body unconsciously rocking to an unfelt swell as these new waves crash over and over around me. What can I really do here for Meryt? What can I hope to find? How am I, or any of us, supposed to face down the silent destroyer who murdered a king's beloved wife and made an entire city disappear?

By nightfall, I'm staring moodily at the rendering of our Thonis islet in the cool storage room. Which is, of course, where and how Bakari finds me.

The muffled slap of his sandaled feet announce his entrance, and he doesn't speak as he settles on the ground beside me. His hands and face are clean, but a layer of sand dusts his shoulders and torso. He must have been riding today.

"Remember when Unika made Hamadi prove himself before she would agree to marry him?" he suddenly asks.

The memory immediately leaps to life, and an unexpected smile tugs at my lips. "He near wrestled half the sailors at port. As if there was any question they would marry." I glance at the soldier. "He wrestled you too. To defeat."

Bakari tries to hide his grin under mock soberness. "I let him win. For his heart's love."

"Ever the romantic. Do tell, soldier, how many of the girls subjected to your poetry do you claim to wrestle for?"

"Soldiers wrestle often in their training," he says innocently.

I roll my eyes at him and his evasive response. "At least Hamadi achieved what he set out to do, unlike your attempts to train a monkey as your personal servant."

Bakari laughs. "How can you remember that?"

"How could I forget?" I counter. "It terrorized the entire islet. Besides, I'm not that much younger than you."

Bakari's smile widens, entirely pleased with his past antics. "You spent much more time in trees than—"

"How better to see what all the older kids were up to?"

Bakari bumps me with his shoulder and his amusement deepens. "A spy even then!" he crows.

"I was climbing. If I happened to see things, then so be it."

"That monkey was quite fond of you," Bakari remembers. "Joined you quite a bit. We called you the two kykys."

The reference to my islet's nickname for me should bring some sort of sadness, but the moment is too warm to allow for much moroseness. From then, everyone but Mother called me Kyky whenever they caught sight of me climbing trees around the islet. Then, I couldn't look at a tree without thinking of how to climb up, of how the view would stretch out from above. My fingers would itch to reach up, up, up to an untouchable cobalt sky, to settle on a lush limb and take in every sight such heights afforded. And it was true, when Bakari's ill-trained monkey scampered up the trunk after me, the others would tease about the two kyky friends in the tree. At least it wasn't much bother when it joined me up there.

"Better in the tree with me than chasing the temple's cats all over the island," I say.

"Or nipping Mother's sacred ibis."

"Your mother could handle anything *except* something touching that bird. We had a bet she'd skin you after you tried to dye its feathers."

"The color washed off easily. Though I truly thought red would go nicely with its natural black tips."

"To think after all the tricks you pulled, it was the monkey that got you sent off the island."

Bakari chuckles, and there's something about the sound, something about the memories we recall that makes the weight over my heart seem just a little bit lighter. When he first sat down, I expected him to launch into another unwanted plea as to why we must live for Meryt, but these moments from the past are much more effective persuasion. These lost moments remind me of living.

For the first time, perhaps, I'm beginning to understand why so many are drawn to Bomani-Bakari, despite his teasing and mischief. There is much to be said about someone who makes others laugh, who knows how to find a way to lighten a burden instead of increasing it. Although that doesn't entirely dispel the fact that he's dragged me into all this against my will.

"I sold the monkey to a sailor on an outgoing ship."

"And took yourself to the palace."

Bakari nods. "What a life that was."

"Do you regret it?"

Bakari shifts beside me, a motion that would rock the painted boat we're sitting in had it been real.

"Mother didn't offer many choices, and I only

picked soldiering because it seemed a less terrible life than others. When Meryt married the king and brought you along…well, it made it easier, because enough of my past had returned to me. I felt I'd even made a good choice."

"Thonis come to Thebes," I muse.

"It proved home was not so far away," he adds. "That others knew what it was to leave our quiet home and start a new life in the palace."

"Although," I point out, "you seem rather comfortable here."

"I've made a place for myself," Bakari says simply. "And I took to horses much better than expected."

"You jeopardize it all by being involved in this. If I'm here, then step back. Return to the security of a life you don't have to risk."

Bakari shifts again so he can look at me directly. "It's worth it, for Meryt, our families, Thonis, and the world that was taken from us. I risk it all and would do so again to find the peace they weren't given."

"Is finding the answer the way to find peace?" I ask quietly. "Even though it cannot undo what's already done?"

"And yet it must be done," he says, determined.

And there it is. Beneath the reassurances and the laughter and the teasing is a flicker of the fierceness that burns deep within Bakari. I lean into the warmth of it, hoping and praying it will be strong enough to rekindle the fire that once burned inside me.

Chapter Sixteen

Day 23

My conversation with Bakari remains vivid in my mind this morning, so for the first time in a long, long while, I sneak over to the training grounds and watch the soldiers at their work.

It's early enough that I'm sure Bakari must still be here, before he's off to get his horses from the stable or whatever else he may be up to, but it takes a few minutes to spot him. When I do, I can't believe I ever missed him. And not just because there are small knots of maidservants fawning over him all about the second-floor side balcony overlooking the barracks' training fields.

A square outline of soldiers frames a dusty pair of wrestlers. The dirt covering the chest and arms and kilts of many of the others makes clear they've been trading partners. A quick glance around the balcony tells me I've managed to come at a rather popular time. I should duck away now instead of hanging around where there are so many people, but seeing Bakari, sweat cutting narrow streams through the dust coating him, grinning wickedly at his opponent, makes me take a step forward instead.

Bakari soon has me admitting he may not have been exaggerating when he claimed he let Hamadi beat him. I'm still certain Hamadi did win on his own, as the two spent much of their younger years wrestling and racing and competing against each other. Unless, of course, someone else came along, then it was Bakari and Hamadi against everyone else. My brother-in-law was a great wrestler, he was quiet and efficient in his movements, but there was also a certain finesse about the way he twisted and held that drew eyes to him. He was certainly someone worth watching.

Bakari moves differently. He's agile but often relies on raw strength. Every once in a while, a deep chuckle rumbles from deep in his chest. Even if he's caught in a headlock. It's a moment when I suddenly understand why he relies so much on humor to live, because beyond his sand-powdered grins and grunts of pain he revels in the aliveness of each movement, revels in living the length and width and breadth of each moment as if it may be his last. To him, joy is an expression of gratitude for each day he's given. I'm now certain this is what draws so many eyes to him, not just a twinkle of the eye or a mysterious smile from a handsome face, but his genuine, infectious celebration of life.

It's not something I noticed or thought much about until now, hidden in the shadows of a balcony at a time I'm supposed to be dead.

I force my eyes away from the action to consider the others watching the soldiers wrestle. Most of the onlookers are men, many leaning against the railing as they discuss form and skill and wager on the winner of each match. Some women stand with them, moving in for a closer look of whatever, or whomever, has caught their interest below. Servants lazily fan their masters with wide palm fronds, while others stretch their gazes as best they can from the spots they're relegated to.

I study them carefully, wondering if any could be plotting and scheming or if the gathering of each group is as innocent as it seems. Even with the betting, there's an easy air about the spectacle, and where two heads bend close in discussion, they do not flinch if a third or fourth joins them. No scraps of papyrus or small sacks of coins secretly change hands. From what I can see, all is decidedly mundane. Still, I stay a little longer, searching for something definitive.

I spot Kemnebi easily, lounging with assured confidence against the railing as he entertains what appears to be a small group of admirers. The difference between him and others is so stark and obvious, I wonder if they're conscious of it as they stand with him.

He doesn't quite have the power of a king, but something about him beckons others to him, a strength that offers the confidence he so carelessly wears. Although I've caught brief glimpses of him walking about the palace with a limp that only he can turn dignified, this is my first chance to really watch him closely, to watch the way others listen to what he has to say and how they seek his approval when they speak.

Bakari was right to question that I didn't immediately recognize his name, but I'm finally beginning to piece together snippets of stories and praise sung about him over the years. Everyone he encounters treats him like an honored friend. A man with such esteem would certainly have his ways, and eager helpers, for making all manner of things come about with no one the wiser.

Which only reraises the question of his non-battle-earned injury and the timing of his arrival at the palace.

A woman just beyond him snags my gaze, one who

seems part of the group and yet above them all, including Kemnebi. She wears the same white linen dress as most other Egyptian woman, but her neck collar is expensively made, studded with enough jewels and sparkling gems to be noticeable from a distance. She stands with one hand on the rail, but doesn't lean against it, as if she supports it and not the other way around. She holds her head high, giving the air of one who could easily balance an overflowing basket of grapes. Her servants hover behind her, ready to spring forward at the slightest gesture.

I'm so caught up in seeing her again, I miss my chance to duck as she turns her head toward me. I tell myself there's no way to be certain she's looking at me, though her gaze is certainly fixed in my direction. A gaze that would most likely know me on sight from the countless times she's seen and addressed me as Meryt's foremost attendant.

Queen Sekhmet.

Kind as she was to Meryt, even she cannot know I'm still alive.

A roar from the crowd and burst of applause mercifully divert her attention.

I scurry quickly from the balcony, not risking confirmation if Bomani-Bakari is the winner they're cheering for.

Chapter Seventeen

Day 24

I finally find something as I'm poking around the room of a lesser court official.

Of course, I hurry out with it and wait anxiously for Bakari in our underground room. When he doesn't immediately appear, I go looking for him. I'm already well on my way toward the training area when I stop in my tracks to think he wasn't in the room because it's still the middle of the day. And I've been walking as though I have nothing to hide. But I must show him what I found.

I duck my head and scurry forward, chastising myself for negligence and willing my legs to go faster in the direction I'm headed. Tracing and retracing my steps will only arouse more suspicion. I flit along the outer ring of the balcony overlooking the training area, listening in to the conversations of observers. Eventually I learn the charioteers are training in the large arena, so I wend my way to the stables and await Bakari's return in the low limbs of a nearby tree.

He arrives in a small cluster of fellow charioteers, strapping young men brimming with force and potential, the pride of our kingdom, chatting and laughing as if "normal" still exists and papyrus isn't burning a hole in my pocket. I shift nervously, hurrying them along in my mind so I can show Bakari what I've found.

Unable to wait any longer, I slip from the tree and flatten against the outside of the stables. Rounding the corner toward the main entrance, I stumble and kick the doors low. A deep thud resounds and I freeze with held breath, certain I'm about to be caught. Again.

But the noise must not be suspicious inside, because there's no pause from the group. I exhale in relief. Making myself as small as can be, I slowly peer inside. From what I can see, most of the charioteers have handed off their horses to stableboys or taken them to their stalls themselves. Mouselike, I dart from wall to wall, keeping low and only popping up long enough to check for Bakari.

When I find him, I quickly slip into the stall and almost collide with a horse's nose. A small yelp escapes me and in the next instant I'm pressed firmly against the wall by a very powerful grip.

Bakari eases up once he sees the person he's caught. "You scared us, Azizi!" he whispers harshly.

I raise an eyebrow at the use of "us," especially as the horse seems just fine. The animal is beautiful with its dark brown coat and white mane. I don't know much about horses, few as there were on our Thonis islet, but this one appears powerful and dignified.

Bakari turns back to the horse and pets its neck in long strokes. "Just a wild little kyky. Nothing to be afraid of."

He continues soothing the horse, completely ignoring me.

"I found something," I blurt out, interrupting him.

That gets his attention. He forces nonchalance as he peers out from the stall, then gestures for me to press farther into the wall and farther out of sight of anyone still here. I suck in my breath as I tuck into a corner of the stall. Now that my mind is finally catching up to my body, I'm terrified to be stuck in a tiny box with such a massive beast. The foolishness of seeking out Bakari instead of waiting is also finally gaining upon me.

I watch Bakari with the horse, watch his easy movements as he brushes it down and barely reacts when the horse's nose leans into him. It's strange to see him like this, to see him so engaged with an animal of the land instead of a ship at sea. When did he change?

"All right," he soon says in a manner as if he's still talking to his horse, "what is it?"

I pull out the papyri I found in the official's room and hold them up for Bakari. He grabs a quick glance, then methodically works his way over to me. As soon as he's closer, he lowers the brush long enough to study the pages.

His brow furrows as he scans them, working through the sporadic, oddly placed sequences of numbers that had caught my attention. The second sheet has lines of script, but there are holes cut through what must be missing information.

"I think it's some kind of code."

He grunts but doesn't immediately answer. Then his brow clears and he looks at me.

"Azizi, you may have just uncovered a smuggling ring right here in the palace."

"What?"

"This is surely something worth discovering, but it's not the secret we're looking for."

"But—"

"Look at how these columns line up," he continues,

overlapping the sheets of papyrus as I hold them so the text aligns with the numbers. "You've seen this sort of accounting thousands of times."

As soon as he shows me, I know exactly what I see, the familiar ledger of a merchant tracking wares as natural as the trees and sky and water. I sigh heavily and slump against the wall, feeling even more the fool for having been so reckless over something so obvious.

"Once more, there is nothing."

Bakari shakes his head. "This may not help in finding our answers, but it may help if we need a favor from the official running this. Even more, it proves that you're finding things meant to remain hidden. So keep digging."

I nod wearily, only relatively encouraged by his perspective.

"Though you'll have to put this back exactly as you found it, so we don't arouse suspicion."

I grumble incoherently as I snatch away the papyri. Bakari grins and goes back to sweet-talking his horse about the antics of wild monkeys.

Chapter Eighteen

Day 25

Fourteen days have passed from when I was supposed to be in the afterlife. Fourteen days since my organs were supposed to be removed and my body salted for mummification, readied for burial alongside Meryt. It's almost a month from Meryt's murder, and we're no closer to finding out who or why than on the day I didn't drink poison.

Most of the notable things we've uncovered are not useful to us at present, though Bakenranef is keeping a list he'll surely wield for his own gain. Otherwise, we affirm no clues are to be found in the boiling pots of water where palace linen is washed. The kitchen, stables, barracks, and training grounds are innocent of murder as well. Which means the clues, if any linger, are hidden deep within the minds or rooms of the ones directly responsible for everything.

I'm despondent the whole morning, thinking of the progress that isn't. By early afternoon, I'm getting fed up with my self-pity and force myself to take a bold step. Enough wasting time with officials not powerful enough to be more than tools or small parts. It's time to focus on finding who's at the top of the pyramid. So I ignore my pounding heart and decide to sneak into the rooms of the second most powerful man in Egypt.

Vizier Omari is away for several days on a trip to the trade city of Kom Ombo near the Nubian border, so I take the chance I've been granted to finally see what he has to hide. I don't believe Vizier Omari has much to gain in drowning Thonis and poisoning Meryt, but the feat of the unbelievable reminds me everyone is suspect. I try to think of every possible motive the vizier could have for damaging the trade of the country he oversees on behalf of the king. He could be angling for increased control through "discovering" a new shipping route or a new niece to marry to the king.

Perhaps he has a "medicine" woman at the temple who must be proven powerful to prepare for a future made-up prophecy. That would explain poisoning Meryt, but not drowning Thonis. Meryt was a life taken once; Thonis was life stolen thousands of times over. I pray this means the two tragedies are not connected after all, but I have nothing stronger to base this on than flimsy, naïve hope.

The vizier could be a Nubian spy, but I quickly push that thought aside. As Bakari pointed out, the queen is Nubian and we're not at war with them now. Besides, I'm pretty certain Vizier Omari descends from one of the oldest Egyptian families, one which only allows marriage to one of pure Egyptian blood. If he harbors hatred for outsiders, the queen would be in his line of sight before Meryt.

Even though neither option rings wholly true, there's no denying the vizier is one of very few persons with the resources and position to do away with a king's wife.

I'm so intently focused on entering his rooms without notice that my head hurts by the time I reach them, my vision narrowing so I only see the door his servants would use. Perhaps I could easily excuse away entering the rooms of a smaller noble or guest with the claims that I'm a new servant who's gotten lost, but the same cannot be said for Vizier Omari's rooms. Everyone who enters is accounted for, everyone knows who resides here. He'll certainly have left some of his retinue behind, but half are easier to evade than all. I shield myself with a great bunch of long flowering white mignonettes, as though I've been tasked with replenishing the fresh scents and flowers of each room in the area.

The stones are cool and grounding beneath my bare feet as I quietly pad down the corridors colored with large floor-to-ceiling paintings. Many include the most powerful of Egyptian deities, and, though Father has cultivated a healthy skepticism toward them within me, I still can't say for certain that green-skinned Osiris or cat-headed Bastet or ibis-depicted Thoth or the falcon-like *wedjat* eye aren't watching me as I sidle and slither closer and closer to my destination.

I imagine their gazes are disapproving not only because I'm sneaking around the Great Palace of Thebes but also because I'm clearly not where I'm supposed to be. I shrink into myself, becoming even smaller as I slink past the imposing figures. I finally reach the vizier's rooms and obscure my face with the great bunch of flowers I carry. A guard at the door glares at me over my overflowing armload.

"What's this?"

"Mignonettes," I reply innocently, softening the shape of the letters so they'll sound less crisp and educated.

"Find somewhere else for them."

"Her most glorious majesty has commanded that every room be decorated in celebration of her holy cat's new litter. We give much thanks to the great goddess Bastet for her gracious blessing upon our exalted queen, may she be blessed with eternal life."

"I've heard of no such order. Besides, the vizier is away."

"The queen said every room."

Unable to see very well over my armload, I can only sense the guard's pause.

"The queen has commanded we show gratitude," I insist.

The guard finally lets me in with a huff, and I hurry past him. I don't stop moving until I'm deep in the rooms, then only stop long enough to ensure I'm alone.

Midmorning sunlight slips between the drawn curtains. I push them aside to provide just enough light for me to work, as I purposely timed the visit for when I wouldn't need a lamp. Sunrays escaping through doorways are certainly much less suspicious, and I will not allow even the slight possibility of errant drops of oil to betray my entry.

I find a few places in the suite of rooms to dump the mignonettes and figure I have only a handful of minutes before someone will question if my prolonged visit is from care or curiosity. I don't bother with the other rooms and head straight for the desk.

Vizier Omari's papers are carefully organized, which forces me to be even more careful as I sift swiftly through pile after pile. More than any other room so far, the vizier's extensive lists and correspondence and detailed notes in his distinct hieratic cursive could very well give us the secrets Bakari hinted at. Because between the details of grain harvests and trade taxes and how many arrows soldiers use in training are all the notes and letters and pieces about nomarchs and noblemen. Even if the vizier isn't involved and is genuinely grieving with us, there's a good chance we'll find something to reveal his suspicions about what's been going on.

I study these papyri most carefully, searching for requests and favors traded, searching for notes of who is feuding or friendly, searching for replies to Bakenranef's multiple requests to memorialize Thonis and his assertions its disappearance was deliberate.

As Bakari predicted, I learn much from the bits I glean, and were I a noblewoman at court, I could certainly improve my status with this knowledge. To know who's arranging marriages with whom. To know who's cutting into someone else's trade. To know who's targeting whom to get a leg up. But I only care to know who murdered Meryt and drowned Thonis.

I allow myself one last stack before I get out. Then I find it.

I'm not even entirely sure what it is at first, but as I start to draw out the papyrus, I realize the length is longer than usual. In the few quiet seconds it takes to fully pull the page out, I know right away what I'm holding.

The plans to King Pa-Ankh-Entef's pyramid.

The pyramid where Meryt will be buried.

The pyramid that will be sealed hours after it's opened.

The perfect place to hide the remnants of a crime.

Beneath the first page is another map, one unfinished and with much less detail than the first. I lift up the long page and squint at the drawing of a single passage and room leading away from the entry hall, the ink faint on the too-thin paper.

I frown and set it aside.

I look back at the main layout

I look back at the unfinished map.

I look back at the main layout.

I lift the unfinished map and place it over the more detailed one.

The room, the palace, everything falls away and a loud rushing fills my ears, as if the placid Nile has taken up the tempo of a frothing sea. I remember the first set of papyri I'd found and how I'd missed something so obvious. My vision focuses so the map before me is all that exists.

I note the entrance, I note the path leading to the king's future chamber, the branch leading to the queen's, and the new one hastily added for the king's beloved wife. I note storage rooms, passages, the grand gallery, every minute detail, right down to the airshaft slanting up and away through the very wall of the pyramid.

Then I trace the plans for the passage and rooms that don't appear on the finished map.

And I know I've found something important. Mysterious. Secret.

Something the king or vizier doesn't want just anyone to know about.

I jolt back to the present with a sense that my time in these rooms has been overstayed. I carefully order the pages as I've found them, take the ones that have caught my eye, and redraw the curtains. I'll return the sheets right after I've drawn a map of my own.

Chapter Nineteen

Day 27

I meticulously copy the sheets well into the night, then fall asleep in the early hours of morning, thereby missing my chance to slip them back into the vizier's rooms when a guard might be less vigilant. Delaying my return risks wasting the advantage of his time away, but a bundle of flowers won't get me back in again. I end up spending a whole day trying to figure out how to sneak in, and in watching the room at least figure out the pattern of the guards.

When I slip into his rooms again, taking care to stay far away from the animal-gods' gazes on the way, I replace the pages exactly as I found them, then turn on my heel and don't break stride until I'm on the other side of the palace. It's only when I stop that I realize how much I'm sweating and breathing heavily.

I'm also in an entirely unfamiliar area, a quiet length of space tucked into a corner removed from the usual palace happenings. I peer past unpainted columns and discover a long, rectangular courtyard basking in the sun. Various plants are placed intermittently along the perimeter, but the place is bare, for the most part.

Hearing the distinct shuffle of feet, I jump behind a pillar, glad I'm barefoot. Not yet seeing anyone and so unsure of their approach, I slink over a few more pillars so a wall is at my back. Only then do I feel confident enough to look for the source of the noise.

I don't have to look long, because at the far end of the courtyard a figure in full sunlight moves through what appears to be a series of stretches. A glint of thrown sunlight reveals a sword in hand, which means he's probably working through various positions.

There's nothing particularly unusual about a soldier finding a quiet place to work through his training, but then the figure spins and lands on his opposite foot with a downward thrust. He doesn't still but picks up speed, executing moves in rapid succession, which greatly rely on control and balance.

He ends the combination and only pauses a moment before he takes a few steps forward, then back, forward and back, perfect and steady. I pull my eyes from the artistry of his movement to get a good look at his face. Then immediately duck.

I should've known.

That grace. That fluidity. That assuredness of poise and movement. Kemnebi.

I scuttle back the way I came, convinced he's right behind me, though I'm sure he didn't notice. It's not until I'm almost back at the subterranean room that fear dissipates under the image that assaults me.

That grace. That fluidity. There is nothing wrong with the commander's leg at all.

****

I show the pages to Bakari when he checks in after his training, and he reacts with an unexpectedly puzzled look.

"Well, surely it's something," I prod, thrown by his reaction.

"It's a pyramid."

"You want me to look for something, anything, and then you dismiss whatever I find."

"Well, you found the pyramid," Bakari concedes, "but if that's what you sought, I could've pointed you across the river."

"Why does Vizier Omari have plans for the king's pyramid?" I question.

Bakari's puzzlement turns to doubt. "He's the vizier," he replies, "so he has papers for everything."

His lack of interest needles me and riles my defiant side to prove him wrong. I *know* these pages speak to something important, and the vizier didn't just have them as a matter of mere record.

"And the secret passage? The hidden chamber? Did you see this when you worked?"

Bakari studies where my finger jabs the map and frowns. The copies are exact, I know because I had an extra day to double- and triple-check, in addition to making a backup set. I even included the overlay on a second, thinner sheet so he can see the pages as I found them.

"Maybe it's the first attempts at design," he muses. "The start of an earlier draft."

"Why keep it? Why draw on paper so thin, to fit perfectly onto the second design?"

Bakari shrugs. "Isn't that for you to discover?"

"Has all that wrestling mashed your ability to think?" I cry in frustration.

Bakari is taken aback by my outburst, but then a slow grin creeps out. "You watched me wrestle?"

"Aren't you soldiers always wrestling?" I mutter, refusing to admit it.

"I did all right, the last match," he says offhandedly, scratching his chin as if he isn't watching me for a reaction.

I ignore him and hide any expression by turning my face back to the maps. "Suppose someone has something he doesn't want found," I begin, "so he hides it in a place that will soon be sealed for decades?"

Bakari blinks and his eyes flit toward the maps. "All right," he allows slowly. "What would they hide?"

I stare at him. "Wasn't that my question when you first sent me to sneak into everyone's rooms?"

Bakari holds up a placating hand. "I'm not saying you're wrong, Azizi," he says calmly. "I'm asking what you think we should be looking for there. What must be hidden in a pyramid, as it cannot be disposed another way?"

I pause, doubt seeping in. "I don't know. It's just so glaringly an ideal place for getting rid of evidence."

"The evidence is Meryt," Bakari says shortly.

His words land like a slap, and I rear back slightly. Bakari stops abruptly and rubs his forehead. The shortness and tone are so unlike him, so unlike even his occasional flares of fierceness, that hearing them leave me too surprised to even form a response.

"I apologize, Azizi. I don't know where that came from."

Awkward silence clunks down heavily between us. I don't know how to respond to Bakari when he's like this, nor do I want to if it only means he'll snap again.

"I'll ask Bakenranef to get extra eyes on the pyramid, to watch and poke around."

I still don't say anything, waiting.

Bakari clears his throat. "Perhaps I thought we'd

have something more definitive by now."

"Well, we may finally be onto something substantial," I say, offering more hope than I've felt in a while. "It will be clear once we find the rest of the pieces."

Bakari shakes his head, as if he cannot see past the thick fog blanketing his mood. "We're grasping at straws. What I asked from you was no simple thing, but I've been certain it would already pay off. Instead, almost a month later we're only finding more questions."

"Ah, you regret keeping me alive."

Bakari's head snaps up, but when he sees my expression, he relaxes and his familiar grin slowly widens again.

"Not in the least," he assures me. "But only because you wanted so much to die."

"No worse than being stuck with only you to talk to!"

Bakari's exuberant laugh cuts through the aftereffects of his previous words, returning him to his usual optimism and the two of us to our usual cadence. The return feels good, something I only realize because of the unsettling discomfort that's suddenly disappeared with his negative mood. We may be grasping at escaping grains of sand, but our work in the last month has helped moor me so I no longer feel adrift as I once did. I still pause at times to catch my breath when I feel the imagined pressure of water burning my lungs, but I'm finally learning how to manage beyond the pain and sorrow that's weighted me since Thonis.

"If nothing else," I tell Bakari, "we can know the vizier had nothing to do with Thonis. Which may also mean he's innocent of what happened with Meryt."

Bakari nods. "True enough, but it's also time we figure out who to watch before they make their next move. If there really is more to all this."

"Kemnebi arrived only after Vizier Omari left," I observe. "People treat him as if he's the second-in-command. And from the way he moves about, his injuries don't seem drastic enough to call him away from duty. He doesn't limp when no one's around."

"Says who?"

"I saw for myself."

Bakari muddles over that a bit. "You suspect him?"

"He's only half Egyptian."

"*We're* only half Egyptian."

"And look at what we're up to."

"We broke tradition for Egypt! All of this is *for* Egypt! And anyway, Kemnebi wasn't anywhere near the palace when Meryt passed."

"Do we know that?" I demand. "I didn't know very much about him until he landed a few days ago. If he's so skilled and loved, he could be anywhere he wants, whenever he wants! Besides, he doesn't have to physically be here to be responsible."

"There is something to that," Bakari reluctantly agrees.

"He's hiding something," I declare resolutely.

"Still pretending you don't have something against Nubians?"

"Every Egyptian has something against Nubians!" I retort. "And what about searching every corner and turning over every stone?"

Bakari studies me. "Then his rooms are next," he says simply.

"Exactly."
"And I'm coming with you."

Chapter Twenty

Day 29

It takes two days to open a path for us to search Kemnebi's rooms. Not only do we have to work around Bakari's duties, but we also have to make sure Kemnebi is busy with something that will keep him away long enough for us to get a good look at his rooms.

The commander finally leaves the palace with a small entourage to assess the work on the pyramid, of all things. I overhear gossip that he'll be meeting Vizier Omari there, as he stops through on his way back from Kom Ombo. I offer a grateful prayer to Father's Divine Force for the events so wonderfully aligned in our favor.

I end up hiding near the servants' entrance to Kemnebi's rooms and wait a good ten minutes until Bakari finally shows up.

"What took so long?" I hiss as he sidles up alongside me.

"There are those who will notice if I'm not around," he reminds me.

"Only because you insist on causing much exasperation wherever you go."

"It can't be helped that I'm so unmissable," Bakari agrees.

"How did you finally get away?"

Bakari raises a single eyebrow, relaying a plethora

of expression in that single motion. "How?" he questions, clasping both hands to his heart. "Jest not unto my love, my rare desert *zahur*—"

I brush right past him and his too-serious expression and quietly enter Kemnebi's rooms. Thankfully, Bakari drops his recitation to catch up.

We stop right in the entrance, listening with bated breath as the door closes softly behind us. We're fairly certain no one is here, and the servants' entrance affords some privacy compared to the visibility of the main door. Still, an unwanted thought warns we might have to revert to some "rare desert flower" poetry if we have to twist our way out of being where we shouldn't. The only consolation is that if one of Kemnebi's servants catches us, he won't know I'm supposed to be dead. Whatever good that'll do.

"This might take a while," Bakari whispers, and only then do I really focus on the large room before us.

It's overflowing with gifts, on chairs, on tables, all along the floor. There's enough to start a small mercantile trade.

"A man very much loved," I remark.

Bakari wanders over to a small golden tray on a nearby table and scoops up a honeycomb. "At least we won't be hungry," he says, taking a bite.

"You can't eat that!" I admonish. "And now you've made your fingers sticky!"

Bakari glances at his hand and shrugs. "I didn't take that much," he defends himself, "just a snack. If you find something interesting, read it out loud."

I shake my head at him. "You always find ways to get around reading."

"Never needed it," Bakari says, flashing a smile I

assume is supposed to make me puddle. I glare back. "Besides, most of the other soldiers can't or don't read, so I'm well ahead."

"And we'll fall behind now that you can't search anything without leaving sticky evidence."

That stops him. I assess the room as he looks for a place to rinse his hands, then head to a desk messy with scrolls and scraps of papyrus papers. I stare down at the desk so opposite from Vizier Omari's neatness. Kemnebi must have many servants who can't read, if he's so careless with his documents.

I methodically pick my way through the pages, peering at the untidy script assisted by the light of high noon. The top pages are simple lists and notes about inventories, household expenses, military drills, nothing unusual. Then there are the invites and requests, which may have been attached to gifts, seeking Kemnebi's attendance at "a small gathering" or "dinner for close friends." These certainly hold some clues as to favors and friends and the delicate balance of court power. Adding to the mess of pages and invites are scraps with sketches of boats and formations. Just a quick look is enough to reveal that even if Kemnebi is officially on leave, his mind is still very much in the navy.

I catch a sudden scent of *kyphi* and seek out its source, digging until I find a half-covered papyrus covered in flowery script. A small rooster is colored into one corner, a black panther the one opposite. Other embellishments include images of jewelry, gold, flowers, the sort of drawings that are supposed to speak to a woman.

I scan the writing and, once I realize what I'm holding, choke down an astonished laugh. It's not fast enough because suddenly Bakari's right before me. Of course, he would be attuned to that.

"What is it?"

"Nothing. A cough."

But my face betrays me as it starts to warm, and there's enough light in the room to reveal it. I don't know if he specifically sees my reddening features but he sees something in my face to tell him that I'm holding something he wants to know about.

"Read it to me."

"No."

"Should I take it?" he asks, wiggling his honeyed fingers at me.

"Fine," I sigh. Then, with the most bored tone I can muster, begin, "*Peret* sees blossoming of you, desert flower. Nubian gold has no sparkle to match the strike of starlight in your eyes…"

I trail off as Bakari breaks out in quickly though barely muffled laughter. He tries to cut it short, but fails.

"Sun rays dance round the dial of time unto evening, the Nile flows gently over your bare feet," I continue stubbornly, a new heat rising from my neck to spread across my cheeks.

Bakari gasps for breath and I stop reading abruptly.

"We've found your love heart poem after all," I manage to say.

"And now I'm sorry I wasn't more eager for reading," Bakari replies.

When I lift my eyes to glare at him, there's something beyond amusement in his, which makes me quickly turn away. When I bring myself to look again, he's looking away too.

"Yes, well, I didn't finish," I say into the awkward

pause, defiant now to read the awful poem through. "In glittering waters, arms, ears, neck bedecked in jewels, awaiting your ship's passing, heedless as the rooster calls against the preying of the panther—"

And then I break off again but not because Bakari's choking on laugher once more. I narrow my eyes at the page. Something's starting to emerge between the written words, as if the letters prettily curving into each other are not quite the words of a love heart poem after all.

Bakari notices my sudden stillness and inches closer. "What is it?" he whispers, as if afraid to interrupt my focus.

I glance up at him, but I'm not really seeing him. My mind is sifting through the wording of the poem, reaching for what I know is hidden there, like the sense of raising my hand to swipe away a spiderweb I can't quite see but feel anyway. I reexamine the other papers on the table, the household accounts, the inventories, the doodled scraps.

"These are the same handwriting," I finally say, pointing from the flowery lines in my hand to some scraps of doodled formations. "This poem was just written with more care."

Bakari steps around the table so he can peer over my shoulder, careful to keep his fingers away from the pages.

"And? Why wouldn't they be?"

"If Kemnebi wrote this, why is it phrased so…oddly? As if it's written to look like it was by someone else?"

Bakari studies the writing again. "Think it's intentional?"

"And what about these words?" I point as I speak. "Rooster, panther, gold. Look how they're written. Bolder and without swirls or connections to other letters, so they stand out. As if to be certain they aren't misread."

"Nile and ships are the same," Bakari adds.

"I may have finally found a code this time."

"But what does it mean?"

"I don't know," I muse, thinking of Kemnebi's arrival at the palace, his exaggerated injury, his connections, his adoration, his bloodline, his trip to the pyramid. "One thing is certain, the much-loved Commander Kemnebi is up to something, and we're going to find out what."

Chapter Twenty-One

Day 31

Early morning alights upon me in my acacia near the Nile, where I've stolen away from our subterranean room for some time to think. Not that I don't have plenty of time and space to think in the palace, which is rather quiet when no one knows I exist, but I'm feeling the waves of Thonis closing in on me, the stars falling from the painted sky, so I have to get out.

Frolicking breezes, gurgling water, and a high tree branch are what my mind needs to sort things out. Open air equals open mind, Father would say.

I turn the words to the poem we found in Kemnebi's room over in my mind. We didn't dare take the original with us knowing he'd be back soon, so we memorized the words that looked different and wrote what we remembered down once we were back in safe quarters. We may have missed some words, but I'm sure they were just fillers.

We sneaked back into Kemnebi's rooms again last night during the supper hour to make sure we'd taken note of every anomaly, only to find the papyrus gone. For the past two days, Bakari and I have been staring at the words we hope we remembered correctly, trying to unlock them without success.

Rooster. Panther. Gold. Nile. Ships.

We've tested all manner of code and symbolism and all we've come up with so far is that the panther is most likely Kemnebi. Gold could be payment or jewelry, and the reference to jewels could be some form of payment as well. But what of the rooster? If it's a reference to someone, it seems the name of a farmer, not anyone at the palace, and certainly not anyone who ever aspired for their child to be a servant at the palace.

Aside from that, as Bakari helpfully pointed out, "Too many soldiers call each other that, because that's how they behave."

I close my eyes to the wind murmuring through the trees, rustling the leaves of the acacia and surface of the Nile, urging them awake for the day ahead. Slews of sleek papyrus skiffs skim along the river this time of morning, cramming in their ferrying and trade ahead of the soon-to-be blazing sun. A quick glance to the dock across the way shows it's still silent of the workers from the Valley of the Kings.

Something akin to joy spreads through this burgeoning moment, the sun rising lazily in the east as the waters lap quietly below, patiently awaiting the strong rays that will soon make them glitter. I can't help but smile at the sight of it all, and, aside from Bakari's mischief, it's the first time in a long, long while that I feel no guilt at doing so.

I open my eyes to the river and a memory shoots above the surface.

A few short weeks after we first arrived at the palace, Meryt was ecstatic, of course, at her new position. I was struggling between my happiness for her and dejection for myself as I adjusted to the new and unexpected course of my life. Being so long away from

Thonis but not sailing toward new horizons was no small matter for me. Still, newcomers that we were, there was much to explore in the great palace, and that at least took my mind off my own self-pity for a while.

The Palace at Thebes is truly a grand place. The main entrance is lined with reaching columns brightly painted in yellow and green and blue and red of gods and kings and doctrine and faith. The palace itself is built around several open-air courtyards with small gardens, and the larger gardens around the palace are lush with all manner of flowers and trees and fruits and colors and fishponds and scents.

Meryt's favorite was the sunken garden, a shallow pond which palace residents could wade right in to cool off on hotter days. Hundreds of pink and yellow and purple water lilies bob above the surface. Meryt once whispered that the king had ordered the garden made for her, in a nod to that first afternoon he'd seen her standing in the waves.

The throne room is quite a sight to behold, with its long steps leading up to the king's intimidating throne lined all the way with fearsome statues of lions, crocodiles, and jackals. Wide ponds sit at the bottom on either side of the steps, lotuses crowding in groups at the surface and glittering fish swimming beneath the still waters. The room itself is as brightly painted as the rest of the palace, but also inlaid with ribbons and ribbons of gold which sparkle in full light.

As cats are deemed holy, they roam freely, though there're always one or two curled at the king's feet on days his precious tiger cub is too rowdy. Somewhere in the palace is a small menagerie of animals, exotic and sacred, treated as royally as the king and his family.

There's also a crocodile pit close to the prisons, though most have been persuaded to believe that it's reserved for traitors who are first beheaded before being tossed in. After all, a traitor to the crown does not deserve to have his heart measured for the afterlife, if he is even allowed entry to such a sacred place at all. Moreover, a heart eaten by a crocodile is certainly not one which can be measured to assess his worthiness.

One hot afternoon, Meryt decided we should go for a swim, delighting in a set of wide steps which lead just out of the palace to a small pool formed by an offshoot of the Nile. We jumped in eagerly, and it was only moments before we'd nearly forgotten where we were. It could have been almost any afternoon in Thonis as we laughed and teased and splashed in the water.

When we finally came out, still giggling and dripping with river water, we bumped right into Queen Sekhmet. One look at the queen and we immediately bit back our merriment. Though she'd been kind and welcoming since we'd arrived, the look she gave Meryt, then me, then Meryt, was anything but.

I remember the moment so clearly, even as words fail to form in describing it. It was as if the queen's dark eyes became deeper, as if within them she held the expectation of a people for beauty and grandeur and above-ness, an expectation that was most certainly not being met. Silenced by her gaze, we wilted, parched reeds left untended to slump against a rotted, abandoned dock. We couldn't move for the strength of her disapproval, though the only thing we wanted was to flee from under her gaze.

There was no doubt in the intention of such a harsh look, either. We, or rather Meryt, was acting in a way most decidedly unfit for the wife of a king. Whoever she'd been before, whatever she'd done before, she was now Lady Tadinanefer-Hatshepsut, and so exalted a woman did not act thus.

We managed to keep our expressions sober until we made it back to Meryt's rooms, where we collapsed in a fresh wave of laughter, although much of it was forced and lacked true merriment. That was the last time Meryt did something like that, the last time she did anything frivolous or without careful thought. From that day she dedicated herself completely to being, and being seen as, the wife of the king. The only time her old, impulsive self reemerged was on the few precious visits to our homes in Thonis.

But though I laughed the incident off with her, I never forgot the feeling of being under the queen's gaze, never forgot what it revealed about what lay beneath the layers of her beauty, grace, and kindness. The queen was not one to be trifled with.

Despite the lingering, withering feeling from the queen's look, the memory makes me want to laugh at our foolishness. I allow a small, quiet chuckle, realizing that for once I'm finally reliving a memory on my own without pain, without an increased feeling of drowning in my lungs. I savor the moment, savor the feeling of living and remembering with joy and without burden.

And then an unexpected voice cuts in.

"Little kyky," it calls up.

I glance down with annoyance at Bakari but quickly hide the expression away when I see it's not him.

It's Kemnebi.

I almost fall from the tree in shock.

"Come down," he orders, and, after the briefest

hesitation, I do.

Not that I have much choice. And, for all the years he's spent on ships, I'm sure the black panther of the king's navy would have no issue climbing up after me, even supposedly injured.

I shimmy down the trunk and kneel before Kemnebi like the insignificant lowborn I'm supposed to be, keeping my eyes downcast as I've learned to do. It's early morning, so there's no kohl around my eyes and I barely took a brush to my hair before I slipped outside. My dress is the now familiar rough material of the lower classes and I command myself not to instinctively itch myself. Perhaps I do look like a little kyky, wild and small and untamed. My heart pounds in my ears with the rhythm of the oars of one thousand warships.

A silence stretches and I risk peeking up to see Kemnebi studying me, though I have a sense that, despite looking at me, his thoughts are well beyond my fathoming. I barely move as I wait for him to speak, grass and small pebbles sticking into my knees.

This close, I know without doubt there's something undefinable about this man. Something strong and magnetic, something that makes me want to be part of the world he inhabits. I don't truly understand the pull, only that it's there. And I have sense enough to understand how it can be used on others to his advantage.

"What's your name?" he finally asks.

"Kyky," I automatically reply.

Kemnebi *tsks*, disapproving.

I dare to meet his gaze, but quickly look back down again. I feel that familiar smothering sense of a wilted river reed. No doubt he shares the queen's blood.

"Truly, Commander," I answer with conviction,

though I stumble as the truth comes out, "as my people called me."

"Where are your people now?" he asks.

"Gone," I say, unable to keep from choking on the word.

He raises an eyebrow, a skilled archer taking perfect aim at his target. I swallow down the lump in my throat.

"All right, Kyky, where did you learn to climb like that?"

"Home."

"Where is home?"

"Home is gone too," I answer, my voice still thick. "Home is here now."

"Whom do you serve?" he questions. "In addition to the king."

A pause which I use to collect myself. I cannot lie to this man, powerful, suspicious as he is, but if I can escape with half-truths, that may keep me safe enough.

"I once served in the rooms of Mer-Lady Tadinanefer-Hatshepsut," I admit. "I am supposed to be reassigned."

"Have they forgotten about you?"

I shake my head, though I know exactly where I'm supposed to be now. "Perhaps they await the burial. I was to help, um, straighten out her rooms, after."

He nods, still watching, assessing.

"Well, Kyky," he finally says, "as you've no new mistress yet, I've a better use of your time. A favor for me."

I stare at his fine leather sandals, unsure how to answer his entirely unexpected and forthright words. I'm also under no illusion that a request for a favor for him is not equal to a command. He must see the look on my face and misread it because he immediately reassures me.

"Not like that. It has to do with climbing trees."

Again, that stops me short.

"I would be very keen to assist the commander however I can," I say carefully.

"I'm expecting something very important," Kemnebi tells me. "Something I cannot risk being delayed. I would like for you to watch for a boat from your tree and notify me immediately when you spot it. Look for other boats arriving with it. Let me know if anyone appears to be watching it. Can you do that?"

"What sort of boat, Commander?" I ask.

Kemnebi gives me a smile I can't read at all. "Just a regular boat, much like any other. You'll know it from the rooster on its prow."

The detail rings loud in my mind, and I can't believe the opportunity handed to me, even if it means getting involved in Kemnebi's affairs. "How long must I watch?"

"Until it comes," he replies. "Within the week."

"Why me, Commander?" I dare ask.

Kemnebi considers me. "We rely so much on the river, but it can trick us. A new set of eyes is wise, especially a pair with such a view," he explains. "Watch in the early morning, as you do now. And while we're away for the Festival of Osiris. Just watch what happens and then report back to me. Understood?"

"Understood."

And just like that I agree to become a spy, again.

Chapter Twenty-Two

Day 33

"That's the second time you've been spotted in that tree!" Bakari accuses when I tell him about what happened with Kemnebi. "You're not being careful!"

"I think better in a tree," I rejoin, even though he has a valid point, "and, besides, see what it led to this time."

Bakari appears torn between admiration and upset, angered at how close the encounter was, yet unable to deny that good progress has *finally* been made.

I flick the coin Kemnebi tossed to me before he left with enough force to keep it moving end over end as it rises then smoothly falls back into my palm. Just as Father taught when I would visit him at the warehouse. I smile to myself. He would have been pleased with the evenness of my toss.

Bakari shakes his head at me. "A spy. For Kemnebi. Spying for the one we're spying on."

I shrug. "At least we'll better learn what he's up to."

"*Possibly* learn," Bakari corrects. "He could be testing you for something else."

"Fine, possibly know what he's up to," I concede. "I'll have a good vantage too."

"If there's anything to see," Bakari mutters.

"A ship with a rooster? It matches the wording of the poem, of course there's something!" I shake the papyrus Kemnebi handed me to "call" him with if the boat shows up while he's away at the festival. One of his servants will be left behind to take it from me. A folded drawing of a rooster. I know because I peeked. "If nothing else, we'll have a boat and a new person to spy on."

"You're not following any boat, Zizi!" Bakari cuts in. "It's not the same as sneaking around the palace."

"Relax and stop calling me that," I say from habit, flicking the coin again. "I'll be up in the tree, remember."

"Only until you climb down."

"At which point I'll come find you," I assure him.

"Promise?"

"I'll come find you as long as it doesn't take too long to find you," I amend. "And as long as you're not at the festival."

The Festival of Osiris is in less than one week's time, and most of the royal palace will be sailing downriver to celebrate at the temple in the holy city of Abydos. Whatever Kemnebi's up to, it would be a perfect time to act unwatched. It will also be an ideal time for a certain spirit to find out more about the individuals she's been watching.

"And if I am?" Bakari presses.

"Then you'll follow Kemnebi when the servant comes with the note."

Bakari lets out a frustrated sound and throws his hands in the air. "Why must you always be difficult?"

"Difficult? You're the one who wanted me to stay alive and spy!"

"And I've had to shave my hair since, so no one could see it graying and falling out."

"You've always shaved your hair."

"What if Kemnebi decides he doesn't need you anymore?"

I should worry about that, but I'm too thrilled to let fear in. I keep my focus on the coin. "I'll think of something, you'll think of something. Something will be thought of by someone."

Bakari snatches the coin from the air before it can land back in my palm.

"Bakari!"

"This is my down payment now," he informs me. "For the barber!"

And even though I'm annoyed that he's taken my coin, I can't help but laugh as he stalks off with it. Then he stops in the doorway and turns around for just a moment, just long enough to flick the coin back, a perfect trajectory as it smoothly sails end over end toward me.

I catch it neatly and he smiles, leaving the room with a parting wink.

In that moment, I realize something very important about Bakari. For all the annoyances, for all the glares and rolled eyes and honeycombs and flowery poems, he's done something I never expected could happen again. Even as he promised we would never forget Thonis, even as he brought the city to life in the painted walls of this room, he's also showed me how to remember without the burden of grief. He's distracted my mind long enough from my single-minded sorrow to let other emotions in, irritation and mischief and fear and laughter. Precious moments of laughter that refill the air in my lungs even if just for a while, long enough to catch a new breath before the too-familiar sense of drowning returns.

Bakari didn't just yank me back from death, he

pushed me back into life. He's reminded me there was a time when I knew without hesitation why I wanted so much to live.

Chapter Twenty-Three

Day 34

I'm feeling bold this morning due to my recent success with Kemnebi, so I finally gather courage enough to search Queen Sekhmet's chambers. I've been pushing off the inevitable for as long as I've been able, but we can't skirt around it forever.

Even if Kemnebi is our main focus at present, no stone is supposed to remain unturned. Besides, Kemnebi is a beloved cousin of the queen, so there's even more reason to wonder at what sorts of things he thinks his connections may allow him to get away with. Not that it has anything to do with the queen's private rooms, assumedly, but today's as good or terrible a day as any other to find out. The queen is scheduled to spend most of her morning in the royal bathhouse in preparation for the trip to Abydos.

I wait until midmorning, when I'm certain the queen will be well along with her preparations, before slipping toward her rooms. A pair of golden carved jackals guard the entry to the royal wing of the palace. I've passed the pair enough times as a servant to Meryt, but then it was always two steps behind and under her protection. Today is the first time I must sneak past them and know well that I'll have no one to protect me if I'm spotted. Taking unwanted flowers to the vizier's room is one thing, breaking into the royal wing quite another. I try not to think of the crocodile pit.

If rumors are to believed, the jackal statues were enchanted by a whole swarm of priests and priestesses. Though I have no way to confirm it, I do know a handful of priestesses was there when Meryt and I first walked past them. Officially as part of Meryt's welcome to the palace, but perhaps their indecipherable chants were actually to make sure the jackals wouldn't harm us. Does an enchantment change its behaviors for a person presumed dead?

I keep my breath very still as I approach them, eyes fixed on the statues that look alive even though made of gold. It may be my own imaginings, but I feel they eye me back. Both are in predatory positions, weight shifted to their hindlegs as if ready to pounce and chase me for my transgression. Maybe it's all in the mind, but I sense the air rustling when I slink between them.

I'm still in a half-crouched, paranoid frame of mind when I creep slowly into Queen Sekhmet's rooms. The audacity of trespass weighs heavy here, well more than in any other room we've rummaged through so far.

Queen Sekhmet stood at the top of the steps leading from the private royal docks when we first arrived. Regal, beautiful, proud as any queen would be, and yet she bestowed the kindest smile upon a very nervous Meryt when King Pa-Ankh-Entef helped her from the boat.

"Welcome," she'd greeted, clasping both of Meryt's hands in hers.

Perhaps she didn't see the young girl the king had brought home as a rival, but I doubt it. Queen Sekhmet knows politics too well for such naivete. Not only was her mother a daughter of Nubian nobility, but her father was the royal overseer of the Nubian king's grain warehouses. She'd grown up well accustomed to the ways of court, which was why her warmth toward Meryt was so unexpected.

"If you ever feel lost or have any questions," she told her more than once, "my door is always open to you."

Meryt had humbly accepted her kind words and the queen had kept a careful eye on Meryt thereafter. She'd advised her on all manner of things and introduced her to many at court. She'd even rushed to Meryt's rooms after Thonis was gone, had shared a cry with her over the loss of the "king's precious children."

Which is to say that trespassing on her rooms feels a gross violation of her kindness. Yet here I am.

Because, despite the love and admiration Meryt had been shown, she was murdered, and the king seems not to know her death wasn't natural. Which casts everyone in dark suspicion. Everyone but those already dead.

A soft scraping followed by the unmistakable sound of ceramic rocking against stone barges into the quiet. Just in time too. My hands shoot out to steady the large vase I've carelessly bumped into. The size of such a piece tipping over and crashing could very well wake the king's ancestors from their valley tombs. Never mind the ensuing questions such an outcome would lead to.

The vase is tall enough to reach my shoulders, and I gape at the unique and breathtaking artistry. Bold and sparkling blue, our beloved Nile spirals around the vase and through a celebration of the three seasons in turn. The top begins with the Nile overflowing its banks, watering the ground for the future harvest. It wraps around until it gradually enters the planting season, farmers plowing the rich soil near the river and sowing seeds for all sorts of grains to grow. Last, the winding river reaches the harvest, where golden fields of grain fall under the scythe. Here and there women expertly carry baskets bursting with purple grapes or piled high with colorful fruit. Deities watch the people at each step, blessing, protecting, guiding the citizens as they work.

The images glimmer in the natural light of the room, and closer examination shows gold and other precious gems melted and crushed into the paints as well as generously sprinkled over the whole design. A very, very expensive piece, no doubt, and surely one of a kind.

As the thought sinks in, I quickly back away from the vase, not trusting myself to linger too long near it after realizing its worth. Despite its size, I'd rather not use it as a last-minute place to hide behind should someone suddenly enter.

Turning my attention to the queen's rooms, I find one wall lined with statues of Nubian deities. I study them very briefly, wondering why the king permits the queen to keep them in her rooms and on such bold display. Does he think it an act of kindness to allow her Nubian pride, or is he secretly angered at her snub of Egypt's many gods? Imagining opposing rows of immobile statues staring each other down makes me appreciate Father's rejection of them all even more.

There are other displays of her Nubian heritage about the room. A large bow, beautifully made but impractical to use, hangs on a far wall. Aside from the large vase at the entry, a collection of pottery is spread across various surfaces in the room. Even a cursory glance reveals most pieces are expertly made, a significant measure more than already expected from traditional Nubian craftsmanship. For most, the middle band between the commonly glazed maroon bottom and black top is inlaid with gold and other precious gems. In a word, the queen's collection is unmatched, being both highly impressive and formidably expensive.

I tear my eyes from the décor and work thoroughly but quickly through the outer rooms, finding little more than the scattered bits left by ladies and maids to a queen. Stitching. Beadwork. Kohl. *Kyphi*.

I sort through a stack of rather well-drawn sketches of people about the palace, wondering what I might find unintentionally captured in their lines. There's one of the king, drawn with an aura of light and majesty. Vizier Omari, stern and serious as usual. I've learned he's a quiet man who speaks more with his eyes and gestures, yet he could be sounding thunder at the way others jump to do his bidding. There's one or two of the soldiers at training, though they're indistinct and seem unfinished. There's several of Kemnebi, always bold and dashing, the artist's feelings seeping onto the paper.

I study a particular one she's drawn of him lounging in that way of his against a railing, calmly confident and decidedly self-assured, convinced it contains some sort of answer about him. A detail captured by an artist but missed by the downcast eye of a lowborn. His head is turned toward the woman approaching to his right, a small smile growing across his face at the sight of her. The sketch is as unfinished as the ones of the soldiers, though I doubt it has much to do with the complexity of capturing men in motion and more to do with the identity of the woman herself.

I think to which of Queen Sekhmet's attendants I've seen sketching to determine who hid herself within the image, wondering if it's truth or fancy that put her in line of Kemnebi's affectionate sight. Is she someone who could provide an opening of sorts? The musing instantly vanishes when I hear a faint murmuring coming from deeper within the queen's chambers.

I freeze and listen, then tiptoe with bare feet toward the source of the human voice. The rooms should be empty. I pray that whoever was left behind is not astute enough to catch me, or someone who knows me if she does.

My rational side orders me to walk away, to not risk everything as I creep closer to the sound.

I press against the wall near a doorframe, noting that the voice beyond is young and female. I listen but can't make out the words she says. Some sort of prayer, or chant perhaps, judging by the rhythmic cadence of the words. Despite my father's indifference toward the Egyptian path of worship, I've learned enough to know this prayer isn't recited in any of the numerous temples.

Slowly, slowly, I peek around the doorframe.

The person is on her knees, her back toward me. Her hair is short and black, her dress the same white linen that all women across every city and status in Egypt wear, though of a decidedly finer make. Gold bracelets jangle at her wrists, blue and red and green glass beads dangle from her ears. Her *kyphi* has the unmistakable scent of—

An unnaturally bright obsidian light flashes before her and a small gasp escapes my lips before I can clamp them down and seal it in.

The girl's head whips around at the sound, but I don't stay to see her face. I'm already darting out of the rooms, bumping that lovely but ill-placed vase again as

I rush out the door. I pray it won't crash, as I've no time to ensure it doesn't totter from impact.

I'm several paces away from the entrance to the queen's rooms, walking swiftly and with my head down, when I bump into someone. I look up to find Rasidi standing over me. I hear my pursuer exiting the queen's rooms behind me. Rasidi can see her over my head, but I don't dare turn around. And then, before anything can be said, a familiar voice cuts into the scene.

"Rasidi."

Rasidi turns and bows low to Queen Sekhmet, except doing so exposes me. The queen sees my face in full before I bow as a good, respectful servant should. I catch how she startles as she thinks about why I look so familiar to her, despite the change in hair and dress and stance and kohl.

I mistimed myself. My lowered eyes widen in fear, a contrast to Queen Sekhmet's which slowly narrow. I may have only been a maidservant to the second wife of the king, but the queen was there when Meryt and I arrived. She saw us both after the swim in the Nile. She's seen me in Meryt's chambers, and she may have seen me that day above the soldier's training ground.

I cannot convince myself that the queen does not know who I am or that I should be dead.

Even as she stares right now at a very alive me.

I can think of no way to whirl or shimmy or skulk away without creating an uproar.

I am caught.

Chapter Twenty-Four

Day 35

Rasidi rescued me, again.

Though I'm still uncomfortable around the supposed medicine woman and her definite use of the dark arts, I have much to thank her for. Especially because I didn't know what to do in that frozen moment when my eyes met Queen Sekhmet's and I know she recognized me.

Rasidi acted first. A quick flick of her wrist loosed a handful of what looked like sand, which sparkled and crackled in shimmering obsidian as it descended. Whatever it was, it made me sneeze. Then I quickly checked that my hands and legs and torso were all intact from whatever Rasidi had done. When I looked up at the queen again, confusion had begun to cloud her brow.

"My queen," Rasidi finally returned the queen's greeting. "What can a humble servant offer her exalted majesty, may she be blessed with eternal life."

The queen blinked, looking from me to Rasidi and back again. I don't know what she saw, but I do know what the queen said.

"I thought she was—" she stuttered with vague gestures of her hand in my direction.

"A new apprentice," Rasidi said quickly. "In training for the upcoming ceremony."

The queen nodded. She didn't say as much, but she looked doubtful. I don't know if the dust muddled the queen's senses somehow or simply made me appear as someone else, or whatever other things a so-called medicine woman can contrive, but I know it shielded my identity in that moment.

"You must be more mindful," Rasidi scolded me. Then, to the queen, "This is the third time this week she's lost her way, Glorious Majesty. Spiritual pursuits are better suited to her than scholarly."

I bit my lip, annoyed at her underhanded jab but more worried my voice would give me away.

"Yes, well," Queen Sekhmet said, "mind the jackals and you'll know where you shouldn't be."

I bowed even deeper to show my obeisance and didn't dare move my eyes from the tiles before me. With that, the encounter petered out, and Rasidi and I left the royal wing as soon as the queen swept by. It wasn't until we'd reached the safety of Bakenranef's rooms that Rasidi spoke again.

"The queen is no fool, though I hope she'll reason away what she saw before I could act."

"What did you do to me?"

"I didn't do anything," Rasidi replied. "Merely clouded their vision so they couldn't distinguish your face anymore. But don't think you can now be careless," she warned. "It will wear off before the day is out, tomorrow at the latest, and the queen will have little doubt if she sees you again."

"I—thank you," I said.

Rasidi nodded. "I know the queen was kind to Lady Tadinanefer-Hatshepsut, but do not think that is all she is made of. She has a firm spine and a hidden streak of an unforgiving nature."

I stared at Rasidi, wondering if she was making reference to that hard look Meryt and I had received from the queen or if there was something even deeper she was warning about. It was one thing to be intolerable of unnoble-like behavior, it was quite another to have a willingly uncontrolled mean streak.

"A servant once tipped a vase, which fell over and broke. She disappeared the next day," Rasidi explained. "No one knows what happened to her."

"Because of a vase?" I questioned, feeling very relieved I hadn't knocked over the beautiful monstrosity in the queen's chamber. Surely no amount of sand would have saved me then.

"The queen is an avid collector of pottery, and this was said to be one of a pair, precious and rare," Rasidi elaborated. "Though one could claim as much about any life."

"Were the obsidian sparks in the sand the dark arts?" I blurted out.

Rasidi eyed me. "Do you truly want to know, considering how you feel on such things?"

"There was a girl in the queen's chamber who also made obsidian sparks appear with some chanting," I said.

"Which girl?" Rasidi questioned, brow furrowing.

I shook my head. "I didn't get a good look at her, but she was the one who chased me. The queen had left her alone in her inner chambers, and she wasn't a servant or slave. She must have the queen's trust."

Rasidi turned thoughtful. "I know the name of each who dabbles in dark arts at the palace. I would know who she is."

"That's all I saw," I apologized.

Rasidi waved my words away. "Never mind that," she said. "I have some tricks to help find out."

I did not ask what she meant by that, little as I wanted to know any more about such things. Grateful as I am to her, a lifetime of distrust toward the methods of such women is not so easily erased. I grapple with separating the actions of a single, vindictive "medicine" woman with this woman of dark arts who has certainly proven herself in some alignment to our cause. And yet, while I see how I may be able to trust Rasidi, I don't think I will ever fully trust dark arts. Not after experiencing both sides of what it could do, not after knowing this path she travels was doomed from the outset.

"You should lie low a while," Rasidi advised as she left. "Long enough for the queen to dismiss what she saw."

I could only nod, unsure of what that should mean to me when sneaking around is what my life has become. The river, the city, any area close enough to walk to raises the risk that someone who once knew me in my life here will see me now and question. I can't help but think it would be better for all if I'd just stayed in my trees back on Thonis to begin with.

Bakari, of course, is less helpful when he finds out what has happened. Rasidi or Bakenranef must've told him.

"Confined to quarters!" he declares as he barges into our room early this morning. "Three days!"

"But—why?"

Bakari fixes a stern look upon me. "That was too close, Azizi. The queen needs some days to forget what she saw."

"I'll avoid any likely path she'd be on."

"And what of the women and servants who were with her? What about the girl in the room? How can you be sure none of them saw you?"

"Rasidi used the sand on them all."

"Rasidi told you to stay away for a while."

"What am I supposed to do with myself down here?" I protest. "I'm no help to anyone if I can't move about!"

"You'll be out soon enough," Bakari assures me, "though with many words of caution and warning to stay far away from wherever the queen, and anyone else, might be."

"And what am I supposed to do with myself until then?"

Bakari shrugs, unmoved. "Write a love heart's poem."

He merely laughs when I glare at him.

Chapter Twenty-Five

Day 36

Bakari must possess some measure of kindness, or pity, as he brings a senet board to our subterranean room when he is off duty this afternoon. I'm bored out of my mind being so long indoors, especially underground and away from any glimpse of sun, particularly now that I can move about without dark grief obscuring my vision. I want to be outside again. I want to climb and explore and swim and enjoy the movement of living.

After spending part of the morning aimlessly walking round and round the painted mural of Thonis, I finally calm myself enough to lie on my back and stare at the stars painted above. It's not long before I lose myself in the past, back to quiet nights in Thonis when Unika, Kebi, and I would stretch out on the sand and Father would point at the sky and teach us how sailors found their way to and from home by the stars. We'd listen quietly in the dark, the sea rushing and retreating from shore as Father traced patterns and stories into the lights flickering above.

Along every little island of Thonis, fathers would be doing the same for their children, instilling a love of sea and sky and sand in the next generation of merchants and captains and sailors. I imagine their silhouetted hands raised upward, fingers pointed to swirl and trace as they gift the sky's compass to the sons and daughters of Thonis.

Perhaps the singular Divine Force that Father believed in was there with us as well. Perhaps it could be found in the bright specks of starlight and the dark reaches in between, perhaps it shone out from the sun and colored the sky and sea he sailed by day. I know to my bones that Father would say it was so.

I've so succeeded in taking my mind from the present that Bakari tiptoes in quietly, thinking I'm asleep. Until I turn my head to his soft shuffle. Otherwise, he'd probably think to wake me with water to the face, a crash to the ears, or even a snake to my toes. I do not ever intend to give him such a chance.

"Poem complete?" he asks by way of greeting.

"I need only a few more eloquent phrasings of admiration for a most handsome black panther," I reply, sitting up. "Is 'most striking and noble and honorable among men' redundant? I've been spending much time musing upon it."

Bakari's lips twitch. "Surely there's enough poetry written for black panthers of late."

"Ah, yes, but not by me."

"You forget he is the queen's cousin, a *favored* cousin."

I toss my hair. "I didn't think you would be one to bother with status."

"And part Nubian," he adds.

"Who are we to begrudge one with Nubian blood?"

Bakari's lips thin and I wonder what he's holding back from saying. "Yes, well, there are other subjects to write about," he finally says.

"Like soldiers?" I tease. "Sing unto brave Bomani-

Bakari…"

"A start of great promise!" Bakari exclaims, face brightening.

I don't say anymore and he looks at me expectantly. "Well?"

"That's all. I reached 'Bakari' and have no more words."

"I render you speechless!"

"Not speechless. Word-less."

Bakari nods, as if he knows just what using his name in poetry can do to a girl. "I may have a way to help inspire you," he offers. "Jest not—"

"One more word of your poetry and I run to Kemnebi!"

That stops him, at least. "We can set aside poetry for something else," he suggests, taking out a senet board.

I readily agree.

"Anything from the queen?" I dare voice the question as Bakari slides out the rectangular drawer which holds the pieces.

The board is unlike Meryt's in that it's unpainted and made from simple wood. It's slightly battered and looks well used, making it easy to imagine Bakari playing with his fellow soldiers well into the night.

"We haven't heard anything," he says, "but you must still be extra careful to avoid her at all cost."

"Of course."

Bakari grunts, part reply, part disbelief that I'll make this any easier.

"Spindles or cones?" he asks, gesturing to the waiting pieces.

"Either."

He sets up the board with perfect alignment, then

brushes off the set of throwing sticks from any dust they couldn't have collected inside their case. He offers them to me, and I immediately toss them to the ground with careless abandon.

One lands on the rounded side, three land on the flat side.

"Three."

"One knocked against the board," Bakari says, collecting and handing all four back to me. "Throw again."

I stare at him, wanting to ask why it matters, before I suddenly recall how seriously Bakari takes the game. When he would play with Hamadi, shouts and curses and pieces took to the air more than once in the heat of their matches. Considering how competitive they always were with each other, I again think that perhaps Bakari hadn't been entirely joking when he claimed to have let Hamadi beat him in wrestling before he married Unika. If that was so, was it a decision that came with a struggle or something he simply did for his friend?

I throw again to humor Bakari, and make sure no sticks bump anything. I still don't take the game much more seriously than that, even as Bakari plays each rule exactly and sometimes argues with himself over which version we're adhering to. In truth, I don't really mind. Our pieces race up and down the rows, and I can play without being reminded with each move that these pieces are our *ka* moving closer and closer to the afterlife. The time moves pleasantly enough and my nerves are temporarily at ease as it passes.

I only interrupt Bakari when he begins setting up a second game. "It's all right, you don't have to stay."

"I want to."

I can't help myself. "Why? You've said there are those who will notice if you're missing. That means you have others to pass the time with."

Bakari shoots me a look, indicating he thinks how silly I am for saying such things. Maybe, but that's not an answer. He sees I'm not satisfied and stops setting up the new game, squeezing the throwing sticks in his hands as he measures out his words.

"The day I left Thonis, you watched me sail," he finally says. "Watched until I couldn't see you anymore."

It wasn't at all what I expected to hear. "I watched a lot of people sail."

Bakari shakes his head. "You watched a lot of people sail to and from the *sea*. You watched my ship sail up the Nile."

"How do you even know?"

Bakari shrugs. "You climbed a different tree. One facing the river."

"For someone who caused so much trouble, you seem to have observed quite a lot more than expected."

Bakari flashes his mischievous grin. "Accumulating information to know how best to cause trouble."

I raise my eyes to the ceiling, but can't help grinning too. I may have spent too much time climbing trees, but even without all the ships to watch, Bakari certainly staged quite a show with his antics below.

"I doubt you put so much thought into it," I counter, "or you have much explaining to do for a lot of incidents you caused."

Bakari laughs, knowing he's caught. "Either way, leaving was no small thing for me, though I wouldn't show it. I made sure to notice as much as I could that day. That's how I saw you switched your view."

"People came and went all the time, but you were the first of our islet to really leave. It felt like something to witness, silly as that may sound now."

"Did you think I'd never return?" he asks, the teasing returning to his voice. "Not even to visit? Or pull a feather from my mother's ibis?"

"I didn't think much beyond the moment of leaving," I admit.

Bakari nods. "Well, it meant something to me," he says. "As if I hadn't just been sent off, that someone would know I had gone."

"Your mother's ibis certainly knew."

Bakari laughs again. "It's in our blood, Azizi. People of Thonis, the families on our islet, we look out for each other. At the very least, we of the Blessed must, for there is no one else."

I raise an eyebrow at him. "At the very least?" I question. "Is there more beyond that?"

He doesn't answer right away. Rather he studies me and it looks as though for the first time he might actually be hesitating to speak whatever words are pressing against his tongue. Finally, he offers a warm smile.

"Another round," he says, and I don't push him, even though I know that wasn't what he wanted to say.

"All right."

"And this time," he adds, "at least pretend like you're playing to win."

Chapter Twenty-Six

Day 38

Unwilling to remain caged in the room below the palace any longer, I steal away to my acacia in the early morning. I relish deep lungfuls of fresh air before I'll be forced to hide away again inside. This is my favorite time of morning, when dawn lifts the veil of mist from the surface of the Nile to reveal the vast possibilities of the day ahead.

When I first became a servant to Meryt, I thought my life was constricting, knowing I'd be foregoing—even if not forever as Father claimed—my dreams to always keep the smell of salty waters close and a sail above my head. At least then I could go wherever Meryt went. I've found a new freedom in being alive when everyone believes me dead, but I will always be constrained in some way around the palace. First my life was limited as a servant; now it is limited in my hiding.

Which is why it's worth sneaking away to my tree for some moments of quiet before I must tether myself to the shadows again, though at least a shadow proves I still exist.

"What appears on the horizon?" Kemnebi soon calls up from below.

I glance down at him, wondering how he could look so neat and polished with the day barely begun. And then

I don't wonder at all because I realize it would make less sense if he wasn't.

I'd seen him well before he even thought to look for me in the tree, seen how he'd walked without a limp to the river's edge, peered the lengths of each direction, before assuming an unhurried stroll along the riverbank. If I didn't already know he was awaiting some sort of boat, I'd be suspicious of his behavior. Not because it's uncommon for any man along the Nile to watch for a ship, but because most who aren't fishermen don't awaken before the sun to do so.

I watched the moment he looked toward my tree and veered from the river toward me. Considering that his limp returned, I'd like to think it wasn't because he saw me watching, but rather that he simply thought to check for me here. If the former, I wouldn't tell Bakari no matter what Kemnebi says to me now, as I'm sure he'd lock me in a sarcophagus to keep me hidden away longer.

I admire Kemnebi as much as anyone else, but only because it would be almost impossible not to. There's a pull toward him that beckons a person nearer without knowing why, a promise that a word or moment or look will be better if it's shared with him. Many cast him in a romantic light, but my regard for him is in the study of his singularity. At times he reminds me of a turbulent, storm-tossed sea, dangerous yet majestic. The king's panther captures me because I'd never met anyone before him who could elicit such opposite reactions. Aside from the king himself, who is our king, after all.

All to say, he surely knows a great many things worth knowing and can make a great many things happen. So, spying deal aside, it's well worth becoming friends with the one powerful individual at court who doesn't know I'm supposed to be dead.

I climb down the tree so Kemnebi won't have to call up to me. It's wise to show him such deference, never mind it avoids questions if someone happens to notice the great commander yelling at a tree. Kemnebi waits until both feet are on the ground before repeating his question.

"All is still this morning," I report.

Kemnebi nods. "It's early yet, but still wise to be alert."

I incline my head in partial acknowledgement, not sure how else to respond. Kemnebi watches me, and suddenly I don't know where to put my hands or feet or eyes. The look in his gaze truly resembles the black panther for which he's named, and I'm not quite sure yet if I'm only a monkey who amuses him or a rooster he sees as prey.

"Tell me, Kyky," Kemnebi commands, and it's all I can do not to jump at the sudden deep rumble of his words in the silence, "what does a little monkey see so high up in her tree?"

I hesitate, examining his expression as best I can to determine what he really seeks to know in his question. His handsome face is carefully composed, but I sense he's willing to listen to an honest reply.

"I see the river stretching and stretching until it turns out of view," I tell him. "I see docks and sailors and boats laden with limestone unloaded at the Valley of the Kings. I see the gold peak of a pyramid sparking in the sun, and should I dare look away, I could skim my sight across the palace to the gardens, then to the barracks and arena beyond."

Kemnebi assesses my answer silently. "That's quite a lot for a little kyky to see."

I turn his words over, wondering what he's getting at, for without doubt there's some meaning beyond the spoken word. Has everyone always talked like this, or do words only gain a shadow once someone takes on a secret life?

"Is it really so much in the length of Egypt, or the width of all the sea, Commander?"

A soft smile unfolds across his lips, more nostalgic than glad. "You speak like a sailor," he says. "Or his daughter."

"My father was a merchant, born in Phoenicia."

"And now?"

"And now?" I repeat. I glance to the tree, then to the river, before my eyes dare find his for the briefest of seconds before dropping. "And now he is gone and this is all I have."

"Not anymore, little Kyky, not anymore."

He raises a hand and gives my shoulder a gentle squeeze. His touch is unexpectedly soft and brief, so I hardly know it was there at all. He turns and limps back toward the palace, and I wait until he's out of sight before I permit myself to fully exhale.

Despite the warmth of the moment, I shiver. On the surface, his gesture is kind, but my stomach churns at the echo of his words. Kemnebi is known for many things, honor, charisma, courage, not kindness. So his words have put me on edge.

I have no idea what he means with them, or how they may yet affect me.

Chapter Twenty-Seven

Day 39

Most of the royal household sails downriver today to Abydos, the city believed to hold Osiris' final resting place. They go to celebrate the onset of *akhet*. So little rain falls in Egypt that the annual overflowing of the Nile's banks, which soaks the farmlands, merits its own season.

"Another god, another festival!" Father would exclaim in disdain.

"The celebrations are fun," was all I could reply.

Before coming to the palace, I had never been to Abydos for the Festival of Osiris, though the royal family, and whoever else can squeeze into the city, travel there every year. Once I came to the palace, I finally had a chance to attend, and the grandeur of the ceremonies in the holy city quickly showed me just how small the festivities were in Thonis. It could be because Thonis relied more on the whims of the sea than the flow of the Nile, but it's also most likely because though Thonis held our whole world, it was really only one small part of the world.

"Today it is Osiris, tomorrow it will be Horus," Father would scoff, "until he is torn apart by Seth. One king builds a temple to the god he deems most powerful, the next king destroys it and builds something even bigger to the god of his choosing."

"Are they not all powerful, Father? Is this not how people believe?"

Father would shake his head. "In many places, but not all. One day, Zizi, you will sail the world and see many temples and celebrations. You will see worshippers and priests and priestesses kneeling before gods shaped by human hands. In all these travels you will come to know that there is a great Divine Force at work in this world, a force much larger than anything these temples and priests can shape."

Father's brother, Meryt's father, believed much the same. Bakari's father, their *chibale*, the kinsman who'd traveled and settled with them and their Egyptian wives in Thonis, didn't disagree. Sure, we'd all attend temple services and religious festivals as a family, but our fathers were playacting. Our mothers bore their cynicism so long as they didn't speak of it in public.

Skeptical as I've become of Osiris and his peers, there's still a pull toward the festivities, a certain anticipation and joviality in the air which makes it seem everyone is one step away from a dance. I'm tempted more than I expected to go into Thebes and find some sort of merriment to latch onto, but, after what happened with Queen Sekhmet, if there's even the slightest chance someone might recognize me, it's not a chance I can take.

As if I hadn't already decided as much, Bakari won't leave without warning me, "Don't get into any trouble while I'm away."

"Your kind of trouble?"

"I'm serious—"

"Ah, so when you—"

"Azizi!"

"I'll be careful, of course, I'll be careful. Don't worry about me, and keep an eye on Kemnebi. Now go before you miss your ride." I nearly push him out of the room. "And keep a love heart's poem at the ready, just in case!" I call after him.

His laughter trickles back to me.

As he leaves, I imagine what I'll be missing, my vision helped by attending last year with Meryt. The king and his entourage will walk from temple to temple, paying grandiose homage in each with chanting priests and priestesses, prayers and expensive gifts. After, all celebrants cast coins, little figurines, and other statues into the Nile, to appease and show appreciation to the gods they believe control its flooding, a flooding which ensures Egypt won't suffer famine in the year to come. Even as I threw with the rest of them, I had to fight back a laugh thinking of Father's words about the fish.

Following the more formal, somber parts of the ceremony, the streets will fill quickly with music and revelers. Meryt twirled with unmitigated delight when the flowers were flung from the rooftops of every household, scented birds with petals as wings for their brief flights. Music will parade through the streets, reaching into every corner and teasing every foot, until everyone is dancing or singing or clapping along. Wine and food will flow freely. The merriment will last for days. And even Queen Sekhmet couldn't ruin our fun with loaded looks then.

Now I wait until the many royal ships have sailed, wait as each line of oars drops in the water and heaves their passengers downriver to the holy city. I'd heard a quiet rumor that the king would be returning early this year, unwilling to participate in a prolonged celebration considering Meryt is not yet buried. Even so, it should be quiet a few days. I turn back to the palace and quickly take advantage of the comparative emptiness. Some guards and servants have stayed behind, but most will soon be partaking in some kind of food and drink and festivities. As long as I don't do anything foolish, or go anywhere near the queen's vase, I should be able to roam the halls with eyes raised.

I return to Kemnebi's rooms. He was among the first to sail after the king and queen, so I figure his remaining servants must have already hastily straightened his chambers and gone off to their celebrations. The only one I'm sure will remain sober is the one I'm supposed to contact should a certain rooster arrive, although I'm also fairly certain he's been instructed to watch the water in the heat of day, unlikely as it is for anything to happen then.

Nothing significant has changed in the commander's chambers since my last visit. It remains the overflowing yet somehow ordered room that we first encountered. I go immediately to the writing table, but aside for updated lines about household items, and some new, uninteresting correspondence, nothing catches the eye. No new poems or unusual letters that might contain hidden messages. I know because I spend a good few minutes trying to decipher a letter from a sister asking about his lazy palace life, which turns out to be just that.

I leave his rooms and hastily search other nobles' rooms before I find myself drifting back toward the royal wing. I should be staying far away, but I want to know if the girl is in the queen's room again. I pass between the pair of guardian jackals with eyes fixed straight ahead, sensing their disapproval as I beeline toward the queen's rooms.

Overly cautious, I open the door only just enough to peek in without entering, then clamp down on a shriek. At my feet, a big mud-green toad hops at its chance of escape. It pulses in place, then croaks blandly. I hesitate. I'm fairly certain Queen Sekhmet does not keep such a creature as a pet, least of all in her private rooms. Then again, what do I really know about the queen?

Sighing, I chase after the toad, which fortunately hasn't yet made it that far. I clamp both hands on top of it, blocking its ability to jump. The skin is bumpy and slimy and gives me shivers, but I pick its sticky feet up anyway and carry it back to the queen's rooms, this time closing the door once I'm quietly inside. I free the toad and it croaks again, though I can't say for certain it's from gratitude.

I stiffen, even though the noise isn't from me, standing still and silent. I hold my breath, awaiting a sign or noise or reaction signaling the rooms are occupied. I wait like that a long while, until I see a quick, bright, obsidian flash, very much like what occurred with the grains of sand that Rasidi threw to confuse the queen. I deliberately blink, but when my eyes reopen the vestiges of the strange dark light are still there.

I have to find out more.

The girl is in a different room this time. Fortunately, her back is to me again, so I risk lingering, praying she won't sense another *ka* has entered. I can't make out her features, but I see the patterns painted onto her arms and the darkness that emits from the handfuls of sand she tosses between chants.

She's surrounded by toads. No wonder she hasn't

heard me.

I watch her as long as I dare, not long enough for the sun to shift its position much on the dial, but enough to confirm that she's responsible for creating the toads. As her back is to me, and I don't dare move any closer, I can't see how each is formed. All I know is that she fills her empty hands with sand and chants, obsidian sparks flash then settle to reveal a bumpy toad.

It seems simple enough, but the wrongness of it sets all sorts of internal alarms to ringing. There's something unnerving about her habitual use of dark arts, especially knowing that each incantation and sparkle sets her farther down the path of darkness. Just another reason to shy away from the dark arts and her maidens.

Even so, there's more to this than what I'm seeing, and though this may not be part of our investigations, there's something to this girl and this sand dust and this dark art that I am determined to uncover. Something that speaks to layers and layers of secrets hid deeper than a subterranean palace room.

With such thoughts burning in my mind, I slip from the rooms to seek out the one person I've tried to avoid but is certain to have answers.

Rasidi.

Chapter Twenty-Eight

Day 40

Rasidi's room isn't on the maps I drew with Bakari, and it takes such a long while to figure out where they are that I don't visit her until morning. It's quiet enough in the palace with so many away at the festival that I probably could've wandered around until I found it, but I'm erring on the side of caution. Besides, I don't want to accidentally interrupt anyone else at their dark arts, so I won't be turned into a toad.

Rasidi's room is in a back wing of the palace, in the same section as other specialists who are too elevated for servants' quarters but not important enough to be indulged with more enviable accommodations.

The space she's been assigned isn't overly large, especially as it has multiple roles as her sleeping quarters, workspace, and indoor herbarium. I have to duck and weave around the small potted plants lining the walls and hanging from the ceiling, effectively curtaining off her personal space from the door anyone can access. Rasidi studies me curiously when I suddenly appear before her.

"The obsidian sparks," I blurt out. "I saw them again."

Rasidi doesn't immediately respond, and I take her lack of reaction as invitation to continue.

"Toads. Real toads. Dozens, maybe. She was just…making them. With sparks."

I clumsily stumble through a description of what I saw, Rasidi's brow furrowing as I describe the scene in the queen's room. When I finish, she's silent a few moments.

"The girl is a ward of Queen Sekhmet," she tells me with a sigh, "an orphan from Nubia. The queen took her under her care as a favor to the family."

"*Nubia*," I hiss.

"They call her Tsillah," Rasidi continues, ignoring or not hearing what I'd said.

"Tsillah." The girl is not named for the absence of light but for what occurs when part of the light is blocked. "It sounds a warning."

Rasidi doesn't disagree, and it's evident she's not pleased about something.

"You've been clear enough how you feel about my practice," she says carefully, "and I won't deny that, for so many, use of the dark arts leads down an even darker path. Yet most do not deny its calling, certain as we are that we can resist falling to its depths."

I blink at her, uncertain that I agree with her outlook. She's telling me she's aware enough to try and fight the pull dragging her to a place of darkness and shadows. However, I also know that death has called to me and that being pulled back wasn't enough to make me want to live without rejecting willful death completely. And that only because Bakari was tugging so hard to keep me here.

Though I walk in shadows, they are vastly different from the absence of light wherein the dark arts feed. To say I have a "feeling" about Rasidi's practice understates the inner recoil of my mind and soul each time I merely think about it. The struggle is not to accept what she does, but to accept the good of her that still remains despite what she does, however long it will remain as such.

"We must watch her, this Tsillah," I say instead of my thoughts.

Rasidi is shaking her head even before the words are fully out of my mouth.

"Not you," she warns. "We don't know the extent of what she can do."

"We need to know what kind of girl the queen keeps close, so we can't let her slip away from us. We have to find out if she is connected to all this."

"I'll watch her," Rasidi says, adamant. "I know enough the shadows she walks."

I suppress a shudder, although I'm also relieved for Rasidi to be responsible for Tsillah. I only hope that with what she's just admitted of the dark arts, she's honest with herself about her ability to navigate that dangerous world. I certainly don't want to think of how we may be forced to keep a close eye on Rasidi one day.

Not that I say any of that to her either. I only thank her for her time, then escape outside to my acacia, intending to watch the river and think about this mysterious presence at the palace.

I climb up and settle onto a particularly thick branch...just as a small papyrus boat with a rooster painted on the prow pulls into view.

Chapter Twenty-Nine

Day 43

I'm up in my tree as soon as it's light enough outside to see, anxious to know what will happen now that I've sent the little square with the rooster on it to Kemnebi. From what I know, the moment I gave it to his servant, he went straight to a small boat at the docks and paddled quickly to find his master at Abydos. As for the boat with the rooster, it's still waiting in the tall papyrus it hunkered between upon arrival several days ago. There hasn't been much movement aboard, so I can't yet figure out what about the little vessel is important enough to call Kemnebi away from the festival.

Kemnebi arrives midafternoon, though the wait makes it feel weeks not days have passed. He barely looks around as his servant steers straight for the Rooster's boat, not even sparing a glance toward my tree.

Between the long branches, I watch Kemnebi greet the Rooster as his boat pulls up alongside his. The Rooster isn't tall, but he looks sturdy and imposing, standing with feet braced against the gentle rocking of the boat. Rows of gold earrings line his earlobes and the colorful feathers of his neck collar flutter against his bare torso. For all Kemnebi's secrecy, this man certainly isn't aiming for subtlety.

A second passenger aboard the Rooster's boat

begins passing crates to Kemnebi's servant. One, two, three, but as the fourth is handed over, the boat suddenly rocks with enough force to upend it.

The force doesn't come from the river itself, so it's either a hippo intent on feeding or something more insidious entirely. Something manmade.

A loud splash snaps me to attention and with a shout I'm scrabbling from the tree. I'm already racing toward the river when I hear a bloodcurdling scream.

Chapter Thirty

Day 44

Metr rushes loudly in my veins, so I can barely distinguish between the sounds inside me and the ones around me. I frown at the wall, struggling to fit the pieces together. It's early enough in the morning that it's still dark, the room lit by a small oil lamp.

Yesterday, I arrived at the river in time to help pull the commander's bleeding body onto the shore. The attackers were all dead, thanks to Kemnebi's servant, Bakari, and the distinct possibility of an enterprising crocodile.

I tear my eyes from the wall when I hear the door open and Bakari enters. I shoot him a questioningly glance and he shakes his head in response. No news yet.

"I asked them to send word here," he says.

I nod. Bakari assisted in carrying Kemnebi to his chambers, where a physician was already summoned to attend him. I hadn't thought much about my feet carrying me to Bakenranef's rooms, but it's prudent to wait here. Our nomarch is still at Abydos, but his rooms are a better place to await an update rather than directing someone to our subterranean hideaway. If nothing else, I may at least be mistaken for a servant of Bakenranef.

I call Bakari's attention to the jug of wine beside me, and when he nods, I pour some for him. He slumps into a chair across from me and leans his head back, the cup loose and neglected in his exhausted hand.

"Good thing you followed from Abydos," I finally say into the silence.

Bakari grunts in response. He tilts up his head and squints at me. "What happened, Azizi?"

I scrub my face, still not entirely sure myself. "I was watching the river, as instructed. When the boat arrived, I sent Kemnebi the message through his servant. Then I returned to the tree to watch."

"In the tree. Where it was safer."

"They were transferring crates when something made the boats rock. I wasn't certain what it was at first, but I heard screaming and ran to help."

By the time I dove into the river, it was clear the two boats had been attacked with the intention of eliminating both owners. The Rooster was killed, as was his servant. Kemnebi was stabbed, but the knife missed the fatal spot below the ribs that would have finished him for good.

"What were you thinking, Zizi?" Bakari asks, voice wavering between shock and exasperation. "Running into the river with your hands bare?"

"I was thinking someone was in trouble."

"You had no weapon!"

He's right, but I'm not about to admit it. Nor would it change anything. I couldn't stay in the tree if Kemnebi's life was in danger, allowing one more person to die when there was a chance to intervene.

"The attackers didn't know that," I counter. "Besides, you were right on time."

Bakari runs a hand over his scalp. He hasn't yet returned to his quarters, so dark bristles are starting to peek through.

"I don't like this," he says. "A new layer on a mystery whose surface we've barely scratched."

"We just saved Kemnebi's life," I remind him, "so we've earned good favor. We're bound to learn a lot more now."

Bakari shakes his head at me, the corner of his lips curved in half a smirk. That seems to be the general tone of our relationship, amusement mixed with raised eyebrows, frustration mixed with twitching lips. I suppose there's some comfort in knowing the feelings are mutual.

"The rooster was called Nkuku," he tells me.

"How do you know? Who was he?"

"A Nubian smuggler who kept rumors about himself swiftly moving," he replies. "Identified by his collar and therefore easy to inquire about."

"What's Kemnebi's business with a smuggler?" I wonder aloud.

Bakari eyes me over the rim of his cup. "You're the one certain we'll be learning all we need to know now."

I hop up and pace the floor, turning the facts over in my mind. I should be exhausted, but I'm feeling restless from how everything's playing out and the slew of new questions raised.

"Those words we noted in the poem," I finally say, "they pointed to that moment on the river. Nile, rooster, panther, code for that meeting."

"If memory serves as it should, there wasn't anything about an attack in it."

"No, nor was there anything about the entirely too large Nubian connection in all of this."

"Now a smuggler is at fault for the sinking of Thonis?"

"I'm merely pointing out an absurdly glaring fact."

Bakari raises his eyebrows, bemused. "They're our closest neighbor to the south. We trade them or fight them. Today we're on good terms, so we trade. Of course, many Nubians are in Egypt just as many Egyptians live in Nubia. It's inevitable, and expected."

"The queen, Kemnebi, Nkuku, Tsillah." I tick the names off on my fingers, visualizing the faces they belong to, wondering at the connection I'm sure must be there, by blood, birth, or bond.

"Tsillah?"

"The girl who practices the dark arts," I explain. "I asked Rasidi about her."

Bakari looks stunned. "You spoke with Rasidi, of your own will?"

"Some things had to be known," I say shortly.

Bakari smirks. "You're growing up."

I pelt him with raisins from a small bowl on the table beside me. I'll have to suggest to Bakenranef that he speak to his servants about leaving food out. Unsurprisingly, Bakari laughs.

"You'll cause me to spill my wine!"

"It won't spill if you drink it!"

Bakari downs the wine, then picks some raisins from his arms and throws them back at me in short bursts. I duck most of them. A knock on the door interrupts us before we manage to turn Bakenranef's rooms upside down.

Bakari silently gestures for me to hide somewhere. I duck behind the door to an adjoining room as he gets up to answer the knock. I hear a brief murmur of conversation before the outer door closes and Bakari's standing before me.

"A messenger from Kemnebi," he explains. "A request to visit tomorrow at our earliest convenience."

I dart a look out the window at a sky that's just beginning to lighten. "What time do you think he means by 'tomorrow'?"

Bakari shakes his head. "Let's at least wait until the sun is up, so they don't usher us out right away with an excuse that he needs to rest."

****

Bakari and I wait until midafternoon to visit Kemnebi, the first time we enter his rooms by invitation. I'm a little nervous about being seen and spend some time trying out small tricks with makeup to make my features appear slightly different. If it only buys me time to hide between first glance and second look, then it should be enough to protect who I am. Of course, I can't use too much or Kemnebi will wonder about my sudden interest in painting my face.

We're ushered into his main room, which, if possible, is even more full of gifts than the last time we snuck in. Vases of flowers burst along the walls with bright celosia, deeper-than-sky cornflowers, and long mignonettes.

"Previously a house of trade, today a festival," Bakari whispers to me.

I smother my laugh behind a cough.

We grow silent as voices drift in conversation from Kemnebi's rooms. I inch to Bakari's left, hoping to blend in, hoping he'll hide me from whoever comes through the doors. He sees the guest before I do, and immediately shoves a joyous array of deep orange, yellow, and red celosia into my arms.

"Wha—" I barely manage to get out.

"Block your face," he snaps.

I raise the bouquet so the long colorful flowers cut through my features. Not a moment too soon, because I've just positioned them when Queen Sekhmet swans through the doors. I quickly dip my chin and cast my eyes downward.

I catch my breath and pray she'll pay us no mind. Then her feet stop before us. My heart races, my *metr* returns to pound in my ears. I have no Rasidi sand to hide my features if she notices me this time.

"Bomani-Bakari," the queen says solemnly, "thank you for what you've done for the commander of the king's royal navy. And my cousin."

Bakari bows low. "All in service to Egypt," he says dutifully. "May the king, may the queen, and may the king's commander merit eternal life."

"I shall remember it," the queen tells him, "and you should remember that if ever you need anything."

"Fulfilling my duty is my only need," Bakari humbly replies.

I'm glad the flowers are blocking my face because I don't think I could endure the unhurried nature of the exchange otherwise.

"Find a place for them," the queen orders. "Anywhere will do."

With my eyes downcast, it takes a moment to realize she's speaking to me. I drop a curtsy and step away, glad for the excuse to leave her prying eyes, glad to keep my back turned until I'm sure she's left the room. As I find a place for the flowers, I briefly wonder if I may yet fulfill my life's calling by becoming a gardener, considering how flowers have twice saved me of late.

"*Zizi*." Bakari's sharp whisper calls me back.

We're ushered into Kemnebi's inner chamber to find him propped on a red chaise, carved lions standing guard at the foot on either side, tails stretching the length of the couch and curving protectively toward his head. He winces as he adjusts to receive us. There's no way a man such as he would ever admit pain, but his skin is notably paler and his *ka* seems drawn.

"I've had visitors all morning," he says by way of greeting, "the king, the queen, both unnecessarily returned early from the festival and full of warnings and worry. The queen is particularly displeased that I've allowed myself to be injured again. You two, however, will be restorative."

"We can return another time, Commander," I offer, unsure if we might anger someone by not allowing him to rest now."

Though I hope he won't ask us to leave. There's too much to know, and the sooner the better. I doubt I can sit still another hour, waiting and waiting and guessing at whatever sort of answers he'll be ready to give.

"I said you're to be restorative," he repeats. "And anyway, I'm only slightly sore."

"From the twenty-two stitches, or have you been battered anew since then?" Bakari asks.

He immediately clamps his lips shut, seeming to fear he's acted too familiar with the queen's cousin and most celebrated commander of the king's navy. But Kemnebi waves his words away with a soft chuckle. Bakari and I share a silent exchange which doesn't go unnoticed.

"So," Kemnebi states, looking from one of us to the other, "you already know each other. Or will you claim you've only just met in the corridor?"

I take a small step forward. "I asked Bakari to keep

watch, Commander. I hope you don't mind."

"I won't say I do, after what's occurred," Kemnebi begrudges. "I've heard about you, Bomani-Bakari," he continues. "I've watched you wrestle a few times. Seen your skill at handling horse and chariot."

Bakari inclines his head in humble acknowledgement of his praise.

"I'm glad you were there," Kemnebi says. "Thank you."

"Glad I was in time," Bakari replies.

Kemnebi nods, then looks between us again before settling his gaze on me.

"You obviously trust him, little kyky," he observes. "But what is your connection, I wonder?"

I turn the question over and try not to let on that I'm sifting through answers as I consider how much to say. I avoid looking at Bakari so it shouldn't seem we're agreeing upon a previously rehearsed response. I figure the truth is best, being the simplest, after all.

"He is my *chibale*," I tell the commander, "from home."

Kemnebi levels a stern look at me, and in it I glimpse what his sailors must feel under his command. Small. Intimidated. Corrected.

"Your home is no more," he says, giving my words back to me.

"Our home was Thonis," I say.

That pauses Kemnebi as the true meaning of such words sink in. He says nothing about my daring to say the name of our supposedly cursed city out loud nor of what that might mean about who I am and whether or not my life should or shouldn't be. Rather, he studies me as he focuses on a single part.

"You are of the Blessed," he whispers with some understanding.

"We survived because we were already in service to our king," Bakari explains, as if that were the blessing that saved us.

Many probably believe it to be so, but if Meryt's murder is truly connected to the sinking of Thonis, then it may very well be our service to the king cursed us three from the outset.

Kemnebi nods and leans against his array of cushions. I don't know what he could be thinking, but no doubt certain pieces are falling into place for him, this explanation enough to give him answers to questions not yet asked.

"Why were you attacked?" I blurt out, sensing I may not get an answer but wanting to move the conversation away from us and our past. "What were they after?"

Kemnebi sighs and gestures with his chin across the room. Bakari and I turn to see three crates neatly stacked. On the lid of the third is a small line of golden shabti statuettes, carved servants intended for burial and meant to serve their master in the afterlife. My breath catches. Are these for Meryt?

"For Lady Tadinanefer-Hatshepsut," the commander confirms.

I eye them from where I stand, unsure if I can move closer, frowning at the stack of crates. There's no question the statues are beautifully carved, solid gold and inlaid with precious emerald and beryl which glitter prettily under our gazes. Looking upon their quality, no one can doubt how King Pa-Ankh-Entef felt about his young wife.

"Designed in Nubia," Kemnebi adds when I look

back at him, a question in my expression. "Very unique."

"Enough to kill for?" I ask, the words out of my mouth before I can think of the wisdom in holding them back.

Kemnebi is silent a moment, and I can't guess if it's to reign in his anger or formulate a response that will reveal little but satisfy all the same.

"Nkuku was a man with many friends," he says carefully, "but he was also a man with many enemies. I cannot know what else his boat was carrying, where he was coming from or where he was going. I only commissioned him for delivery, because I trusted his speed and silence for the value of what he carried for the king."

The answer makes sense, even if I'm certain some servant may have been equally capable. Why trust a smuggler over an emissary with armed guard? I cannot believe whoever staged this attack was only after Nkuku. I saw when the boat arrived. I know how much time passed until Kemnebi sailed up. Whoever did this was waiting for the commander, aiming to get rid of both men at the same time. I wonder what information the odd pair might share that someone wouldn't want to get around. Kemnebi splays his hands as if to ask what more I expect of him, as if to say he's told me all he knows.

"The thing about secrets," he says evenly, "is they keep best when buried deep. What Nkuku knew is silenced with him."

He could be reassuring me the attackers have done what they set out to or offering a note of caution to me and my questions and my watchful eyes. Chills ride down my spine and Bakari stiffens, sensing some darkness in the words, though he keeps his face from betraying his discomfort.

We may have the favor of the queen and the black panther now, but that doesn't mean either can be trusted. That doesn't either mean he isn't suspecting we may now be holding a secret he wants to bury deep.

We wrap the visit up a few moments later. I'm following close on Bakari's heel as he leaves, but a deep voice calls me back.

"Don't go too far, Kyky," Kemnebi says. "The river won't watch itself."

"Is there someone else I should be looking for, Commander?" I ask innocently. "A sheep this time? Or a duck?"

Kemnebi smiles, crinkling the corners of his dark eyes. "You saved my life," he says simply. "I am not so quick to be rid of a messenger from the gods."

I nod, relieved he still sees me as having some use to him, hoping this means I don't have to be watching for him over my shoulder just yet. Bakari waits just outside the room when I stride out. He shoots me a questioning look, but a slight shake of my head tells him, *Not here.* We don't speak again until we're safely back in our subterranean room.

"What did he want?"

"To keep spying for him, I think."

"You think?"

"He didn't say it in so many words, but I believe that's what he meant. He called me a messenger of the gods."

Bakari barks a laugh.

"My life for a handful of raisins," I mutter.

"Too much. You're only worth about half of that!"

"Forget raisins. Rocks."

Bakari ignores me, plopping on the painted ground, his back to a bustling market packed with stalls of colorful wares.

"What else could that man be up to?" he muses, returning to the topic at hand.

I settle beside him, a palm pressed to the wall behind me, seeking the warmth and laughter of Thonis, willing it to rush through my *metr*, revive my *ka*, and renew my strength for the days ahead.

"Important individuals will have their secrets."

Bakari snorts. "Secrets best kept buried deep, as he said."

I sit up straighter. "You think he arranged the attack on Nkuku?"

Bakari turns the question over a moment before shaking his head. "Why order an attack if he could just do away with him himself? Especially anywhere else along the Nile less likely to have witnesses."

"To make it look like he had nothing to do with it."

"Even if he doesn't know that you shouldn't be here, whose word could hold water in accusation against his?" he reasons. "Besides, he surely has any number of excuses ready for why he could kill Nkuku in the name of the crown, smuggling foremost among them. Plus, despite his fortitude, that cut on his side nearly gutted him. Kemnebi isn't foolish enough to play so loosely with his own life."

I slouch back against the wall. "So the attack was really aimed at both of them."

"Most likely."

"The question to be asking is what Nkuku was carrying that would tempt someone to the point of murder."

"Kemnebi showed us the shabti. They're expensive, but I doubt unique enough for such measures."

I don't respond right away to Bakari, and he turns to look at me. I'm not looking at him though because my eyes are fixed on the opposite wall, on the ships carrying goods to and from Thonis.

"Uh-oh," Bakari intones. "What are you thinking?"

It takes a moment to order the images in my mind so I'm sure of what I'm seeking. Everything happened so quickly, after all, so I have to be as sure as I can. Then again, what I saw, what I know without doubt that I saw, was in the moments before the rush began, before the boat rocked and the scream sounded and the blood flowed. I finally turn to meet Bakari's gaze.

"Kemnebi showed us shabti sitting atop a pile of three crates."

"Ye-e-e-e-s," Bakari says.

"I saw the crates as they were passed to Kemnebi's boat."

"And?" he presses. "Kemnebi seemed at peace enough to show us what they held."

I shake my head at him. "That must be because there's nothing to hide from those three crates. The secret must be in the one that wasn't there."

"What?"

"I know what I saw, Bakari. What happened to the fourth crate? What could it possibly hold?"

Chapter Thirty-One

Day 45

Two thoughts won't quit circling my mind like a predator sizing up unknown prey.

First is the mystery of the fourth crate. The more I focus, the more certain I am that it reached Kemnebi's boat before the attack, which means it wasn't lost when Nkuku's sank. Second, Kemnebi's boat never overturned. It only tilted enough to upend the two passengers who were already standing, but not the cargo. I'm sure of it.

It's possible the crate still made it to the bottom of the Nile, which would align with Kemnebi's words about buried secrets, but a newly awakened defiance won't accept this option. The river is too deep to dive or dredge, but there's also no need for it. The three crates Kemnebi showed us are proof his boat's contents made it to shore.

Then comes the final thought, that if the attack was over the crates, the fourth one won't be easy to find.

"Two weeks," Bakari announces when he pops into our underground room for a quick visit. "Kemnebi must stay abed two weeks before he can even think of walking the lengths of the palace again."

"He'll be up in less," I bet.

"He swears it'll be only one. If this fourth crate is important enough to hide, he'll either keep it in his rooms or check on it the moment he's moving on his own again."

"Or bury it deep," I remind him.

Bakari's brought me some lunch and I take a handful of grapes, biting halfway into each to test for firmness and how far they'll spray. Father taught us to eat grapes like this. Well, Mother insisted we bite into them when we were very young so we wouldn't choke, and, because we didn't like to, Father found a way to convince us. I'm sure Mother was glad none of us were choking, but she didn't entirely enjoy how we turned eating grapes into a game.

Bakari hands me a cup of beer and shifts out of the line of spray. "All guards and even soldiers are to be on extra lookout," he reports. "Extra rotations, extra men at the river and at Kemnebi's door. Even if sneaking into his rooms was an option, there are too many eyes now for anyone to get in unnoticed. Too many eyes watching all over the palace for you to be sneaking around much."

I scrunch my nose, showing what I think about that. "That leaves us with sitting around and trying to guess what sort of secret a rooster and a panther could share. A secret potent enough to murder for."

"No end to the options there," Bakari warns, "but as this is the news of the day, no one's overly suspicious of my questions about Nkuku."

"All we need is to wrestle some information out of Kemnebi."

Bakari grins at me. "He seems to trust you, little kyky. Just go and ask."

"And maybe stick your head in the mouth of a hippo!" I exclaim, squeezing my last grape in his direction.

Bakari looks shocked at my outburst, then bursts out laughing, and I join in.

"Meryt would always say that, before she married the king," I finally say when we catch our breaths.

Bakari's laugh becomes a chuckle. "We all said it," he says easily, "though I think Hamadi preferred lions to hippos."

I smile, thinking of my brother-in-law, whom I knew longer as a friend. "That sounds like him, choosing a more noble animal."

"He was a noble sort," Bakari agrees. "A good man, but entirely too serious about so many things."

"Someone had to keep you in line," I counter. "Imagine if there were two of you about our islet?"

"No ibis would be safe!"

"Nor any cat, dog, or monkey!"

Everyone knew Bakari was a terror to animals, unmindful of their sacred status as he sought to train them for odd jobs or pulled their tails and teased them like they were younger siblings. That's part of why we were all so surprised when word reached us that he had become a charioteer. And not the one shooting arrows from the chariot, either, but the one driving it, the one who had to speak to and cajole and honor the animals that pulled it. Somewhere between Thonis and Thebes he'd discovered a gentle touch with horses, and suddenly outgrew his former treatment of animals.

Bakari nudges me with his shoulder. "You came through all right, little kyky."

"Because I was too high up in a tree for you to reach!"

"You think I can't climb?" he challenges.

"It only matters that you didn't climb any I was in."

186

Bakari gives me a mischievous look. "Thank Hamadi. If he hadn't had his eye on Unika and specifically forbade it, things would have been different!"

"Again, Hamadi proves the noble one. And now he's got naught but a troublemaking charioteer and a little monkey to avenge him."

"My parents, your parents, Meryt, the entirety of Thonis only has us."

I shake my head at him, at the enormity of what lies before us. "Only a force beyond this world could see us through."

"True enough," Bakari agrees. "And we'll have our fathers to thank for preparing us to trust in that."

Chapter Thirty-Two

Day 47

A few days of steadily turning the words over like a lamb roasting on a spit finally begins to form an idea of what Kemnebi might have been referring to about deeply buried secrets.

Bakari and I are meeting with Bakenranef in his chambers after his return from the festival. We relay what's occurred as far as we know it, and our nomarch fills in some missing bits from the knowledge he gained due to his position.

"The second boat sank pretty quickly, so its cargo now belongs to the Nile," he confirms.

"The boat sank or someone sank it?" I question.

Bakenranef looks between me and Bakari. "You didn't see either way?"

I think back to that moment. *The boat rocking. The scream. The splash. Kicking up water as I run straight into the river.* I see each moment play out, but when I try to focus, the images blur.

"If it's gone, someone made sure of it," Bakari insists.

"So they were after the men and whatever they carried," I conclude. "But why attack a king's commander right in front of the palace? Especially one so favored and cousin to the queen."

"It's a perfect cover," Bakenranef explains. "Even the most beloved of the king's ministers have those who would rejoice to see them gone."

"Either way, if the attackers did take anything, they stole from a smuggler, so it's doubtful there's any trail," I add.

"Do we have any leads?" Bakari asks.

Bakenranef shakes his head. "Aside from Kemnebi and his servant, no one else survived. The one attacker who was recovered can't be identified because his face was slashed."

Bakari looks sheepish but not apologetic. "It wasn't exactly a time to worry about a clean cut."

Our nomarch waves his words away. "Probably a hired man anyway, one of a thousand faces who could have been there that day."

"So once more our most promising lead has been cut off."

Bakenranef nods, thoughtful. "Kemnebi is a shrewd individual and celebrated not only for his family ties. If anyone knows what's going on, he does."

I exchange a glance with Bakari, who leans toward me. "Can you can get something from him?"

"He asked me to *spy* for him. That proves he finds me useful, not trustworthy."

"As you've pointed out, we saved his life, and that's bound to mean something. Besides," Bakari adds, "I'd wager the commander has taken a bit of a shine to his little kyky."

I roll my eyes and ready a retort about Bakari's ridiculous imagination, but Bakenranef interrupts before we can descend into bickering. "Azizi, find a way to visit him again, and soon."

I nod, glad enough for a plan that won't lock me up in our subterranean room, wasting more time hiding when we've finally begun to uncover *something* undoubtedly big and unexpected.

I replay Kemnebi's cryptic words about buried secrets, sure there's a clue for us in there. I start from the beginning, not just from the moment he found me in the tree, but well before that, the moment I watched him standing on deck to this moment now.

Why would someone wish him harm?

From the outset, it was plain to see Kemnebi is the kind of person who turns heads due to his grace, bearing, and overwhelming presence. His *ka* is so strong, it enters a room before the rest of him, filling and surrounding the space so others can't help but notice him. Which is to say, he's the kind of man who always has eyes on him. So if he does want to move about without notice, he has to be very, very good at it.

Additionally, we'd seen his rooms, the many gifts evidence of the respect and admiration others hold for him, of just how many friends and followers he has. Which is also to say, Kemnebi has an untold number of connections, and thereby access to a great many things. A man like that could do almost anything, even without having to actually do something.

There must be a hint as to the motives of such a man tucked away in the quieter parts of his self. The answer is certainly just beyond what we've been able to see so far.

And that's when my mind snags on something we've overlooked from the day we first found the poem. The reason we were able to sneak into the commander's room to begin with.

Kemnebi had gone across the Nile to see the work on the pyramid, where Vizier Omari would meet him. In other words, we knew Kemnebi wouldn't be there because of where he would be instead.

A series of disjointed facts merge into a single clear image, so obvious now that I see it.

Pyramid. Shabti. Buried.

"Something's going to be buried in the pyramid with Meryt!" I burst out.

Whatever conversation Bakenranef and Bakari were having immediately cuts off. They stare at me with widened eyes.

"Think about what Kemnebi said," I urge. "What better place to bury a secret than with the dead? *He's* the one who'll be sealing something in the pyramid!"

Now that I see it, I can hardly consider anything else, particularly considering the map we found and the commander's meeting with the vizier. Whatever's been going on, with Thonis, with Meryt, I'm even more certain we'll find the truth of it in that pyramid.

"What would he possibly want to bury there?" Bakenranef asks.

"That's what we have to find out."

Bakari shakes his head at me. "Are we supposed to search a *king's sacred pyramid* that's crawling with workers, when we're acting only on a hunch?"

"Yes."

"Surely you're the one now stricken with madness."

"And you're the one who kept me alive without even knowing what we were looking for or our chances of finding anything at all," I rejoin. "The workers don't have to know we're working on suspicion. We need only sound certain we'll find something."

Bakari looks to Bakenranef, and then we're all looking at each other, expectation vivid in my eyes, doubt evident in theirs. But I won't back down. I'm sure of this connection, at least. I stare hard until their doubt wavers.

"I'll see about getting some workers to search it," Bakenranef reluctantly says. Keeping a maidservant alive is one level of tradition-breaking, but turning over a pyramid is sacrilegious. "Though between the ever-present guards and the thousands of workers, it won't be easy to break rank for some exploring."

I glance at Bakari, who shakes his head.

"I've been reassigned from the work shift to prepare for the upcoming race, so I doubt they'll see reason for returning me." He looks to our nomarch. "Surely we have enough men in a single work unit to do some looking around?"

Bakenranef nods absently. "We'll figure it out," he reassures us. "We'll search."

Bakari returns the nod, satisfied. I accept the answer for what it is, though I'm anxious to row across the river and begin the search myself, desperate for solid proof to confirm what I suspect.

"We haven't much time left," I remind them. "The mummifying is almost over."

"We have over two and a half weeks," Bakari says.

I blink. I should have had that number at hand, probably would have too, had I not been so caught up in murders and secrets and climbing. Two and a half weeks seems like a long time, but that means it's already been almost seven weeks since Meryt was murdered, and just over five since I was supposed to be dead too.

So much has happened since then. So much more

192

has been uncovered. And yet, even with leads but without definitive answers, the past few weeks don't look to have amounted to very much at all. Worse, it's starting to seem two and a half weeks won't be nearly enough time for what needs to be done, and then what?

Meryt will be buried with Benerib and Madu to serve her. Thonis will remain sunk and forgotten from fear of saying her name. And we will be left in the land of the living with hands empty, vengeance and answers lost in the unyielding current of time.

Chapter Thirty-Three

Day 48

It's difficult to keep my focus as I nervously await news from the pyramid. Whatever they find will answer so much of the unknown we've been grappling with the past while, and I'm eager to know so we can move forward.

I drift aimlessly through the royal gardens, sticking to walls and corners and paths lush with overgrown limbs that hide me. It seems a waste to risk searching any more rooms when this path feels so sure, yet my hands and mind itch with determination to uncover more.

I end up arguing with myself outside the door to Kemnebi's rooms, tucked behind a column from where I can watch the comings and goings in the area. As expected, many gifts and notes and well-wishers arrive. Some visitors are let in, some are not, but even those who enter do not stay long. About two hours later, I sternly tell myself I'm being ridiculous and should just take a chance. Before I can think a way out of it, my feet take me to the servants' door.

I hover near the opening until a small knot of servants appears carrying fresh linens and refreshments. I fall into line and slip past the guard with them. As they move about their tasks, I stand against the wall a moment, catching my breath, bewildered at how reckless

I've been.

When I look up, it's right into the eyes of a servant.

My breath leaves me, but as there's no immediate response, I look closer. It's the servant I gave the picture of the rooster to when I spotted Nkuku's boat. The same one who was in the boat with Kemnebi, and whose arm is now in a sling from whatever injury he sustained. I guiltily realize that I never asked after him.

His gaze flickers over me, then deliberately continues panning the door, the walls, as if to show he doesn't notice me. When I just stand there, he catches my eye and quickly flickers his gaze to his right before resuming whatever he's about. There's something to be said about being a spy of the black panther.

Quietly, I thread my way through the now familiar rooms, moving in the direction the servant indicated with his gaze. I find Kemnebi on a couch in the corner of a balcony overlooking the Nile. The shabti statuettes are lined up on a nearby table where he can study them, brow furrowed in deep thought. I don't say anything. I sink to the floor behind the table and wait.

He spots me within seconds. "Hello, Kyky," he says with a slow smile. "How did you get here?"

I keep my expression innocent. "I walked in."

Kemnebi tilts his head. "Simple as that?"

"Yes, Commander."

"I can rely on no one, even most trusted Gahiji," he says with a deep sigh.

There's something about his tone that makes me sure he said something to his servant about letting me pass should I come round. Something about the way he says his name that seems an offering, should I need it. Or him. A black panther does not just let his guard down, after all, not even for a little monkey. I suspect Gahiji is much more valuable than the mere servant I thought him to be.

"Any interesting animals on the Nile today?" Kemnebi asks.

"Nothing that can't be seen from here."

"Current conditions have resulted in being a bit on the peripheral of where I'd like to be."

So Kemnebi is also itching to get about and discover something more. That doesn't indicate if he has any leads on his attackers. His continued resting is evidence that the blade cut rather deep, though the wholeness of his *ka* already appears better.

"I do hope your scratch is healing well," I tell him.

Kemnebi inclines his head. "Would you believe I've survived worse?"

Considering Egypt hasn't been in an official war in at least twenty years, no. Then again, I know little of the work a highly regarded commander does for a king to ensure that such a peace remains so.

"I believe there isn't much you wouldn't survive," I say quietly.

Something in my response must catch him, because he unexpectedly says, "And what of what you survived? Tell me, Kyky, what was it like?" Then, off my confused look, clarifies, "Thonis. When she disappeared."

I recall the memory with as much remove as possible, seeking words to describe it without cutting too deep. The rising wave. The dark foreboding. The force that paddled us down the river without rest. The absolute silence that swallowed us. *The nothingness.*

"Sudden," I finally say. "All of it there and alive and then…not. No trace, no remnant, as if she'd never been."

Kemnebi shakes his head and leans back. This may not have been his first time getting stabbed, but his grimace says the pain is still fresh.

"I was sent to search the area after," he tells me.

"There was nothing to search."

"There was nothing to search," he echoes. "She was a beautiful city. I sailed from her shores many times."

I nod, unable to say anymore. I wonder why he's bringing this up now, what he can hope to learn from talking about this, of all things, with me. If he was there, then he knows there wasn't even anything left to look at. He knows what it was and he knows what isn't there now.

I glance at the shabti, hoping to move the conversation away from home.

"Have you ever seen the like before?" he asks, noticing my focus.

"The craftsmanship is very fine," I say.

"Among the best."

"Although, Commander, Egypt has very fine craftsmen too. Why send to Nubia for something which can be made here?"

Then, realizing I'm questioning the king's favored commander, I quickly clamp my mouth shut and drop my gaze to the floor. Perhaps he will be merciful if he sees immediate remorse and humility.

Kemnebi is quiet a few agonizing minutes, and when he speaks again, I have no idea if he's going to send me to the crocodiles or formulate some answer to my question.

"There is a legend," he says, "of a set of shabti created by Osiris himself, a gift to the first man to die and cross to the afterlife. When the man was reborn, the shabti returned with him. However, they were eventually stolen from his possession when word spread that the one buried with these statues is assured of being reborn in this world alongside Osiris."

I dare lift my eyes and look at him warily, fortified by a healthy dose of my father's skepticism. I may have seen the dark arts for myself and thereby know there are ways to tap into forces beyond observable nature, but that hardly means I believe in such myths and manmade deities.

"There are others," Kemnebi continues, as if my face doesn't betray what I'm thinking, "who claim that the Shabti of Osiris are a protection against death and destruction, an assurance that the kingdom that holds them will stand and thrive forever."

My face contorts even more, my doubt increasing with each new branch of the tale, with this twisting distraction he's offering instead of a straight answer.

"And then there are others," Kemnebi finishes quietly, his gaze now on the shabti, "who believe that too many people have been murdered chasing false prophecies, so whatever power such statues possess, they are best lost or buried where no one will find them."

My heart plummets at the familiar language, but Kemnebi makes no indication this is the second time he's spoken of buried things. He stares at the shabti, as if unaware that he's finished speaking. I take advantage of the moment to study him for any sign of what he means by telling me this tale, for any trace that he knows the secrets Nkuku took to his watery grave or the answer to the biggest secret in the palace. His gaze betrays nothing but distance, and pain.

"Are the shabti of the dark arts?" I interrupt the

silence.

Kemnebi's eyes snap back to me. "No," he says firmly, "but the craftsman who made them was a skilled practitioner."

"Was?" I question, snatching up the last word, annoyed once more that the dark arts are ever present in stories of unnatural death.

Kemnebi blinks, and that slight motion slams him back into the present, onto a balcony at the Great Palace of Thebes with a little spy from a cursed city sitting across from him. He shakes his head and smiles.

"So many questions today," he muses, deflecting.

"I only intend to act as your eyes and ears, Commander," I say simply.

Fortunately, this makes him chuckle, eyes crinkling at the corners, laughter spilling into the grooves engraved from hours squinting against the bright sea-sun. Having grown up around sailors, traders, and merchants, I know those lines well. I consider if perhaps part of my regard for Kemnebi isn't entirely because of who he is, but also because of those he reminds me of.

"Eyes and ears for me," he agrees, "not to question me."

"Even to ask after the extra guards who should still be at your door?" I may be pushing too much now, but that same recklessness that brought me here is muddling my judgment.

"I sent them away. The assassins got who they were after."

I bite my words back in time, but my heavy silence says even more. Kemnebi raises an eyebrow, as if to say it would be wise not to question him or his assertions.

"Whoever sent those men should tremble all the

more for daring to act on the very banks of the palace," he adds.

"Wouldn't be the first time," I mutter, realizing too late I spoke aloud.

"What?"

The word is sharp as the crack of a whip, and I jolt from impact. The intensity in his dark eyes grows, blackening his pupils even further, strong enough that I have to look away. When I turn back, those eyes are still watching me, unrelenting.

"What?" I choke out.

"What do you mean it wouldn't be the *first* time?"

The tone, the expression, the enormity of the man yielding it make it difficult not to spill everything right there. I bite my tongue. I don't know if I can trust him, but I do know that I can't hold back against that look. And so the words tumble out of me, controlled as much as they can be, not the truth about myself, but only about Meryt. That her death wasn't natural. That she was murdered.

"Lady Tadinanefer-Hatshepsut. Nkuku. You," I list. "Assassins do not tremble being so close to the great palace as they should. And who can guess who might be next?"

Kemnebi mulls over my question, his expression dark. "How does a little monkey in a tree know so much?"

My body wants to tremble, but I fight it until my heart pounds from exertion. "I served Mer—Lady Tadinanefer-Hatshepsut," I remind him.

The expression that crosses his face tells me clearly he noticed how I tripped over Meryt's real name. I'm certain he's figured everything out, that his next words will be accusations and condemnations for not dying with Madu and Benerib.

Instead, he says, "Someone is trying to strike at the king through those closest to him."

My eyes widen. "*The king*?"

Kemnebi doesn't immediately offer reassurance, which is worrying. "We can't really know unless we can surmise their purpose," he muses to himself.

"The queen, the vizier, either could be in danger. How many will they strike at in trying to reach the top?"

Kemnebi eyes me, no doubt already mapping out any number of strategies. "I will discuss this with my cousin."

I want to add that he shouldn't mention me, but then realize he can only speak of a girl named Kyky if he does. Though he wouldn't know much about handling spies if he did name me, even to the queen. I wait expectantly, but he doesn't say anymore, which could mean that he doesn't know, doesn't want to say, or is already making plans for how he will soon know even more than me. It could also mean that he's in on it, and that I've just revealed how much we know. The suppositions and counter-suppositions make my head spin with their unending circling.

"What can we do to ensure the others will be safe, Commander?" I ask, attempting to draw out more information.

It works somewhat, as Kemnebi returns his attention to me, but only to say, "Leave it to me. Tell no one. Don't even speak of it here."

So I don't tell him who else knows. Or that, just as he's roped a girl who was already a spy to be a spy for him, I've now accidentally roped a most powerful military official into the web of this secret about Meryt.

We wrap up the visit a few minutes later, with no more said on the subject. As I get up to leave, Kemnebi throws one last question at me.

"Kyky?"

"Yes, Commander?"

"Think your soldier friend a safe bet to win the chariot race?"

The question's so unexpected it takes a moment to decipher its meaning. In the flurry of everything else, I've forgotten all about what's coming up. The race is part of the week's long celebration leading up to the Opening of the Mouth Ceremony, all part of the official burial of the beloved Lady Tadinanefer-Hatshepsut.

I even forgot Bakari would be competing. If he wins, he'll be invited to join the long mourning procession preceding the lavish funerary banquet as it crosses the Nile into and through the Valley of the Kings.

"I'd bet on him any day," I say with the conviction that those words hold true well beyond the race.

I leave his quarters with my mind a whirlpool not only from his curious, parting question but also from all he's shared with me, and what I let slip to him. Even more, I can't figure out why he chose to share those stories about the shabti with me, why he would tell three different versions of a tale that hasn't ever been proven to hold a shred of truth. Was it a hint as to the contents of the fourth crate? Or had the stories merely been called to mind while looking at the golden shabti deliberately brought from Nubia?

Perhaps there was no specific intent, the tales nothing more than shared musings. But his words about the supposedly legendary shabti causing too much death give me pause. I can't decide if he's enamored of the tale or through with it. One thing I do know for certain is that something's shifted between us. Sure, he's still the well-loved, charismatic commander and I a mere servant to him, but after my visit this afternoon I have a sense that he's testing the waters between us, gaining a sense of the current and seeing if I'm cut of the same cloth as Gahiji.

I don't know if that leaves me in a better or worse position, considering we don't yet really know what Kemnebi is up to. I can't even guess if the injury that brought him here was ever that severe or if what I unintentionally revealed will be to our detriment. Nor can I fathom what benefit such a powerful, well-admired, honored individual could possibly see in keeping me close.

I'm so lost in thought I almost stumble upon something I shouldn't and give my cover away. I missed the voices I almost came upon and only pull back into sharp focus of the world around me at the sound of high-pitched, girlish laughter.

There's no corner to hide me in this open courtyard, so I quickly duck into the shade from a cluster of young pomegranate trees. I peek through the branches and stumble back in shock.

Bakari stands with a fellow soldier and three women, both men appearing capable and strong with their military postures and muscled torsos exposed to the sun. Peering closer and most certainly *not* spying, it looks like they've been stopped by the wives of court nobles. I don't see each clearly, but I've been at the palace long enough to identify most of the women by voice and mannerism.

And there's no mistaking their manners or intent in

stopping two young soldiers of the king's army. In an open courtyard. Where anyone can see what transpires between them.

The too-friendly smiles.

The suggestive demeanors.

The giggles burbling up like the bubbled breath of fish in the river.

I grit my teeth, thinking of my father and what he would say, why he never wished us a life at court.

Then I hurry away from the question of why I grit my teeth at all, as if whatever Bakari does is any business of mine.

Chapter Thirty-Four

Day 49

"I looked for you in Thonis last night."

Bakari's voice cuts into the jumble of my thoughts, my conversation with Kemnebi, the moment I wasn't supposed to see, each piece merging into a muddy mess that's clouded my mind all day.

I struggle to focus on his face and the smell of horses and feel of the stall wall against my back as he brushes down his beautiful horse from this morning's training for the race.

It even takes a moment to remember why I'm here, to remember that I awoke with the memory of Kemnebi's question about betting on Bakari and next found myself in the stall, ducking behind the horse to keep out of sight.

"What?" I ask, forcing myself to look at Bakari.

"I looked for you last night," he repeats.

"I was on the roof." My eyes are already straying back to the horse.

"I looked there."

I shrug, still not meeting his eyes. I'd hidden on the roof until I was sure he would give up looking for me and return to his barracks. "We must have missed each other."

A long pause, then, "Is everything all right?"

"Aside from the usual situation?"

Bakari sighs. "Yes, aside from that. Something happen yesterday?"

"Yesterday," I echo, an unwanted image of a blooming courtyard filled with coy laughter and stoic bearings sprouts to memory. I push the scene away, telling myself it doesn't matter, reminding myself there are quite a few more important things to focus on.

"Did you find anything new yesterday?" Bakari prods. "Were you seen by someone?"

"I visited Kemnebi."

The brush pauses in Bakari's hand, but he doesn't immediately respond. Eventually, his hand resumes its long strokes along the horse's back. I watch, mesmerized by the motion.

"You're becoming a regular visitor there."

That snaps me to full attention. "Didn't we agree I was to try getting more information out of him?"

"Of course we did," he says tersely. "It's just, the stabbing—surely there's somewhere less conspicuous."

It's the tone of his voice that breaks the dam I've been trying to build. "Conspicuous," I snort, my own tone sharper than expected.

Bakari stops moving, his hand frozen midair. Slowly, he lowers it and turns toward me, a mix of shock and confusion on his face.

"What are you so upset about?"

I want to bite back the words I've unleashed, berating myself for being so foolish. But, of course, it's too late, so I may as well speak and get this wreck over with.

"I saw you in the courtyard yesterday," I accuse, "you and another soldier, when I was returning from my visit."

Bakari's brow furrows, trying to pinpoint where I might be headed.

"Certain...women were there too."

It's a moment before Bakari's brow clears in understanding, and I'm slightly surprised when his next reaction isn't anger or even embarrassment but resignation. He nudges the horse's nose so he can duck around to my side of the stall and look me straight in the eye, clearly showing the intent of honor and honesty in his.

The moment is intense, and I break it by glancing down and noticing how his hand has tightened over the brush, a hand calloused from the chariot's reins, the same hand which brought a forgotten city to life with ink and paint. I've never thought about such things before, or what they might mean about the kind of man the carefree young troublemaker from Thonis has become.

"I won't deny that such an...encounter is not uncommon," he says, his voice rough, stilted. "Certainly not for a soldier, especially not for a favored one. Wasn't the first time and probably won't be the last either. I also won't deny that for a young soldier it's rather flattering that pretty women seek him out, even without encouragement."

His gaze fixes on me, but neither of us can hold the other's eyes for long, not with such words filling the air between us. It's odd, but before six weeks ago I don't think this conversation would have played out the same. I don't know if it would've happened at all. If I'd have spoken or if Bakari would've felt an urge to explain instead of tease or deflect or call me difficult.

But much has changed since then, and there's a burn

to his *ka* now, a sense that it's less about excuses and more about something he wants me to understand, an undertow to his words that speaks to a care that I see him right. I don't know if I welcome it, unable as I am in the moment to pinpoint what this newness is.

"Azizi, I remember Thonis. It isn't easy, but I do not forget when I shouldn't."

He pauses but I don't chance a glance at him, unsure if he's finished or what I might see if I meet his eyes. The pressure settling hard against my heart has returned, though it's less a sense of drowning and more a sense I can't completely identify. Perhaps it's the return of feeling to someone who's escaped death, who wants to live enough to allow what's alive in this life to mean something to her again. It's possible this feeling isn't a pressure but a fullness, a fullness that swells in the reassurance that when a whole city becomes a curse, someone else remembers how it was once a blessing. Even more, he remembers how sturdy were the homes that raised us, how enduring were the ways our fathers showed us.

"Besides," Bakari adds, his voice lighter, "just because I don't really write love heart's poems doesn't mean I'm careless and free."

I keep my gaze fixed on the horse behind the soldier, suddenly afraid to look up, afraid he'll start again with his rare desert flower poetry if I do, afraid he might be teasing. *Afraid he might not.*

The moment passes as he turns back to the horse and resumes his gentle brush strokes. He doesn't press me for a response, and I don't trust myself to give one until I'm sure that any will be out of place for its delay, so I can avoid it after all. I move along the wall, toward the door of the stall.

Only then do I look up, but not at Bakari or the horse but outward, toward where the Nile runs, flowing constant and sure.

"Is it odd to deal so much with horses?" I ask, hand ready on the door. "When so much of our life was the sea?"

Finished, Bakari steps away from the horse and stands beside me. He opens his palm to reveal a thick carrot nestled inside. He slides to the side as I take it from him, then gestures with his chin toward the horse. Hesitant, awkward, I offer up the carrot.

The horse neatly snatches the treat between its teeth and quickly nibbles down. I jump back with a small squeak when its lips reach my fingers.

Bakari watches with a fond smile. "It's surprising sometimes, isn't it, how quickly we can adapt to something new."

He opens the door for me, but doesn't let me go without a parting wink, which follows me as I leave the stables and step back into the sunshine.

Chapter Thirty-Five

Day 54

Bakari and I are intercepted by Kemnebi's servant as we're making our way to Bakenranef's rooms to find out if there's any update from the pyramid. I recognize him immediately as the one who did not stop me from visiting Kemnebi just days ago. I search for the name that's slipped into memory, Gahiji.

His appearance is so quiet and so sudden, we have no time to react in any way but blink in confusion over where he came from. My first thought is that I understand how Kemnebi could be so sure of finding out what he needs to know with such a man in his service. And if this is only a servant, who could say what the master can do?

"Commander wishes to see you," he intones in his deep voice. "Both of you."

I exchange a quick glance with Bakari as Gahiji turns to lead the way, certain we'll follow. I only have enough time to relay with a look that Bakari's guess is as good as mine in regard to what Kemnebi could want with us this time.

Surprisingly, Gahiji doesn't walk us to Kemnebi's rooms or any other room in the palace. Instead, he leads us outdoors, weaving at an odd angle through a quiet, well-maintained orchard of fig, jujube, and even some peach trees heavy with fruit adding an enticing dash of red and orange.

"Where are we going?" I mouth to Bakari.

He answers with a shrug, as much a stranger to this part of the palace as I.

We move away from the orchards and cross through a less cultivated patch of land. Within minutes, we're nearing a figure who has his back to us and a bundle at his feet. Several more steps and the figure turns. Kemnebi. As we approach, Gahiji crouches and raises the bundle up as he straightens. I start. Not a bundle, a man.

"Kyky, Bakari," Kemnebi greets us shortly.

A glance toward the man Gahiji roughly grips. A glance toward the area behind him, which rolls away from us at a steep downward incline. The curve of the land indicates a circular impression in the ground, and I step forward to take a closer look.

"Careful," Kemnebi warns calmly.

One glance down reveals why. Long, scaly green creatures mingle at their leisure in the hot sun. The crocodile pits. They exist, here, at the Great Palace of Thebes. I immediately back away.

"Why are we here?" Bakari asks before I can form words.

Kemnebi looks at us both evenly. "You've been investigating a murder," he states.

We nod.

"And here is your murderer," he says, gesturing to the man Gahiji restrains.

A nod removes the gag from the man's mouth, but all he does is spit in our direction. I step to the side and out of range, just another step in the odd dance this scene is turning into.

The man is lean, bloodied and bruised in several places. His legs barely manage to hold him up. Dried blood flakes from his fingers, his chin, his swollen eye. No doubt he's been beaten, probably tortured, even starved. Yet he is defiant.

"How?" I stutter.

We've been looking so long, we'd been so lost, floundering without even a clue of where or how to begin. How did Kemnebi manage to solve everything so quickly?

The commander purses his lips, a sort of answer to say that he has his ways. "Thank the queen for the expediency."

I stare at him. "You-you told the queen?"

Kemnebi nods. "Her Glorious Majesty may be at heightened risk, and as you see, the decision has proven wise."

"What about the king?" Bakari asks.

Kemnebi doesn't immediately answer. After a pause, he finally says, "The king, may his life be eternal, has entrusted me to do what must be done."

His answer is vague, and, I suddenly realize, without limits. Unease creeps in and slowly dampens my relief. Something tells me I would be a fool not to become even more wary of Kemnebi, despite his capture of the poisoner.

I turn toward the man who took Meryt from us and glare at him with a look I wish could kill. "He confessed?"

"Eagerly," Kemnebi confirms.

"Why?" I ask the man. "Why did you do it?"

He grins, revealing bloody, broken teeth, then

merely shrugs, a response more infuriating than almost any he could've said. The only reason I don't pound him into the sand in that moment is because Bakari places a restraining grip on my shoulder.

"Did you know she carried the king's heir?" I accuse, harsher. "You murdered a woman *and* a child!"

The corners of the man's lips slip very slightly before his self-assured grin returns in force. Something flickers in the eye that can still open properly. Perhaps he didn't know. Or he didn't think we did. Or he didn't care. Bakari's hand tightens on my shoulder.

"Thonis," Bakari says to the man. "What do you know about what happened to Thonis?"

The man looks at each of us, and his smirk grows wider and even more malicious. Black panther. Little monkey. Charioteer. He surely knows this is the end of him, that his life will not last past this encounter or only be extended long enough for him to wish it hadn't been.

"This is only the beginning!" he cries.

Then, before anyone can move, he twists violently away from Gahiji, catching him off guard long enough to yank free.

With a running start, he recklessly flings himself into the crocodile pit. Bakari and Kemnebi and Gahiji are right behind, but they are not quick enough to stop him. They stand a moment, perhaps watching as the body falls, but turn away at the dull *thwack* and the sudden roar of awakened predators. The sound of dozens of snapping jaws rises from the pit, followed by an unearthly scream abruptly cut off by a gut-churning *crack*.

I can't move, overwhelmed by disbelief, anger, hurt. I catch Kemnebi's eye as he turns back. What happens now?

Kemnebi sighs. "There is naught to be done now but hunt down every accomplice and wipe them from Egypt." He nods, as if his assertion is closure enough. "This will not be a beginning but an end."

He signals to Gahiji and the pair stride off, leaving me and Bakari alone near the crocodiles. The feeding frenzy has ended, but the sickening sounds still echo. A cynical part of me wonders if Kemnebi hasn't left us here on purpose, some sort of threat or warning or promise or…who can even know the thoughts of so favored and shrewd a commander.

Bakari and I exchange a glance. I'm about to speak, but he shakes his head, as if to say, *Not here*. Then, perhaps alerted to something in my expression, he puts a hand to my elbow and steers me away from the pit. We don't stop until we're safely tucked away in our subterranean room. The moment Bakari's hand falls away, I whirl on him.

"What just happened?"

Bakari shakes his head and rubs his scalp. "Could it be that simple? All we've been looking for, done?"

I frown. "We didn't learn *anything* from him! Even if he did poison Meryt that doesn't tell us who sent him or why. Nor does it explain how Kemnebi and the queen found him in *days*."

"We should be satisfied the murderer was caught and punished."

"But I want to know *why*!" I shout. "I want to know what happened to Thonis!"

"As do I." Bakari squares his jaw. "If anything, we need to watch Kemnebi even closer, because if he finds anyone else who's connected, we must speak to him on our own. Or we may never know the truth of any of it."

I shake my head, refusing to allow such an option to take hold. The only thing worse than all the merciless death is the unknown, the lack of reason for any of it. The reason might be even worse to hear, but at least it will be something to hold onto. At least we needn't feel so lost.

"This does not grant me peace. This does not reassure me of justice," I insist. "If anything, it makes the questions stronger."

"So we keep looking for answers."

I nod but stop midway as a new thought begins to form. "For all we know, that man may have been the poisoner or someone our esteemed commander used in his place. Note how the assassins are killed during their attack, then the poisoner throws himself to his death."

"Certainly convenient for whoever else may be involved," Bakari agrees.

I press a palm to the painted walls of Thonis, reassurance and vow that I am not satisfied, that I have not forgotten them.

"Kemnebi may or may not be innocent, but the poisoner was right about one thing," I say, "this is only the beginning. And we will not reach the end until we know what Kemnebi is hiding in that fourth crate."

Chapter Thirty-Six

Day 55

Rasidi is already in Bakenranef's chambers by the time I arrive for an update. At first, I'd thought we'd been summoned because of what happened with Kemnebi at the crocodile pit, but as soon as I see the now familiar figure waiting, my stomach sinks.

I may have found a level of regard for the medicine woman, not least for saving my life twice, but that doesn't mean I'm comfortable around her. Or when seeing her I think of anything but poison, the precipice of death, and dark, dark arts. Dark arts which almost killed me once, and have saved me since. I'd like to believe there's more to Rasidi than the path she's chosen, but past experience and perception have made me conflicted and pretty sure my heart has not remained untainted.

Bakari enters right behind me, and as soon as we're all accounted for, we relay what occurred at the crocodile pit. The nomarch frowns as we speak.

"That's it?" he asks, bewildered. "An assassin found and gone?"

I nod. "We could only confirm his confession before he threw himself over."

"What answers of Thonis?" he presses.

"There were none," Bakari answers. "Only

intimation of more to come."

Bakenranef's frown deepens. "Something isn't right," he murmurs. "Too tidy, it leaves too much unknown."

He's spoken our thoughts exactly.

Bakenranef falls into troubled silence, and instead of saying more, he breaks his thoughts and looks toward Rasidi. The rows of bracelets along each arm chime softly when she moves.

"I inquired after Tsillah," she begins, catching my attention entirely. "She was trained by a rather powerful priestess in a temple in Kerma where she lived before the queen took her in."

"And?" I press, seeing the loose ends of yet another set of questions just beyond reason's grasp.

Rasidi shifts in her seat, eliciting another musical chord. I don't know her well enough to read her, but I would say with confidence she looks unsettled. Something thuds deep within me at the thought of such a slight girl causing Rasidi disquiet.

"The path she walks is notably, ah, absent of light," she replies.

"Speak plain, Rasidi," Bakenranef urges.

"She's very powerful," Rasidi says straight. "She doesn't move about much, but I've been keeping an eye on the queen's chambers, so I can watch for her when she does. There isn't anything obvious about her actions, walking the gardens, gathering a plant here or there, eating the same food as the rest, if smaller portions. But for those who know how to spot the subtle gestures, how to listen for the words spoken under a breath, she's steeped in the dark arts. I suspect she's capable of things I've only ever heard of."

"Have we any protection against her?" I ask.

Rasidi frowns. "Powerful or not, the dark arts is limited in what it can create and what it can affect."

"Could she poison a queen without actual poison?"

Rasidi shakes her head. "No," she says firmly, "she cannot. Someone had to administer the poison, so if that man confessed, he may have spoken true."

"What about Thonis?"

Rasidi opens her hands wide, showing such is beyond her capacity, but not ensuring it's beyond *anyone's.* "That would require some tremendous power indeed."

I slump back in my chair, mulling her mixed answers. I find some comfort in her confirmation about the accused man, yet I'm still very troubled about Thonis, about this girl and her shadows. At least the shadows I've been forced to cling to were signs of life. I cannot claim the same for the queen's ward.

"Where does this girl, this ward, factor into all this?" Bakenranef asks to the point.

We all glance at each other.

"Maybe she doesn't," Bakari suggests. "At least not yet."

"You suspect the queen might be saving her for something?" I pipe in.

"Maybe," Bakari replies. "Though she may just be a ward, and knowing of her powers, the queen requests spells for her own protection. Whoever has orchestrated all this death obviously has no care for rank or status. Anyone could be at risk."

Rasidi nods. "King Pa-Ankh-Entef was persuaded to give me a home here for what I could do, so it's entirely likely this all comes down to a familial favor by

Queen Sekhmet. Such a move is not unusual across royal courts and noble homes."

I'm shaking my head even before she's finished speaking. Perhaps kings and queens and nobles offer a home to young women with certain powers, but it's too simple an explanation for the queen's ward. I may be influenced by prior perceptions, but I *know* the girl is up to something.

"It's the Nubian connection," I insist to Bakari, but he only shakes his head at me.

The topic of Tsillah falters, not least because there's only so much help and knowledge the rest of us can offer about her. Rasidi will continue to watch her, and Bakari and I are happy to leave her to her task. That decided, there's another important question to address.

"What news from the pyramid?" I turn to Bakenranef. "It's been a week without update."

Our nomarch runs a hand over his shaved head, a habit I've noticed he leans on when he has news he doesn't want to deliver. I've spotted him often enough at court with one of several wigs, but he's free from such weights of fashion here. Kemnebi is one of very few people who doesn't bother with a wig at court, nor did we spot any in his rooms. Perhaps the hair tangles in his rows of earrings, but I doubt it. Everyone here has earrings, and everyone seems to find a way around such hiccups. Perhaps it's merely that a panther doesn't need to prove the blackness of his coat.

"It's been more difficult to get someone in to search than anticipated," he says. "With so many men working each lighted hour of the day, there's heightened challenge in slipping away from the workforce without being noticed or without a work station suddenly falling short in its progress."

"So we've no hope there," I conclude.

"I didn't say that," Bakenranef corrects. "Over the last week, our friends on the job have managed to nab a few quick peeks."

"Anything suspicious?" I jump in. "Did they find the missing crate?"

Bakenranef shakes his head and is soon running his hand back and forth across his scalp again.

"Nothing unusual," he says quietly.

His words are so simple, yet they pin me to my seat. I was so certain something would be found, so certain the pyramid was the answer to the hint Kemnebi tucked into his words, the final link in a chain of disjointed parts. Could I have imagined all of it? Conjured a clue and a solution because I've grown so desperate to find anything that will mean something?

"Breathe, Zizi," a voice drifts on a whisper into my ear.

I don't realize how lost I am in shock until I'm swimming toward those words. I finally focus enough to realize Bakari is crouching beside me, coaxing me to regain myself.

"There you are," he says, when I meet his gaze. "I worried you'd swallowed some mandrake again."

I stare at him and he laughs when I blink, a sound more relieved than joyful.

"I was so sure," is all I can say.

Bakari nods. "I hoped we'd finally find some answers there as well."

I slump in my chair. "Will we ever take a step forward without losing two more falling back?"

"Investigating after something occurs means we're

already starting off behind," Bakenranef says. "And though Kemnebi may have caught the man we've been looking for, his efforts have interfered in our work."

"We still have time, Azizi," Bakari reminds me, "and we do know more than before. At least we know someone has paid for Meryt."

"But we don't know what any of it means," I counter, "or how any of it is connected at all!"

"We still have time," Bakari repeats. "We have time."

I'm not entirely reassured by his words. Not after so much time has passed and we're floundering in a sea of more questions than answers. From when I was brought into this little group of spies, I've tried hard to remain patient before the unknown, to propel myself forward with the conviction that we would succeed. But it's moments like these, in the void of unfulfilled expectation, when despair rears up the strongest, sweeping through my *metr* and dragging me down.

I repeat Bakari's words over and over, a mantra and a promise that as long as we have time, we have a chance. I cling to them, the only raft I have left in this darkened, tumultuous sea of broken lives and deception.

Chapter Thirty-Seven

Day 56

I sit quietly tucked away from the world on a branch of my adopted acacia tree and bite into a peach. It's warm and sweet and I lean forward so the sticky juices drip away from my chin and hands.

I know I should be elsewhere. I know I should be spying and slinking and skulking between shadows, using the little time we have left before Meryt is buried to the fullest, but I can't bring myself to care. I'm allowing myself this pocket of time to detach from the mysteries and secrets and death. So much so that this moment of sunshine dappling my face and this sweetness dripping from my hands is so far removed from my current life it's almost ludicrous it could be real.

In this precious cocoon of quiet, I look anywhere but across the river to the Valley of the Kings and the mastabas and pyramids and tombs. To my left is Thebes, the capital city, a swirling mass of movement and sound as men and women move about their day. To my right, well beyond the reaches of the palace, are the first hints of farmland dug deep into rich soil and close enough to the river to be watered when it overflows its banks. Within a few months, those long rows of deep brown earth will puddle, then turn into fields of wheat, ripening gold in the sun.

There weren't many farms in Thonis, as the small islets that made up the whole of the city were too small for much plowing or even grazing. We were also too close to the sea, which could hardly be relied upon to water grain as the Nile does. Many families cultivated small garden patches for beans and lettuce, garlic and leek. All across the small chain of islands was dotted with fruit trees, wonderfully leafy and heavy with orange peaches and browned jujubes, red pomegranates and dark black plums in their seasons. The walls of several houses were also home to wide-spreading grape vines or cascading jasmine, coloring the sandstone bricks green and purple as they bloomed.

I miss my beautiful city so much it hurts.

To my right and to my left and even on the river before me, where boats glide past carrying wares or passengers, an untold number of lives are being lived. To each are joys and sorrows, secrets and celebrations, triumphs and failings, but not one is prevented from leaving footprints in the sands. Rather, that's a lone privilege belonging to me, a spirit in a tree who sees so many lives and yet cannot take part in any.

I finish the peach but remain in the tree, ignoring the sun's journey across the sky as I embrace the anonymity. This isn't simply about grabbing a few moments to ground myself in small blessings, to remind myself of the little details that add sweetness and richness to life. I just don't want to return to the palace. Not to the futile fight against the unknown forces moving against us, already so many steps ahead. Not to the memory of a city that became a curse, to survivors who were called blessed, even though one is now murdered and one was bound by duty to follow into death. Not to the emptiness of a justice served without answers, explanation, or satisfaction, nor the undercurrent of a palace's web of connections and favors and debts I can barely keep track of. I want to stay on this branch forever and forget about everything but the rush of the river, the rustle of the leaves, and the sear of the sun on a narrow strip of desert land.

Mother would say I was being defiant. Father would hide a wink behind a somber expression. And Bakari would say—

"You're being difficult."

The soldier stands at the foot of the tree, one hand on the trunk, ready to climb and drag me back down if he must.

"Don't you ever have somewhere to be?" I call down.

Bakari looks right and left with exaggerated inquiry. "Is this not somewhere?"

I roll my eyes, though I doubt he can see it. "Don't you have a schedule or training or wrestling to get to?"

Bakari unleashes his infuriating smirk. "You want to see me wrestle again?"

"I want to stay in this tree," I enunciate.

"I'm giving someone else a chance to win."

I peer at him, considering. "By not wrestling?"

Bakari drapes himself in false modesty. "It would hardly be honorable to go easy on an opponent," he says. "But, if I'm not there, then it's impossible for me to beat him."

"So sing the praise of humble Bomani-Bakari!" I proclaim. "Won't your adoring fans ask after your whereabouts?"

"They're no doubt thinking I have some very

important business to attend to, or are insanely jealous of who I might be spending time with."

"Ah, I am ever grateful you allowed Hamadi to win that day."

"Not that Unika would ever have me anyway."

"Unika was smarter than the rest of us," I agree. "What about the race? Do you also plan on not showing up?"

"My pride would not allow me to go so far," Bakari says easily.

"But it takes skill and not pride to win a race," I caution.

Bakari barks out a short laugh. "You sound like my father."

He inclines his head, measuring my distance, squinting as the sun stripes across his eyes despite the black kohl around them. He grabs hold of a limb, testing.

"Will you come down or must I climb up?"

"If you're here to give me a talking—"

"I wouldn't dare."

"Or to write a poem!"

"I'm just here, Zizi," Bakari says simply. "That's all."

That stops me, the frankness of it, the candor infusing his words. I lower myself down a few branches, but not yet all the way down. I'm still above Bakari, but within reach so we needn't shout.

"I needed to break from feeling helpless," I explain, giving him honesty in turn, "a break from feeling that I've abandoned Meryt, and even Benerib and Madu, to the afterlife without evidence to hold and explain why. What if—"

Bakari's shaking his head even before I've finished

speaking. "Don't go back down that road," he warns. "There's no end to it."

"But that's no answer."

Bakari sighs. "You think I never wonder what would've been if we hadn't left Thonis earlier than planned? Or if I'd persuaded my brothers or mother or father to finally come with us to Thebes and see the palace for themselves as we'd always planned?"

He pauses to slow the anger that's building as he speaks. His grip strengthens around the limb, muscles straining briefly as he pulls himself up to sit across from me in the tree. "They'd been promising to visit for months," he continues, "and what if they finally had?"

"And what if our fathers had been away on trade?"

"Or if you'd brought Kebi to Memphis as she wanted?"

"Or if the king had never seen Meryt?"

"Or if I had beaten Hamadi that day in wrestling!"

I laugh, but it's more to release the strangling tension than from any real sense of joy.

"Such questions could go on forever," I muse. "And then promptly circle back on themselves."

"Which is why it's best to stay away from such thinking," Bakari emphasizes. "Rather, focus on what's known and what steps we can take, however small they may be. At least we're moving forward."

"For example," I begin, "I know that if I throw this pit as hard as I can, I could land it much farther than you can."

Bakari raises his brows. "And where is my pit?"

"There is only one pit."

"So there is only one throw."

"Exactly. I throw farthest this way."

A wide smile stretches across Bakari's lips, reaching up his cheeks to crinkle the corners of his eyes. "You've taken some tips from my wrestling credo," he says in admiration.

"As long as it doesn't get me in a headlock because I was distracted by a feint."

"You have been watching!" Bakari is entirely too pleased.

"I was watching for suspects while you happened to be training below."

"Call it as you will, the facts remain. Now, will you finally join me on the ground below?"

Instead of responding, I climb down the rest of the way and brush myself off at the bottom. Bakari follows quickly behind.

"Much better." Bakari nods when we're standing across from each other.

I look at the tree with a mind to climb right back up again. Then I glance in the direction of the palace and sigh. "I suppose there's no running away from it."

"That's a cry to lead an army to battle."

"We don't need an army, just answers."

"Then let's find them," he replies, gesturing for me to lead the way, perhaps afraid I'll whip right around and dart back up the tree.

I start toward the palace, musing over how many things have changed since Meryt turned the king's head, so very many in so short a time. I pray to Father's Divine Force that we'll need even less to turn things around.

Bakari falls into step beside me once it's clear I'm really walking back. I watch as our bare feet fall into pace together, as we wade through a short path of wild purple and white daisies, deep blue anemone, and white flowering myrtle marking the outer boundaries of the palace.

It's a few moments of silence before he says something, and even then it's so quiet, I'm sure he's talking to himself. Except, I hear the words he says and know they're also for me.

"Don't ever regret choosing life," he whispers, "for that isn't very much life at all."

They sound like words our fathers would have said if they'd had the chance. Instead, Bakari is the one to say them. Bakari who never ceased to live each day and who knows how important they are for facing whatever comes next.

Chapter Thirty-Eight

Day 60

I resume the motions of listening and sifting and lurking, but it takes time for me to find the rhythm again, fighting as I am to keep despair at bay. Dark thoughts linger, waiting and watching and warning of failure in the deep recesses of my mind. Over and over, I forcefully push them aside. They cannot subvert my attention if I don't allow them to touch me at all.

I visit Kemnebi in the morning, his *ka* nearly returned to him in full health. He didn't quite look himself that day at the crocodile pit, but I thought then it was only because of the man at his feet. Seeing him, I realize what a struggle it must have been for him to stand and appear strong when his body was still healing from a missed blow of death.

The visit is pleasant but wholly unremarkable, which is odd enough, all things considered, yet there is no one moment or word to tease and tangle my thoughts after. We play a few games of *senet*, during which I concentrate enough to scratch out a win, and we pass the time without a single mention of roosters or secrets or shabti or murderers or even trees. I had hoped the commander might reveal something more about the assassin or whatever other investigations he's conducting, but, true to his warning to never speak of the murder in his rooms, he acts as though none of it has ever happened.

Rather, he speaks about Nubia—Kush as they call it—how his family would travel south during *peret* season to visit with his mother's family at their large estate. Queen Sekhmet's family would be there as well, so they spent much time together during childhood. Kemnebi hadn't considered joining the navy until it became evident King Pa-Ankh-Entef would make Sekhmet his queen, which was how he was able to enter the king's service already an officer.

"Did you hesitate to join the Egyptian army?" I ask, praying the question won't be considered untoward.

Thankfully, Kemnebi shakes his head in response. "Marrying the queen seemed signal enough of the king's intent to keep peace between our two countries. Some spit on me for signing on, but others commended me for finding a way to stay close to the queen."

"On the seas?"

"Sharp for a little kyky," Kemnebi observes.

Suddenly, I fear I've gone too far, forgotten the distance between our stations in the seeming innocence of the visit, and am about to feed a pit of hungry crocodiles. Kemnebi must see something in my look, for he smiles without sharpness. Knowing him so little, I may be reading him wrong, but I sense an openness in his look. Not a guarantee of blurred lines and absolute honesty, but something that suggests I'm allowed to ask the right sort of questions this once.

"Power," he explains. "Each victory, each time I distinguish myself, my Nubian family brags about how we are holding the navy together. How we are proving that we too can be a force on the water, not just with archers and chariots. Besides, everyone knows a successful commander is a favored one."

"Can a man really speak of such things aloud?" I whisper.

Kemnebi glances around, not a servant in earshot, except Gahiji. "You know what it means to balance the love of two countries."

I glance at him, startled, and his smile widens, squinting his eyes so he looks to be charting his course at sea.

"Kyky of Thonis, you may dress and speak and act Egyptian, but Phoenicia is written in your eyes."

I stare at him, floundering for words.

"You forget," he tells me gently, "how much I also have seen commanding men and sailing seas."

We return to the game and Kemnebi returns to his stories. I don't understand why he shares these with me, stories about trying to capture a stray cat with the young queen in Nubia or about their uncle who policed with a trained monkey. And yet, it seems natural for these stories to flow, to share something of the world beyond the palace while we toss the sticks and move the pieces around the board. Though Kemnebi's younger than my father was, I can almost hear his voice in the tales the commander tells, the deep chords speaking of other lands returning me to a place that's kept alive in the last two remaining hearts.

The only words that give me pause at all is that sharing his childhood with the queen means they are much closer than we accounted for. Although, if that means the queen knows of her cousin's dealings with smugglers, or if the panther knows of how his cousin once made a servant disappear because of a broken vase is difficult to determine. It certainly explains why he went himself to the queen with the news of a murderer. Through his stories, I sense him tying threads together for me, even if I can't say what or how. He doesn't offer any startling information, yet I feel I understand more, somehow. It leaves me in quite a place of in-between, my suspicion of him warring with this carefully curated friendship he's given me.

After the visit, I'm finally feeling like I may be returning to myself when I'm summoned to Bakenranef's rooms for a late-night meeting. I try not to let it interfere with the rest of the day, but a meeting in his rooms can only mean something very, very good or something very, very bad. There's no other reason to gather us back so soon after our last meeting.

I enter Bakenranef's rooms a step behind Rasidi. Bakari's already there, leaning against a wall with a look that doesn't foretell good news. He appears slightly worn, probably from training for the upcoming chariot race, as his body speaks of a tired *ka*.

A dusty young boy stands beside the same table Bakenranef leans over. I rise on tiptoes to peek at what they're studying so intently and catch sight of the design for King Pa-Ankh-Entef's pyramid. The one drawn from the papers I found in Vizier Omari's room, the hidden passage and chamber added onto the same page in a different color to distinguish it.

A boulder tumbles into my stomach as I join Bakari against the wall.

"What's happened?" I whisper.

Bakari glances over at me. "You were right," he answers, though the look on his face says he isn't entirely thrilled with it.

"About which part?" I ask, half in jest.

Before Bakari can say anything, Bakenranef glances up and notices the rest of us there. He looks directly at me before clearing his throat and running a nervous hand across his scalp.

A second boulder thumps down to join the first.

"What happened now?"

Bakenranef clears his throat again. "Azizi was correct," he echoes the soldier, then gestures to the boy beside him to speak.

He appears intimidated, but some light prodding from our nomarch finally buffers him.

"I greet you," the boy says, bowing to each of us. "May you *ka* shines bright and you lifes be eternal." He swallows, pushing back the small tremor in his voice. "I comes from the pyramid. I runs to brings the message to the headman and brings water to the mens when they works. I am *shaduf*-boy."

"Tell them what you saw," Bakenranef prompts.

"In the nighttimes," the boy continues, "two moons ago, I am late to the sleep because I have lost *shaduf* for water bucket and the headman is very angry if I cannot finds it. The mens cannot drinks if there is no *shaduf* to scoops the water. So I looks for it nears the pyramid but no one is there because it is too much dark for more workings."

"Did you find the *shaduf*?" Rasidi asks kindly.

The boy nods. "I finds the *shaduf*, but I also hears mens is coming. I am too much small so they do not sees me, but I sees them."

My voice catches in my throat, but I manage to scratch out, "What did they do?"

The boy looks directly at me, light brown eyes

friendly and utterly without guile. "I sees them carry a crate. They brings the crate insides the pyramid."

My breath stops completely. I grab Bakari's arm and squeeze, exultant. "The missing crate! It's found!"

Bakari shakes his head at me. It takes him two tries to speak. "That's the thing, Azizi, they couldn't find it."

I know something is wrong if he's calling me by my full name.

"What? Kemnebi said, 'The thing about secrets is they keep best buried deep.' So it has to be there."

"Our men have searched everywhere," Bakenranef explains, "but they can't find a thing. Not even an errant footprint. The crate's disappeared. Again."

I shake my head at him, at the boy, at everyone in the room. "No-no-no-no-no, it can't disappear. It can't disappear if he saw it. It *can't*."

"Azizi—" Bakari tries, but I cut him off.

"*No*," I insist, "they must have missed something. They had to have missed something!"

Bakenranef jabs at the papyrus on the table before him. "They didn't miss anything!"

"The hidden chamber!" I try, but my nomarch cuts me off.

"There is no hidden chamber!" he exclaims, exasperation evident, though if it's for me or the results or the entire situation is anyone's guess. "They looked everywhere. They know everything on this page, and off. It's gone, just gone."

I slump right to the floor, defeated. How can we find something that won't stay seen? How can we catch up to someone who keeps vanishing? Is there no end to the number of times we'll grab hold only to find our hands empty? This was supposed to be our chance at answers.

"What does this mean?" I ask in a quiet voice.

"It means," Bakari says, eyes fixed on me, "little as I like or agree with such conclusions," he darts a look at our nomarch, "that someone might have to go into the pyramid."

"But it was searched and nothing was found," I repeat.

Bakari shakes his head. "Unless a great feat of dark arts was performed, that crate is there somewhere. With enough time, without anyone around, someone could actually find it."

"What you're saying—?"

"What we're saying," Bakenranef interrupts, his voice firm, his hand steady and away from his scalp, "is that in five days, the mummification will be complete and work will cease on the pyramid for a long while. As such, it will be the perfect opportunity for someone to get a good, thorough look at just what's been placed inside."

"You're going to lock someone in the pyramid? Alive?"

Bakenranef waves his hand at my exaggeration. "It will be during the Opening of the Mouth ceremony and funeral banquet. No workers, everyone's distracted, easy to slip in and out before the door is sealed."

"A priest or priestess would be least suspicious," I suggest.

"A priest cannot be bought," Bakenranef says.

"That's not true," I rejoin, "and everyone knows it."

"We need someone who can disappear without notice," Bakenranef amends.

I nod toward Rasidi. "Surely you have some sort of sand for that?"

Rasidi shakes her head. "Even if I did, who wouldn't

notice someone suddenly turning invisible? Or someone missing entirely?"

"What if that someone gets caught? Or trapped inside?" I demand.

"It won't happen," Bakari says firmly. "But if it does, we'll get that someone out."

"And what sort of someone could be persuaded to search a pyramid readied for the dead?" I question, though the threatening avalanche of boulders in my stomach hints well enough to where this conversation is headed.

"Someone who knows what should have been packed away," Bakenranef says pointedly. "Someone who can immediately spot if something is added or missing or out of place."

I look at each of them accusingly, driving home what they're asking of me.

The boy looks away quickly, perhaps already wishing to be away and back in the simple world of his bucket and *shaduf*, of ladling mouthfuls of water to workers so they don't collapse under the hot sun.

Bakenranef stares back at me, a hard set to his eyes not uncommon to leaders, forced as they are to make decisions that may sacrifice one for the good of the greater whole. And what more expedient sacrifice than one who's already accepted what such decisions entail?

Rasidi looks back at me, unexpected sympathy in her expression. I look away first. I don't want to see it.

And Bakari, well, Bakari's dislike for the situation is plain for all to see. I never want to look away from this remaining link to all I ever cared about, but I do, as mercy for him.

"There is only one someone who can do this right,"

Bakenranef says quietly.

"Someone who won't fear dying because she's already dead?" I nearly spit.

"Someone who needn't be accounted for," he says simply. "Someone who always knew where to look."

"Someone who must show her face in the very tomb she escaped being buried in?" I ask, but no one responds.

I also don't add that the very thought of it freezes my legs and churns bile in my throat. How can they ask me to return to Meryt's tomb after they so brazenly dragged me from it? How can they ask me to be alive in a place sacred for the dead? How can they ask me to go inside if they cannot ensure they can get me out again?

I'm back in that lower storage room in Father's warehouse. Bakari is beside me now as he was then, but the others are all Chisisi, unrelenting as she tries to steal the air from our lungs and suffocate us between the walls of a tiny, underground room. That's why I cling so tightly to my trees and sails, both need sun and space and the sweet snap of wind to dance and fly.

And yet, who else can disappear for so long without question? Who else is better suited to this risk?

I feel above my body when my mouth opens and I hear myself confirm in a low voice, "Someone like me."

Chapter Thirty-Nine

Day 62

Bakari was wise enough to leave me be after the words that sealed my fate two nights ago. Nothing could have been said anyway and I've since lost myself to the space he's given me.

He eventually seeks me out and finds me sitting in a painted boat on the ground in our subterranean room, staring at the painting of our little islet, wondering if death has come for me after all.

In many ways we've come full circle, him approaching me in the same room where he first asked me to cheat death and defy tradition by not drinking poison. I hadn't wanted to then, but I'd allowed myself to be persuaded. As time passed, I'd come around to his side, to the desire to live and laugh and know the reason for what happened to Meryt and our families. And perhaps, I may even have allowed a dim outline of a mast and a ship on course for the horizon to sail into the image of my future once more.

I was foolish to think I'd cheated death when I'd only been given a temporary stay. My heartbeat turns leaden and ominous at the very idea of entering the pyramid, as if it knows that what I've run from these past few weeks will finally claim me there. We escaped death in Thonis and became the Blessed. I avoided death in the palace and became a spy. Now death looms again and I may well end up dead after all. It's one thing to have left Meryt alone in the afterlife, but to desecrate her tomb on the day of her burial, or any day thereafter? I cannot fathom it. Even Father cannot dismiss such an act with his usual scorn for the gods of Egypt. No Divine Force would look kindly on this deed.

Bakari doesn't greet me as he slides into the boat beside me. He crosses his legs and waits with perfect posture against the wall, but I have nothing to say. It's several long moments before he breaks the silence.

"We won't leave you there," he says.

"Don't even try, Bakari," I snap.

"You were the one certain something was hidden there!"

"And they looked! What chance have I to find something where the others didn't, and in so short a time? What if I'm trapped inside? How can you guarantee you'll be back in time? And you more than any know why any minute stuck there will be excruciating."

"We *will* get you out," Bakari insists. "We have to."

"You can't break into a pyramid while the priestesses are keeping watch," I counter, "which they always are. And you'll hardly be able to convince them why they should reopen a door they've just sealed. Will you resort to more dark arts then? How many uncertainties am I expected to find comfort in?"

There's hardly any inflection in my speech, not anger or sorrow or fury or despair. My *ka* feels deflated, a sail without a wind to lift it and let it fly.

"We'll find a way," Bakari is adamant. "I will not allow it to be otherwise."

"Think of me when it's time to celebrate the Festival

of the Valley."

"You'll be there to celebrate it yourself," he says firmly.

"We'll see," I say, though he's sounding like he'll uproot trees if he must to get me out.

Even so, I don't see what assurances he can offer when so much has been out of our control from the outset. No one could have stopped the wave that swallowed Thonis. No one could have stopped the poison in Meryt's *metr*. No one will dare stop this new step we're set upon. How much power do any of us really have over the continual flow of life?

None, Father would say, in a nod to his singular Divine Force. So best give in to the current and embrace wherever its pull leads.

We lapse back into quiet.

"What are you thinking?" I finally ask.

"Nothing."

"Whatever it is, just say."

"No."

"Why not?"

"Because saying is an admission that I may not see you again, and I will. Not saying provides plenty of incentive to make sure I do see you again, so I won't have to live with the regret of what should have been said. I'm thinking only of what will go right, not what could go wrong."

I study him, trying to decipher what else he means from his expression, but he gives nothing away. I give up with a sigh.

"I may be difficult, but you are a fool."

Bakari smirks. "Quite a pair of Blessed ones are we."

"Much good that's done us."

"It may well take a fool to see what a wise man cannot."

"And what, Bomani-Bakari, can a wise man not see here?"

"A great risk that may prove incredibly worthwhile."

"A fool's answer."

"But is it better than no answer at all?" he challenges.

"No," I say simply, at which Bakari lets out a short laugh.

Seconds later, he scoots closer to me, the heat of his body drawing nearer. I don't know when this shift happened, but I needn't look to know what he intends. I rest my head on his shoulder and we sit like that a long while, soaking in the memory of Thonis.

We've never sat like this before, and yet the motion and gesture are somehow so familiar. Perhaps because we've been offering each other a shoulder for longer than we realize, at least since the day I jumped into the boat behind him to paddle like mad to where our homes once were. Or since the day I watched him sail up the Nile to become a soldier. We didn't notice at first, when there were still three of us, when my time was still bound to Meryt, but it's been some time since our small group became just a pair.

So really, we've been leaning on each other's shoulders for months, lending strength and reassurance to ride the new wave that threatens to drive us back down. This is just the first time we're admitting without teasing or argument what has been true for a long while.

Chapter Forty

Day 63

I don't know where to put myself.

There seems no purpose in searching the palace anymore, with the murderer found and killed and eaten, and the key to our answers somewhere across the river. Yet there's no way to search there any sooner. I'm tied to a thread at the end of the pendulum of time, swaying back and forth and forth and back without any hint of finding center.

As a new day dawns, I avoid the few people who know about me. Not that any of them specifically seek me out, as they each have their regular schedules to keep to. Which only makes this harder.

When Bakari first roped me into this mystery, I didn't know of the others. Though I still don't know of most, I knew they were out there, searching too. When searching and listening and spying on my own, I was alone, but part of a whole.

Not anymore. This thing they have asked of me, this thing I have agreed to, singles me out in a way I'd rather not think about. I must enter the pyramid alone, and may very well die alone, right where I should have been from the start. A mighty Force from beyond this world has certainly led me to where I should have been all along. There is no solace in thinking of the others determined to uncover the truth, as no others will be required to stare down the fate they escaped.

I don't want to climb, I don't want to miss Thonis, all I want is noise and people and distraction.

So I tag along behind a group of nobles to the chariot races, which seemed too frivolous before but may be just what I need now. I've skipped all the other celebrations leading up to the Opening of the Mouth ceremony, but watching now is the least I can do for Bakari, a sort of full circle to his initial journey to becoming a charioteer. If nothing else, I should have a good report to give his family if I see them in the next life.

The arena is loud and packed with people, a moving mass of life that pays little attention to someone like me. On the track, I instantly recognize Bakari as the third from the right, reins loose in one hand as he raises his other in a fist for the adoring, cheering crowd. I marvel at how calm he appears, his *ka* oozing confidence, his stance one of poise and command even though I know what sort of worries and secrets are buried deep behind his charming smile. Knowing as much, I see how in every way he is the Bomani-Bakari people at the palace so readily praise.

I detach from the group I shadowed and cast around for the right sort of place to tuck myself into, hidden yet with view enough to watch the races. I would try to sneak a seat beside Kemnebi, whose physician finally agreed he could be out and about today. Not that not having permission stopped him until now. Except, there are too many people around the honored commander, and his seat is quite close to the queen.

Queen Sekhmet looks especially beautiful today. Her white dress is knotted over one shoulder, and a thick, heavily gem-studded collar drapes her neck. Her wig is plain, but the headpiece of layered gold coins over the dark hair glistens so brightly rumors may soon begin that the deities have gifted her a piece of the sun.

Next to the queen is Tsillah. A dark cloud passes over me despite the clear day.

I duck into the shadows near the pole of a raised canopy and watch the royal party from an angle. It's the first time I get a clear look at Tsillah, though I mainly see her in profile. She's a small girl, and her narrow build doesn't help to make her look any older than a probable fourteen or fifteen. I can't put my finger on it, but there's something about her interactions with the queen that indicate the queen's not merely allowing her to tag along as part of her duty as guardian. It isn't unlike the way it was with me and Meryt, in that I was her cousin as well as her servant. Except, Tsillah doesn't seem much like a servant and the queen addresses her with regard, as if she too is of royal blood.

My focus is pulled away by loud shouts and fierce cracking of whips. There are four chariots in this contest, the start of an event that will include several foot, horse, and chariot races. At sunset, two hundred servants with torches will perform a closing dance. It's evident the king has spared little expense in expressing how he feels about Lady Tadinanefer-Hatshepsut.

Meryt would be pleased at the fuss being made over her. "About time!" she would exclaim, in a way that would have us laughing, even knowing she wasn't entirely joking. Growing up as the fourth of five sisters, Meryt was often, unintentionally, overlooked. Then she was spotted by the king himself, in a moment of notice beyond what any could have imagined.

The chariots shoot from the starting line, kicking up dust as they race down the long lane marking the track, which follows an elongated oval back around to the start. The horses run neck and neck for the first stretch, and it's all I can do to keep from calling out encouragement.

As they take the first bend, a now familiar dark brown coat with a white mane starts pulling ahead. By the time the first circuit is complete, Bakari has pulled out in front and doesn't seem willing to relinquish his spot in the slightest.

Even from this distance, even between the swirl of dust and the rush of movement, I see his face furrowed in concentration, though not devoid of his trademark mischievous grin. Watching as he continues to gain speed in the second circuit, I have clear answer of why he would take so well to horses, why he would choose chariots when his whole life had been the sea.

He's enjoying this in a way quite unlike any delight he may get from the long pull of an oar or even a wind-filled sail. Something about the challenging balance of control, speed, and even recklessness suits him well.

I flick a glance to Kemnebi, wondering if he bet on Bakari, and how much he would think it worth. The way he leans forward, eager yet restrained, says he probably did. Keeping in the black panther's favor is another reason to pray Bakari wins.

Looking at Kemnebi proves a mistake because my eyes immediately shift to the queen and her ward. The queen seems interested in the race, but there's something unnerving about the way Tsillah sits and watches. She also leans slightly forward in what could be anticipation as the riders round the bend again, but she stares more than watches, as her head doesn't always follow the circuit of the chariots. I tell myself I'm too far away to see clearly, but I study her long enough to be convinced that she's moving her lips. Or it could be something else entirely. I cannot even guess what.

Maybe she's sounding out the letters from papers in her lap. Maybe she's reciting prayers, a habit formed from living so many years in a temple under the care of a priestess. Maybe she's reciting some other things the priestess taught her. Could she be doing something to sabotage the race?

The thought is abruptly discarded as a rousing cheer overtakes the arena, signaling a winner has been confirmed. I look back toward the center, but the mob of cheering people, stomping, clapping, whistling, has become so wild I can hardly see what's going on.

Finally, the excitement abates long enough to allow me a glimpse of the track. The four chariots are lined up, but their drivers are in a grouping with some officials trailed by their scribes. There's a low murmuring of anticipation and then the mass breaks loose and Bakari is pushed forward from the others. He takes a step and kneels before the king.

"Bomani-Bakari," King Pa-Ankh-Entef loudly proclaims, "you are truly of the Blessed!"

A raucous cheer erupts from the crowd, drowning out whatever the king says next. Roses and gold coins shower down into the arena, the onlookers' gift to their champion. The king says something more, but I'm hardly listening as I'm already slipping away. I have no need to watch the other races, and I prefer to save this day in memory as the moment of Bakari's victory. I've a sense that though I could never quite feel that the palace was home, such is not the same for Bakari. He'll be all right here if I am also soon gone.

At least I know that as victor he's earned a seat at the ceremony across the river. If nothing else, I'll know he'll be nearby when I sneak into the pyramid.

Chapter Forty-One

Day 64

Meryt's mummification will be complete tomorrow and we will reunite at her burial as was always expected.

It's a sobering thought, especially because I don't know how this will end for me, and a foreboding voice tells me I can no longer outrun what was meant to be. I enter the pyramid without a guarantee of finding anything or of not getting caught, maybe even sealed inside. If I die inside, I may never be found before all that is left of me is dust and bones. I have no idea what awaits me, and the uncertainty of being alone in a dark, lonely place plays morbid tricks on my mind with thoughts of shrinking rooms and suffocating breath. It would be best to shake away such thoughts, but I feel tomorrow is a reckoning for all the death I've escaped.

I am not prepared for the waters before me and don't recognize the flow of this current at all. Still, for Meryt and for Thonis and for the thousands who will not be named, I will do what no one else can. I will trespass on the sacred to find proof of the profane. Then, with something worthy in hand, I will beg forgiveness for my transgression.

I want to steel myself for what's ahead, but only wonder if Meryt had the chance to peek into the future would she still ask me to accompany her to the palace?

Would my parents still encourage me to go? Had either known that I would defy tradition in their name, would they still call this an honor?

The questions plague me so I barely sleep. Tension makes my muscles too stiff to relax and it feels like a school of fish is wriggling in the river of my *metr*. It also seems a waste to sleep with a high chance of so little life left to live. Even the compromised life I'm living now.

Each night I lie awake and stare at the painted stars of Thonis, dreaming for the hard wooden deck of a ship beneath and a course set anywhere waters can take me. Extra care is evident in the painting on the ceiling, and I imagine the creases of Bakari's callused palms as he carefully replicates the map of the sky above Thonis. The ground may shift under my feet, but no matter where I am the compass of the stars remains the same. As long as I can see them, I can always find my way.

I'm lost in such musings, tucked against the far wall, gaze fixed between the painted sky and our islet, when Bakari arrives.

"Thought I'd find you in a tree," he says at the doorway.

"I was, before."

Silence, weighty and meaningful. Bakari doesn't yet enter the room.

"So," I break the quiet, "how goes the life of a victor?"

Bakari shrugs. "Still have to care for my own horses, though I prefer as much anyway."

"Kemnebi must be pleased."

"The whole court is mighty pleased," he mutters.

"What a dreadful life to be honored by so many powerful people!"

"Yes!" he cries seriously.

"You were hardly unnoticed before."

"Perhaps," Bakari concedes, "but before, their praise was for excelling in training, now it's for winning them jugs and jugs of money."

"It isn't the first time you've raced. Or won."

"More and more jugs then," Bakari says bitterly.

I chuckle at his annoyance. "A vain man can never be a happy man."

"Stop quoting my father!" he exclaims, but a laugh bubbles out of him, releasing some of his tension.

When the quiet falls again, it's much more settled, comfortable even.

"I brought you something," Bakari tells me, finally entering and moving toward me.

I sit up and study him, amused. "Now's hardly the time to increase my possessions."

Instead of answering, he crouches and offers up a small leather pouch in his palm.

"What is it?" I ask, taking it.

"Open carefully," he warns as I tug at the tie cinching it tightly closed.

I undo the lacing of the cord and slowly draw the pouch open, keeping it nestled in the palm of one hand for ensured balance. I peek inside and frown.

"Earth?" I peer closer, my frown deepens. "Sand."

Bakari holds up a hand, a dam to stop what he knows will come. "From Rasidi."

"No," I immediately reply, pushing the bag back toward him. "I'm done with the dark arts."

He stops my hand firmly, one eye fixed on the positioning of the pouch to make sure it doesn't spill over.

"I know you don't like it. I don't either. But, Zizi, take it. Just in case."

"What am I supposed to do with it?" I question. "How am I to use dark arts if I will not touch dark arts at all?"

"I don't know. But if it may help, or should you need it, then I'd be glad to know you have it. I would not reject it, whatever it is."

"You have always been more forgiving." A pause, then, "How does it work?"

"She said you've seen her use it before," Bakari replies, miming throwing a handful in the air.

I stare at him, unable to answer, unable to wrap my brain around this moment and what it means. A thrum reverberates from the soul embedded deep within my heart, a warning against taking any part of this.

"Please, Zizi," Bakari nearly begs, "please."

My frown deepens, as I make no attempt to hide my displeasure. Still, I tie the pouch closed and put it on the ground beside me.

"Thank you," he whispers, visibly relieved.

I don't know if he realizes I'm placing it on the ground in hopes of forgetting it there. I have no desire to cross into the world of dark and shadows Rasidi spoke of, not least because I remember well my father's warning, remember in my lungs that suffocating sense of a collapsing room without air.

Another silence, this one lined with anticipation. Something big is happening in less than a day. Meryt will finally be sent to the next life, and I? Who's to know?

"What do you want to do on your last night?" Bakari asks, settling in beside me. "Before what's sure to be the start of many others," he quickly amends.

"What would you want to do?" I turn the question around. "If you could choose."

Bakari studies me, then looks back toward the mural on the wall across from us. I've seen it so many times, it's as clear in my mind as the memory it preserves, but Bakari observes it in a way that makes me wonder what message or detail he's hidden in the bold strokes and swirls of paint.

Our whole islet is on the mural as planned. I'm up in the tree as promised, Meryt and Unika and Bakari and Hamadi are on the shore. Kebi plays with some of the younger children in the surf, and our mothers watch them while washing clothes or shelling beans or any other mundane activity which ensures the comfortable running of a home.

Bakari even painted in his mother's ibis preparing to fly, long black beak and neck raised aloft, wide white wings with black tips spread to ride the wind. His father is stepping into a small skiff, the ledger he always carried tucked safely under his arm, his younger sons crowding around to see him off. Meryt's father is already in the boat, oars at the ready. My father's back is to us, but his head is slightly turned, catching one last glimpse of our islet before they depart. His ship awaits them in the sparkling sea beyond.

"Everyone is here," I say quietly.

"And were this my final night, I'd have all I want," Bakari concludes.

It's no poem, but he's spoken well the words I hold in my heart too. I flick a glance up at him, sitting so close to me I can feel the warmth of his *ka* on my skin. The expression on his face as he looks into our past leaves no doubt this charioteer has not gone far from the sea. I return my gaze to the mural across and go over each person in turn, pulling up memories, not scenes or stories, but motions and acts, moments of being alive, the sparkle and feel of life.

We did the best we could for them. Tonight, at least, it will have to be enough.

Chapter Forty-Two

Day 65

Today marks seventy days since Meryt's death, the day she is finally ready for the afterlife. Benerib and Madu have also been prepared, though as servants, even to a king's wife, their mummification ritual was much shorter.

Meryt has been wrapped and wrapped in rolls of linen, wards and prayers and incantations chanted at each turn. Her personal items have been neatly packed for use in the next life. The royal cooks have been preparing a lavish feast for days and days in honor of the burial ceremony. Everything is in order to row across the Nile and escort her to her final rest.

I've finally exchanged my itchy lowborn garb for the simple white dress of a priestess. All makeup and kohl are scrubbed from my face, any last bits of jewelry are removed. I am as plain as the purity of my heart should be. Bakari holds my belt for me, the one with the small pouch and smaller knife and chisel, just in case. There can be no hint of anything but white about me if I'm to pass as a priestess.

"At least you'll have some food with you," Bakari comments as we move toward the skiffs waiting to be rowed across to the Valley of the Kings.

"I'll be missing the feast, remember?"

"True enough," Bakari muses. "We'll have to do something about that."

"Now's hardly a time for honeycombs."

He chuckles softly as we split up to weave through the hundreds of people who have turned out from the palace and Thebes itself for the procession. We can't go together, as Bakari will surely be recognized and greeted by many. It'll be safer to meet once most of the boats push off from shore.

Most of the people gathering at the shore now will not cross the Nile but will remain standing on the banks in mourning until they can no longer see us. Already, some lament, some wail loudly, many send well-wishing flowers into the water, so it becomes a colorful floating garden. The current swiftly carries most of them away, fittingly up toward Thonis, but some are scooped up by people already in boats to be taken to the valley.

The highest ranks have turned out in their best of dress. Vizier Omari, the royal scribes, nomarchs, royal officers, nobles, mayors, and priests. A few favored wealthy merchants. The heads of royal warehouses and livestock. All the people whose secrets we've pried into over the past few weeks, the accumulation of power we could never make use of.

Somber as the occasion is, it's somewhat festive too. We certainly never had such sendoffs when someone died in Thonis.

We find Bakenranef and signal across several heads that we're ready. We can't get too close to him, as we're specifically keeping out of sight of Kemnebi and certainly the king and queen. I can't be certain what passed when Kemnebi told the queen Meryt's death was a murder, but even if he did say the information came from a maidservant, he doesn't know my real name. I needn't give him a chance to point to a face the queen will immediately recognize.

Our nomarch's boat is filled with friends and servants, so, instead of trying to slip in unnoticed or stow away, we board the small skiff beside his larger one. It shouldn't take long to row across, but there's no use risking even that short time if it means someone might recognize me on the larger vessel. We settle in and Bakari makes sure the oars are properly locked in place.

"Good to see you doing some work for a change."

"Look well, for this is the last you'll see for a long while," he rejoins, then quickly falls silent as he realizes what he's said.

I tap his knee to get his attention. "I'm not upset, though I shouldn't say as much because I'd rather watch you squirm."

His gaze snaps up to mine. "Difficult as always." He smiles.

And I smile back because, really, I can't not.

Moments later, the first of the boats begins to cross the Nile and we patiently await our turn among the last. We're quiet as we row across, though there's really not much we could say over the growing noise of the gradually assembling mourning parade. Music has started up somewhere on the opposite bank, with voices rising up to join the dirge. Mourners and priestesses, dancers and nobles fall into line and prepare for the procession to the pyramid. As the sarcophagus is unloaded, priests follow, holding the canopic jars containing Meryt's organs, save the heart that's been kept inside her. My own heart is pounding so loudly my *metr* strums like an instrument with its echo.

256

By the time our skiff reaches the opposite shore, the procession is already under way, weaving a sorrowful yet still somewhat joyous trail to the pyramid. After all, today is not just mourning a life gone but celebration of the life that will begin after this one. I wonder what our families will say when they see her, when they learn the truth that her honored life in the great palace was cut short and that she has left the last of us "Blessed" behind. I hope, at least, she'll be with her baby.

Then I wonder if she will even see our families, as they were never buried, their hearts never measured. Can the sea act as a giant tomb for bodies that may very well have disappeared?

Father would chastise me for spouting nonsense. He would say his Divine Force doesn't need a mummy or a heart or canopic jars or chanting and wards to usher someone into eternal life. I don't know where Father built his beliefs from, as they seem a combination of different lands he sailed to. Either way, they bring me comfort now. After all, I'd much rather think of everyone being reunited than of Meryt truly left alone in the afterlife.

The parade flows through the valley, past stubbly mountainsides speckled with holes marking the entrance of tombs. We pass a mastaba, the step-shaped pyramid much blockier than the one we're headed toward, like layers stacked upon each other where one strong tap at the top would flatten the set into a neat square.

Soon, King Pa-Ankh-Entef's pyramid casts a pointed shadow on the sands. The white limestone lining the slanted sides is almost blinding in the light of the searing desert sun, and the triangular gold-capped peak sparkles with flashes of glittering light.

We reach the pyramid just as they begin the Opening of the Mouth Ceremony, raising the mummy up so all senses can be returned to Meryt before her entombment. Priestesses lead the ceremony with anointments and spells, their voices rising and falling on the wind of funerary music which hasn't let up. King Pa-Ankh-Entef speaks about Lady Tadinanefer-Hatshepsut, more a farewell to the "golden gleam" of his eye than a eulogy.

Queen Sekhmet sits in a place of honor, the elegance of her movements softening the fierce royal that lies beneath. Her gracious expression makes it easy to believe she's here to mourn the loss of a friend and not a potential rival. She listens with dignity as the king eulogizes a wife he came to favor over her. The wife he may have made queen had she borne him the heir she carried.

Tsillah remains behind the queen, the hunch in her posture making her small frame even less noticeable. Like most other times I've seen her, she seems to be attempting to fold her body into itself, as if her already petite stature is too big and gangly to live with. Perhaps she finds solace being even closer to the ground, just as I find it high up in a tree. One would think a girl shown such favor by the most powerful woman in Egypt would sit up straighter, or at least lengthen her neck to hold her head higher.

For once, she isn't murmuring as she remains apart from the ceremony. Still, a chill shivers down my spine as I watch her. There are no toads around, as far as I can see, but I doubt that signals anything safe about her. I wish I could more directly pinpoint an action or a word to prove my suspicions of how dangerous I suspect her to be.

I purposefully move my eyes away from her to travel over the crowd, picking out faces I recognize, taking account of those who've been included in the day's festivities. I find Kemnebi, and Bakenranef, who does little to hide his grief, which no one would fault him for. More than one person casts him a pitying look as another part of the city once under his guardianship is sent to the world beyond.

It's no secret he was a much more powerful nomarch when he still had the might of Thonis, thriving trade city and gateway to Egypt, as a pedestal to stand upon. Without the bustling port, with the city's name an unmentionable curse, he's lost quite a lot of his standing, and much of his political pull too. He still has enough allies to make sure his circle is never entirely quiet. After all, there are other cities along the shore, and the new gateway to Egypt is also under his domain.

The king finishes speaking and Meryt is finally brought into the pyramid with great ceremony. Madu, Benerib, and her many possessions are already waiting for her.

I choke down an unexpected swell of tears, feeling my cousin is being torn from us once again. Bakari gives my shoulder a gentle squeeze, his face solemn, understanding that I cannot yet celebrate her journey to the afterlife. The king invites all gathered to partake of the funerary banquet and the festivities begin with renewed life. It is also our signal to slip away.

"Sure you don't want something to eat?" Bakari presses.

"We don't have time!" I insist, moving quickly toward the entrance.

Bakari shrugs as we keep our heads down and

quietly sidestep the feasting, keeping to the edges of the crowd as we sidle closer and closer to the pyramid. We keep to shadows as best we can, but, in truth, the sun is still too high to provide enough shadows to hide in, though the rest of the people are too busy to notice us. Or so we hope.

We stop some lengths from the opening, far enough out of sight to properly examine our options. A few guards linger as the last few crates and personal items are brought into the pyramid. The supplies for sealing up the pyramid are stacked to the side, ready and entirely too close at hand. We quickly recognize from their demeanor that the men at the entrance are part of the small staff of guards and priests that live in the valley to protect the tombs and watch over the sacred sites.

Bakari points toward a pile of bricks, mere paces from the entrance. I nod in understanding and ready myself to duck behind them until I have a clear path to scuttle inside. My heart is thundering loudly enough to join the other instruments at the feast.

Before I set off, Bakari presses my belt into my hands, then steps out alone toward the guards. I understand what he's doing quickly enough, as he greets them heartily. He'll have their attention for several minutes at least, if they're as much a fan of Bomani-Bakari, recent royal racing champion, as everyone else seems to be. I tie my belt tight and don't waste any time staying low and scurrying behind the pile.

A shout goes up, making me sure they've spotted me by hearing my heartbeat. There's the distinct scuff of sandals on sand, no doubt a solider moving in my direction.

"What is it, good soldier?" Bakari asks loudly as he

reaches them.

"Something there," the soldier replies.

I shrink against the pile, sure I'm about to be found, wondering if I have enough time to hide somewhere else. Despite the heat of the desert sands, I carefully remove my sandals, hoping to quiet my feet for whichever direction I'll have to run.

"A rat drawn to the food," Bakari says dismissively, and I can almost see how he waves in my general direction, wiping any suspicions away.

But then there's another, unmistakable, sound, and a creature emerges from somewhere behind me. I almost shout in fright, but a second look reveals a small figure, *shaduf* boy. He nods without looking at me, and saunters over to add his treasured ladle and bucket to the distraction.

"I greets you, soldier-mans! May you *ka* shines bright!" he calls to the guards, who undoubtedly recognize him, and take his *shaduf* with hearty appreciation.

There's some murmuring I can't make out, and then Bakari's unmistakable voice cuts in with something that makes the others laugh. I wait several long beats before I dare peek around the pile to find Bakari captivating the soldiers with his trademark good humor and charm.

I'm so low to the ground I'm almost flat on my stomach, every muscle tense as I wait for his signal. It comes when he circles his hand and points to something behind him, focusing every eye away from the entrance. He jabs as if to emphasize whatever story he's spinning for them, but I know that gesture is for me.

On quick and quiet feet, I beeline for the entrance and slip inside the pyramid. The air inside is cool and refreshing after so much time in the midday sun.

I should find a place to hide, to make sure I'm not seen by any remaining slaves or workers, or at least follow the memorized map in my mind to one of the deeper chambers where I'm less likely to be spotted. From there, I can easily work my way up, eliminating each room instead of weaving a confusing, less efficient route.

I know this plan to be wise and yet I stop only a few feet into the entrance, gazing open-mouthed at the wonder of the grand gallery. I've heard about the beauty of the pyramids. I've seen almost all the grandeur of the Great Palace of Thebes. And yet knowing the exact rooms on a map, or calculating the wealth of a king on display hardly compares to the unmatched artistry before me.

Light from the entry illuminates the room while torches placed at intervals add a warm flickering glow so the entire space, floor to ceiling, sparkles. Little can measure up to the mural of Thonis in our subterranean room, not just for the skill of the painter but also because of the value and realness it holds. Yet what I see now is something vastly beyond comprehension altogether.

What the draftsmen stenciled, what the sculptors etched in copper and bronze, what the painters brought to life with bold color and silver and gold is a room unlike any I've been in before, not in the palace, not in a temple, not in any story of faraway lands my father told. In the sparse light, the floor gleams silver water, rippling across the chamber and gently flowing in all directions. Stars shine down from the ceiling, not unlike those we colored to dance in remembrance of Thonis, though these glint with the help of precious gems. Painted pillars line the room, granting the entire setting a high, majestic air. Decades of care have been chiseled into every square of this pyramid, and it shows.

Voices from outside jolt me back from the immobilizing beauty. I frantically look for a place to hide, and dash behind the closest pillar. My heart is pounding again, challenging my focus as I overlay the map we carefully copied with the room I'm standing in. I'm suddenly aware of how little time I have to search an entire pyramid and not only find something but also smuggle it outside. For all our plans and talk, we hadn't thought of what might happen if I found something too big to carry.

I push the thought away and refocus on the task at hand. *One step at a time.* It isn't easy to search from behind the pillar while remaining mindful of any movement from the guards outside. I can't even guess if Bakari is still there or if he knows he can't distract the soldiers forever and has finally joined the feast before someone starts asking for him.

I peer through the dim light, seeking each passageway and identifying where they lead. The King's Chamber. The Queen's Chamber. A narrow air shaft which casts little light. An ascending passage to Meryt's room. A descending passage to a subterranean storage chamber. A passage that wasn't on the first map but the second, the one that leads to hidden chambers.

If someone hid something in this tomb, it's most likely there.

I keep close to the wall as I move slowly toward where the chamber should be, pacing out what I assume to be the right spot. I turn expectantly, but instead of an opening, I come face to face with a larger-than-life painting of Osiris. I stare at his green face, his white atef-crown, his narrow, pointed beard, and the glittering golden scale he lords over. Other deities surround him, hieroglyphs decorate the space above them, but my eyes are drawn back to Osiris and his scale. The scale that measures a heart for worthiness of being reborn in the afterlife. Or so they say. Father would certainly scoff and say something about souls being weightless and beyond a manmade god's measure.

I tilt my head to study the image, a gnawing doubt growing alongside a rising horror as I question my certainty of the map for the first time. No artist would exert so much time and care to paint so important a deity over a false opening. I run my fingers across the image, searching blindly for any seam or crack or intimation of a false door, but find none.

And yet, I know what I saw on the diagram. I know something was hidden in the pyramid's design.

Desperation giving way to recklessness, I run to the other side of the room, heedless of who may see me. I stop directly across from the looming depiction of Osiris, reassuring myself I've simply swapped the map in my mind, mistaking directions, even though I know my way. This wall is also thickly painted with deities and hieroglyphs and bold and glittering colors. I press my hand gently against a cool stone and press.

Nothing happens.

I move a few paces to the side and try again. Nothing. I press high, I press low, but nothing moves. I frown at the stubborn wall of this too-beautiful chamber.

"Will you not show me what you hide?" I ask in a low voice.

Just then I hear a noise, a faint thud that has me

casting about frantically, deciding between possibly running outside, right into a guard, or risking an uncharted run deeper into the pyramid. The noise comes again, closer now, I imagine, and my feet choose the path for me. I fly toward the end of the entry hall, away from the opening of the pyramid and the light streaming through. I press into the corner, willing myself to disappear into shadow. I listen and wait.

There's another noise, more a thump than a thud, but an uncommon sound for a supposedly empty pyramid. I strain to hear, pressed into the corner as I am.

It sounds even closer than before, and I realize why when I turn my head to look for it. I've moved so far through the hall, I'm right up against the ascending passage.

My breath leaves me. *Why is there noise in Meryt's room?*

I tell myself it's only the servants organizing the last of her things. I tell myself to move away from the passage because they'll be on their way back down. I tell myself and I listen, slinking deeper into the shadows where the torchlight cannot find me.

I slow my breath and wait and wait.

Every second feels like one thousand and more before a lone figure emerges from the passage. One, not several. One, not a slave. One, with a posture of command. I follow the retreating figure at a distance, his short kilt marking him as a man. He keeps close to the wall as he quickly strides toward the entrance. I'm not fast enough, while being so cautious, to catch more than a glimpse of a muscular back and the tips of a blue-and-gold ceremonial headdress. I can't even see if he's wearing a wig beneath it, because of the unsteady light.

I glance over my shoulder, uncertain if someone else will emerge from the passage and catch me stalking the first someone. Caution wars with my desire for answers, desperation nudging out reason in this chance to catch a hint of the man before me, to finally catch those who've been acting unseen. But my timing isn't right and the risk is too great to expose myself now. In other words, I gain very little knowledge outside of a most glaring fact. Someone was in Meryt's chambers.

As the figure exits, he nods toward the guards at the entrance. They jump into action as if commanded, though I can't see what they're up to from where I stand.

I can't exit now, so I retreat to the mouth of the passage and decide it's safe enough to go up. No one else has come through, and I haven't heard any other strange noises. I debate taking a torch with me, knowing it will reveal me before I emerge, giving the advantage to whoever might be above, but soon conclude I can't risk not having some sort of light. So I nab a torch from the wall and carefully but quickly make my way up to Meryt's chamber.

Without a sun or dial or obelisk to check, I don't know how much time has passed since I've entered. I only know I don't have much more of it.

I pause in the entry to the chamber, casting a cursory glance around for other unexpected visitors. Once I confirm the room is clear, I step inside and avoid looking at Meryt, who now knows I haven't joined her, forcing my eyes to instead find the crates of her belongings and take stock. I whisper a request for forgiveness for what I may have to do.

From what I can tell, everything is as it should be. I test the lids of the boxes and find them undisturbed. A chair and a table and the *senet* board have been left out, and I smile, thinking of Meryt playing with her father when they meet again. I recognize right away the neat line of shabti on a shelf, the shabti Kemnebi had shipped up from Nubia.

I stand in the middle of the room and frown at the unknown, making a slow circle as I try to determine why everything looks to be in place and yet something is undoubtedly amiss. It could be my own intrusion into this sacred space, but I know what I saw. I know what I heard. *Someone* was here, and that someone was here for a reason.

I pause in my circle as the torchlight falls on the four sarcophagi. Meryt. Benerib. Madu. And what should be me. I stare at them a long time, outwardly calm in body yet unable to control the tremor swimming through my *metr*. It's only when I sniffle that I realize I'm crying, silent tears tracing narrow streams through the dust coating my face.

I should be serving Meryt in the afterlife, even if I was called upon to grant her a greater service in this one. Surely someone else could have found out what I did. I should not have left Benerib and Madu to die alone. They were so young. We are all so very, very young.

Before I know it, I'm kneeling before Meryt's sarcophagus, hand on the richly painted cover inlaid with gold. Tears fall freely. I silently pray that her heart's measure will see her warmly welcomed to the afterlife. I ask her to forgive me for staying when she left. I ask her to hug my family, her family, all our families, and beg them to watch over the last two left behind. I tell her it truly was an honor to serve her, and I would not trade our time at the palace if that meant she would have been here alone. That she would have died without family or friend beside her.

My hand hovers over the lid as I ready to stand back up. A faint thud and a small thought echo in my mind. I stare as my hand moves of its own accord to the space where the top connects with the bottom.

I realize what I'm doing in time to snatch my hand back, then stumble to my feet and away from Meryt. My body shakes as I think of what I was about to do, as I understand what I've almost been driven to. A break from tradition, a tread upon sacred ground, but to stoop to something so sacrilegious? There would be no forgiveness for it.

And yet, I'm now convinced of what I heard, know without doubt what caused the noise.

My eyes shift from Meryt to Benerib to Madu to me.

I can't shake the sound now that I know its match. A lid closing.

Someone did something here with purpose, something that someone wanted to remain hidden and buried deep. Like all best kept secrets must be.

I take a shaky step closer. I plant the torch into the soft sand. I stretch out both hands. And slowly lift the lid of my sarcophagus.

I gasp when I see what's inside, falling back so the lid thuds closed, just as it had before.

I take a deep, steadying breath and reach back out. I raise the lid again and force myself to look and study and *know* this buried secret.

Not a person, not a mummy, but three golden shabti woven with black thread. I reach a trembling hand out and a warm buzz greets me. The bright black thread I soon realize isn't thread but neat rows of glowing obsidian sparks. Obsidian sparks like the ones Rasidi creates from sand and Tsillah uses to make her toads. There are so many the shabti glow with them.

I stare in wonder, in puzzlement, then a story filters in pieces into my head. A story about mythical shabti whose possession may guarantee the eternity of a kingdom. A story told in Kemnebi's voice, the same voice that said perhaps these shabti should be buried so no more lives are lost over them. The same voice that spoke of secrets best kept when buried deep.

The contents of the fourth crate. These are why Nkuku and Kemnebi were attacked that day on the Nile. The suspicion of a Nubian connection isn't much stretch after all, though all these really seem to prove is Kemnebi's innocence in Meryt's death and Thonis' destruction. Surely someone who went to such lengths to procure and hide these is not seeking Egypt's destruction but preservation.

As the thought sinks in, a new awareness kicks me into action. A rush to get out of the room and back into daylight. I've found enough to tell Bakenranef and Bakari that I was right and herein are secrets buried deep. The rest can be figured out another time. But, as I struggle to stand, another thought begins to form, one so horrifying and bone-chilling it slams me back to my knees in the sand. I can't move my arms to close the lid again. I can't find my feet to stand. I can't take up the torch to light my way out.

Whoever put these here *knows* that someone is missing from the sarcophagus. Knows that someone who's supposed to be dead is still alive. Knows that absent someone is me.

Kemnebi knows who I am.

Kemnebi knows and has not spoken.

Kemnebi, the only one who knows the contents of the fourth crate.

The thought rocks me.

Could that have been him leaving the passage? I didn't see enough to know. Did he limp or am I only imagining an uneven gait now? I didn't check before sneaking in if there had been others slipping away from other rooms and passages.

Time I don't have passes while these thoughts roar through my mind, blocking out all else. I only know that it's a sudden thought that finally jolts me back, which finally gets me to close the lid, snatch up the torch, and move as quickly as I can down the passage.

Hiding the shabti here proves that Kemnebi has chosen his Egyptian half over his Nubian, that he believes in the legends he told me. These are the shabti supposedly carved by Osiris, a protection against death, an assurance that the kingdom who holds them will stand forever. And this must be connected to his meeting here with Vizier Omari that long-ago day.

But, if this is so, that also means that he could view what Bakari and I have done as treason of the highest order. And if he knows I'm alive, then he knows that Bakari is part of this. He knows how much we trust each other. He knows we've been investigating Meryt's death. He heard me call him *chibale*.

As I hurry to the main entry, I suddenly realize it's grown darker. More time has passed than I accounted for, and if the sun's already setting, most people will have begun to return home. At least, I think, if I miss a boat, I can always find a place to sleep and then swim across in the morning. I can only imagine Bakari anxiously watching the entrance, ready to admonish me for being so difficult by cutting it so close.

Crossing through the grand gallery, the reason for the quickly growing darkness, that nod to the guards at the entrance, abruptly becomes painfully clear. I drop all caution and race toward the exit, the very one they've just finished sealing, trapping me inside.

Death has found me after all.

Chapter Forty-Three

Day 66

Trapped.

In a closed space. Without sunlight or air. My mind flashes to Father's warehouse and the woman who nearly killed us in it.

Am I still breathing?

I was a fool to think I could escape once more.

There is no time in this sealed place, no day or night, no sun or moon or stars for light or to map my way. All thoughts and sense flee my mind; knowledge is crowded out by fear so great I know nothing at all. My only certainty is that someone who shouldn't knows I'm alive, that I've indeed found the secret I was sure would be here, and that I may well now be buried in this place before I can reveal the many answers I've finally found. Well, as I may not be alive much longer, my first worry may soon be irrelevant. The second allays suspicions of a most powerful commander of Egypt's forces. And the third means the satisfaction of being right will not leave these walls.

I sit in the middle of the grand gallery, drop right to the floor where I stood numbly once I knew I wouldn't be leaving the tomb. I sit and I sit and I sit. Unsure, unfocused, unable to form a thought of what might come next. Unable to believe that everything that's happened over the past several weeks, the discoveries, the near misses, the progress, has crashed to a halt with poor timing and a sealed pyramid door.

I imagine what the others must be doing now, try to imagine what they can be doing with the burial fresh enough to ensure the pyramid will not go unguarded for a while yet. There's no way they can linger without arousing suspicion. There's no way for them to return without raising serious questions, which will reveal me. Is it better to be trapped in a pyramid or locked in a prison en route to a crocodile pit? Even if I have discovered something important, the desecration I've committed and trampling of sacred customs will not allow me to live. What else could the king do were he to find that I never joined his beloved Lady Tadinanefer-Hatshepsut, especially as we haven't truly proven her murder but only Kemnebi's innocence?

For a brief moment, I allow myself to see Bakari demanding the entrance be opened, flashing his name and victory and whatever else he can so the guards listen and obey. It's a scene only real in my thoughts, for there is no way the guards who live in the Valley of the Kings are as irreverent as we. He can hardly claim to have left something important behind from when he worked here, never mind that a girl who's alive but shouldn't be is hardly a reason to break open a tomb.

"Good," they'll say. "The gods have put her where she should have been from the start."

I close my eyes and offer a prayer to the Divine Force of my father, praying I will be heard, that my father was right to believe in a singular entity much greater than the totality of Egypt's many manmade gods. I have only this Divine Force to trust for somehow getting out alive.

I doubt any of the gods I never believed in would help me run away from what obeisance to them demands. Even as I think such things, I don't yet open my eyes, fearing to see the deities painted on the walls staring in accusation and condemnation.

When I finally do pry my eyes open and regain focus, I notice the air in the pyramid has cooled, a lot. I can only surmise it must be night or early morning, as a risen, heated desert sun would surely warm up the stones so it wouldn't be so cold. Which means I have to get moving.

Distantly, I hear torches hiss, casting the room in further darkness as their oil burns out. My breaths turn to gasps as I imagine the room growing smaller in the dimmer lighting, sure a vengeful Chisisi has come back to finish what she started. Death has many agents to send after me.

Grab hold of yourself, a strong voice speaks sharply from a corner of my mind, and my body instinctively listens.

Only then can I force my heart to calm and remind myself that of all the people who could be trapped in here, I'm the only one who knows both the layout of the tomb and what's been packed away. Most of those are Meryt's personal items, her clothing and headdresses and *senet* board, but there are other things we anticipated she might need in her next life. Things like dishes and a cradle and…an oil lamp.

I reach for a withering torch and carefully make my way back up the passageway to Meryt's room. I try not to cause too much disorder among her possessions as I rummage around until I find what I'm looking for. A small golden oil lamp, the one she kept in her bedchambers, a gift from her mother on our last visit to Thonis. Simple but finely made.

I fill the lamp from a small cruse and offer it a flame from the torch. A softer, steadier light illuminates the room, and were I anywhere else I'd say the glow is warm, welcoming even. I measure the weight of the cruse in my palm and figure I must have enough oil to last another day if not two, granting about two and a half days to find some sort of evidence and figure a way out. Because I can either wait around to be rescued, or try to chip away at the mortar sealing the door with my little knife and chisel, or I can allot some time to searching, to wring some benefit out of this unfortunate twist, and then get to chiseling. I only pray I make it out before I collapse from hunger and thirst.

I turn back to the crates and take out Meryt's beloved leopard shoulder cloak. I ask her forgiveness one more time as I wrap it tight around myself to ward off the cold. I bite off a bitter laugh, seeing myself as I am, a wayward servant, dressed as a queen, sealed inside a pyramid.

Then, with heart thumping loud in my *metr*, *ka* flickering as the light of the lamp, I descend the passage back to the grand gallery.

I extinguish some of the remaining torches, hoping to save what little light they may yet give should I need it, and leave the rest lit to signal my way back to the gallery. There's a moment of darkness when I extinguish the last torch I've chosen, a moment when I'm standing in the large room and deciding which way to go, that I feel something skitter across my bare feet. I suck in a breath and barely glance down, moving my head as little as possible.

Dull color. Hard shell. Sharp pincers.

Scorpion.

Were I not so frightened, I would roar with laughter at this new threat to my life.

You think you have a chance? I yell in my mind at the small creature. *Are you here to finish what I never did?*

I stand rigid as the minutes tick by, body tense, breath shallow, until the scorpion finally scuttles away. I watch it move toward the King's Chamber and immediately move in the opposite direction, down toward the Queen's Chamber.

I pick my way down the descending passage carefully so as not to chance stumbling and spilling the lamp. Plus, I want to make sure I give wide berth to any more scorpions or other dangerous creatures locked in here with me.

Unlike the majesty of the grand gallery, the walls of this passage are bare, the way ahead a close space carved into rocks which, according to the map, leads to the Queen's Chamber and subterranean storage even farther below. Small rocks dig into my feet, indication there was no hurry to finish this area yet. I swallow back my instinct to yelp as they dig in, certain that even the faintest noise will signal the scorpion to me.

The Queen's Chamber is empty, the walls unpainted. Not much has been done to prepare the room for its future inhabitant. Perhaps the assumption is that it needn't be worked on until the queen passes, which shouldn't be for years yet. Meryt's rooms were hastily made ready in the almost three months since she was unnaturally taken from us.

Still, I look in every corner and press every few

stones, just in case I find something that shouldn't be there. My stomach growls from hunger and the rumble echoes like a tiger in the empty space. I try not to think about how dry my throat is or how much longer I'll be able to last without food or water if I don't find a way out soon. I estimate I'm probably already into my second day without food, or however long ago was my light breakfast the morning of the burial, and the very thought turns my limbs leaden. The tomb won't be open again until the dead are visited during the Festival of the Valley, and that's quite some time away yet. I once heard from a caravan driver that one way to trick the dryness from the mouth is to suck on a pebble. I wonder how many hours it will be before I'm forced to try that, before even a scorpion will look edible.

As I turn to leave, my foot kicks against something light, sending it sliding across the packed dirt floor. I bend to the floor with my lamp and let out a small shriek when a small creature looks back at me. I hold my breath, waiting, but the creature doesn't move. I move closer and see that, though much of the skin and color have eroded away, the petrified form that remains is unmistakably that of a toad. It looks as though the body was salted and dried for mummification then forgotten before it could be wrapped.

It could be happenstance, but there's only one person I know of with a preference for toads.

I reexamine the floor of the chamber and find three more toads in similar condition. They aren't evidence enough, but I'd say they're a glaring sign Tsillah has been here at some point and left some of her friends behind. I'd guess it to be at least some months ago, considering the state of the toads, which would be well before Meryt was murdered.

When Thonis was drowned.

Why ever would a queen's ward be casting spells in a pyramid?

I search the chamber again and again but find nothing else to support my new itching suspicion.

Finally, without much else to look through to warrant another search, I leave the Queen's Chamber for the extra storage room below it, thinking on how it would be an ideal spot to hide evidence. I take to the descending passage again, though it soon becomes even narrower and rougher hewn.

Someone's made use of the subterranean storage, littering it with various tools, chipped pieces, and other debris not fit for the tomb of a king. As the rest of the intended residents of this pyramid are added, the area will probably be cleared to make space for all the things they'll be bringing into the afterlife. In the meantime, it gives me something to look through, so I'm glad for the tools and chipped stones, among other things.

I place the oil lamp in a safe spot away from most of the items and get to sifting. I don't let my mind wander as I work, afraid of what sort of worries it will call up if I do.

It doesn't take long to go through what's there, and my sifting only confirms that the haphazard piles when taken apart are just as they seem from the outside. Namely, they hold mere bits and pieces and nothing more.

Learning from my visit to the chamber above, I examine the floor by the light of the lamp, but don't find anything unsavory down here, not even remnants of toads. It would seem at least one room is just as it should be in this pyramid, which is more than I can say for anything else I've seen so far.

A sudden wave of tiredness washes over me, and my hand shakes so badly I fear I cannot keep my grip on the lamp. The light's burning too low anyway, so I turn back toward the passageway and make my way back up, not stopping until I've returned to Meryt's chamber.

I settle the lamp on the floor and kneel before it to carefully refill it. Then my tiredness leads me to sit completely. I just see the light awakening as my squinting eyes shut and, despite the worries and fear and need to find something to hold onto, I fall into a heavy sleep.

Chapter Forty-Four

Day 67

The sputtering of the lamp yanks me awake with a frantic image of spiders and scorpions crawling all over me. I shake out each limb fiercely before I'm satisfied, though I see no creature skitter away. Then I remember the dying light and refill the lamp, using the last of the oil in the cruse. Did we assume the afterlife too bright to need more than one small jug of oil?

Considering the oil in the lamp burned down, I assume I slept a few hours. I must find evidence before this light burns out completely or figure out a way to see in total darkness. At this point, I can't say for certain which would be easier.

I try to stand but dizziness forces me back down again. I lean against the wall to collect myself, to convince myself it's no matter my mouth is dry as the desert and I'm about three days without food. Bakari will figure out a way to break in and soon rescue me with gleaming, sticky honeycombs. Thinking of Bakari, my hand slides to my belt, and my fingers trace over the three pouches that are attached. I hadn't thought to check each before entering the pyramid, but I know right away there're two more pouches than planned.

I slip my fingers into the first one, and nearly cry when my fingers press against something soft. I pull out the few slices of dried fruit, smiling past my slightly tilting vision as I slowly press a piece into my mouth. I want to swallow them at once, but force myself to chew thoroughly, not least because my *ka* is dwindling so my body is too tired to move much quicker.

A muffled laugh escapes my closed mouth as I think of how Bakari must have included this pouch as a joke. He might have saved my life with this bit of mischief, or at the very least prolonged it. Of course, a few mouthfuls of dried fruit are hardly enough to sustain me long, but it's the thought as much as the bite of food that cuts through my emotional exhaustion and gets me on my feet, anxious to make good use of the lamp's remaining oil.

I make my way back down the passage to the grand gallery, which echoes loudly with each shuffle and breath. I turn toward the King's Chamber, fiercely praying the scorpion has either burrowed under the sand or found somewhere else to be. I certainly hope it isn't hosting family and friends.

The walk to the King's Chamber is slower than it should be because my tired feet won't move faster despite my commands. Considering the state of the Queen's Chamber, I don't suspect I'll find much here, but then again, I've already uncovered two unexpected finds in two different chambers. On top of the toads and shabti, the King's Chamber could well uncover something new.

I finally exit the gallery into the King's Chamber and all is just as I suspected. The room is bare aside from a large granite slab that will one day be honored with supporting King Pa-Ankh-Entef's sarcophagus. The unpainted walls are inefficiently smoothed from the inside to hide the imperfections of the stones diagonally stacked on the outside.

I search each corner anyway, looking for more toads or statuettes with mysterious obsidian sparks while keeping a wide eye out for scorpions. I tap on some stones on the wall just to be sure, but the room is as empty as it looks. Somewhere in a diagonal above my head, an air shaft stretches through the stones to the outside of the pyramid, but it's hardly a place for hiding things.

I stand directly beneath the elevated ceiling of the chamber and take in the room from there, seeking an angle to spot imperfections or unexplained raises or dips or really anything at all in the unadorned space. My eyes slowly, carefully scan each section, and it's only then that I notice an opening toward a passage to my left.

Leading with the lamp, I peer inside only to find that the walls of the passage are much closer and rougher than the others I've been in so far, even more than the ones leading from the Queen's Chamber to the subterranean storage. I attempt to squeeze in, but my lamp immediately begins to sputter in the tight space, so I back away quickly, suspecting the light is warning it will not have enough air in a passage that must narrow further as it goes. If there's not enough air to feed a flame, there's certainly no space for me.

I back away from the passage and glance around the chamber once more, verging on desperation. From what I know of the map, aside from the unfound hidden chamber, I've looked through almost every room of the pyramid at this point. If there's nothing here, then it may well be the shabti are the only buried secret, in the end. And yet…

Those toads are nagging at my mind. They just don't make sense. I'm so sure they're an indication Tsillah was here, which could mean the queen herself was here, but for what? Kemnebi was the one behind the glowing shabti, so what could have led the queen down here months before construction had to be rushed? What could a queen or her ward have lost in a barren, unfinished tomb?

I stare straight ahead as I think, my eyes unwittingly boring into the wall across from me, which is the only reason I notice something wrong with the corner where it meets the next wall. An anomaly easily overlooked by someone not thinking to look for it at all.

I cross the chamber and raise the light to scan the opposite wall. As suspected, there are nooks and crevices that immediately swallow the light, instead of a clean surface alight from its glow. I lean in until my nose is almost against the stone and see that the stones which make this wall are smooth and carefully stacked. But they are not sealed with mortar. I push one, hard, and feel it shift slightly. These stones, this section of wall, is not permanent. And it could very well be none of it was meant to be here, either.

My eyes widen with the discovery, and my hungry, thirsty, tired senses snap to full alert.

I set the lamp down some paces away in the hope that a misguided action won't blow it out. Then, carefully, I press and press against the highest stone I can reach, until it eventually thumps out the other side. The few stones above it shift down, but those are soon easily removed. Now, I have enough space for my hands to work and, stone by stone, remove the fake wall blocking off the opening.

By the time I've moved enough stones away to create an area large enough for me to pass through, I'm exhausted but fueled with triumph.

The wall was blocking a staircase leading up.

I found the hidden chamber.

I take up the lamp and step inside.

Chapter Forty-Five

Day 68

I stumble into consciousness some unknown time later. It's bone-deep cold and complete, almost paralyzing darkness. My slowly starving body feels beaten and bruised, as if I've been viciously hurled down several flights of steps. Which, I realize with a start, is what happened.

I fumble for the wall closest to me and eventually drag my body into an imitation of a sitting position using it as support. Then I seek to calm my pounding head, my gasping *metr*, to collect my scattered, frightened thoughts into a coherent picture.

I stepped through the opening in the stones and followed the narrow passage up, away from the King's Chamber. As I neared the hidden chamber, a soft dark light appeared in the passageway, discordantly illuminating, warm, and foreboding. I knew right away I had found whatever we'd been searching for, something even Kemnebi or the vizier didn't know about. But that knowing did little to prepare me for what lay within.

I shrieked when I stepped on a petrified toad in the doorway. The soft crunch of a body pressed to ash was even more frightening in the silence and anticipation.

It jolted me so I stumbled into a room alight with a now-familiar obsidian glow.

The memory starts to blur, so I clutch my hands to my head and struggle to focus on what I found. To recall in exact detail the truth I finally discovered.

Piece by piece, I remember a table in the middle of the room, surrounded, aglow, infused by a great haze of obsidian light.

The power in the light was evident and inexplicably overwhelming, even if I didn't want it to be real. Then I looked beyond the haze to what the table held.

Serene, sedate, a glowing replica of Thonis.

Suddenly I couldn't breathe as the once-familiar sensation of deep waters pressing against lungs surged over me. I felt as I had the moment we found what the wave had taken, that sense of drowning with my vanished city. I gasped for breath against the unforgiving currents; I floundered to find my footing even though I was standing. I pitched forward, losing my lamp and the little oil I had left, instinctively flinging out my hands to break my fall.

I crashed to the floor, and my hands scraped against shards of something sharp. Something broken was scattered on the ground before the ghostly city glowing and glowing like a dark blessing too bright and beautiful to ever be a curse.

Dazed, I examined my cut hands in the obsidian light and saw they'd been sliced by pieces of broken pottery.

I gathered some pieces into a small pile, only to uncover a new horror in the slivers and emerging pattern of something familiar. The pottery was inlaid with gold and gems, a sure sign of an expensive piece. I sorted the pieces into an approximate pattern, then stared in shock at artistry I'd seen before. I recognized enough to know the pieces had been taken from something larger, an image I could finish in my mind.

The reassembled shards showed citizens of Egypt celebrating the onset of *ankhet* season at the shore of the Nile, anticipating the flooding that would soon water their crops.

This was only one scene of several on a large vase with a winding Nile River.

A vase whose twin sat at the entrance to the queen's rooms in the palace.

It hadn't been carelessly broken by a servant after all. It had been smashed with deliberation.

I grabbed the pieces to pack into one of the pouches but stopped when I noticed writing on the underside of some. I flipped the pieces over, refitting together a puzzle of the word that had been broken.

Thonis.

Before me was the true curse that had turned my city from the gateway of Egypt, from a thriving port city, from a blessing of prosperity, into silence and nothingness. This piece had been intentionally shattered in channeling the power of a dark, dark art to execrate my city and extinguish every life it held within it.

Recalling the moment nearly splits my head in two, the pain of such malicious destruction too great to fit inside my mind.

I regathered the broken pieces and shoved them into the pouch emptied of its dry fruit, the first real evidence that I would keep close for however and whenever I was found.

When I was finally somewhat upright, or at least not bent over in pain but able to raise my head somewhat, I took a good look at the table, choking down the bubbling sobs threatening to overwhelm me.

Thonis, her beauty carefully preserved, her glory carefully detailed, her gemlike glitter a match for the sea that surrounded her. The city that was more than just a place, the place that was more than just a home. The foundation of my life, the pillars that held me up, all rooted deep in our little islet on the sea.

I couldn't resist reaching out to her. I felt my hand move through whatever force gave her shape and lit her in that strange glowing obsidian. As I touched the mound for our island, something unseen snapped. A sudden surge roared over me, as if a dam had broken and the water was crashing in breakneck haste toward the replica.

The invisible force was so great it threw me backward, back through the door and into the passageway, slamming me so hard I tumbled down, down, down, until I must have stopped where I now sit.

No wonder I hurt so much.

A deep inhale stops me short as I realize that, strangely, my lungs no longer feel as if they're underwater and I only gasp from pain and not a perceived lack of air. I no longer feel that imagined sense of drowning with my people.

I must have done something when I reached through the haze. I may have even set something free when I touched my fingers to my lost home. It's the first time in months that I no longer feel the pressure of not being able to rise, of being powerless against the great sea holding me down. If anything, the sense has been replaced by anger, confusion, and a renewed determination to get out of here and tell the world what I found.

For the first time I have an image and proof of the

destruction. For the first time I can imagine faces in the place of the mysterious unnatural force that destroyed my city. For the first time my blood burns with a desire for vengeance.

That thought shatters all others from my head.

I have to get out of here.

How?

I raise a hand to wipe my eyes but only get sand and dirt in them. I rub my hands to clean them off, and startle when obsidian sparks appear. I immediately stop. When nothing happens, I peer closer at my hands, though I can barely make them out before me in the dark.

Understanding dawns quickly, and I reach for the third pouch Bakari tied to my belt. It burst open from my tumbling fall, but there's no mistaking it held the grains of sand from Rasidi. The one I didn't want to take. The one Bakari made sure I had anyway. That mysterious sand that could do so many little things. And it's all over me now.

What had he said when he'd brought it to me?

That it might be my way out. That I would know how to use it. That it may help and I should not reject it, even as I placed it on the ground beside me, hoping it would be left and forgotten, this perilous sand of dark, dark arts. My only option now.

Feeling ridiculous, I gather what little I can and toss it in the air, focusing on the singular thought that I want to get out, and fast. Some obsidian sparks flicker as the mixed grains of sand fall over me. Nothing happens.

I wait and wait and wait.

Just as I'm about to despair and stumble back to the grand gallery, something eerie crawls over me.

I can't explain the feeling, can't explain the

strangeness of what suddenly blankets my *ka*, but I feel myself shifting, my body closer to the floor, my eyes changing, my view changing, the smell of the room increasing. Suddenly, I don't feel as lost in the dark, because it doesn't keep me from knowing my way.

When the odd sensation is over, I exhale deeply. A forked tongue hisses out of me.

I turn to examine myself, but instead of a neck, my body coils back.

Snake.

I've been turned into a snake.

I want to shout but I have no voice, only an angry, vile hiss.

What cruel trick is this? What have these dark, dark arts done?

I don't even know how long this will last.

The only comfort is that this new body has no hands or feet to carry the aches and pains and bruising of my human one, or I'd hardly be able to use it. I'd hardly be able to move at all, considering the bumps and bashes I sustained on my way down.

So, turning into a creature without arms and legs and a different kind of body altogether is certainly helpful to keep away the pain, but how does that help getting out? Am I expected to burrow deep underground instead of trying to chisel my way through?

And that's when it hits me, the true genius of Rasidi's unwanted gift.

I had thought the only place I hadn't investigated was the hidden chamber, and only because I hadn't found it yet, but that's not entirely true. I had only investigated every place a human could fit, but a snake could search far more.

Like an air shaft leading from the King's Chamber directly out of the pyramid.

Good thing I'm not afraid of heights.

So I do what any snake would. I unhinge my jaw and swallow the pouch with the pieces from the vase. Then I slither toward the wall and make use of every nook and cranny and uneven surface, climbing upward, ever upward, racing against time and an unfed body as my new form churns to digest what I've swallowed, slinking toward that long narrow shaft and the freedom just beyond.

Chapter Forty-Six

Day 69

I emerge from my slow and painstaking slither through the air shaft into the cold light of early dawn. From my vantage, I have a clear view of the glowing strips of yellow and orange and white that mark an awakening sun. Around me is the most breathtaking vista I may ever see, more than any tree or mast can afford. I'm high enough to imagine I'm in the sky itself, that I've found the steps to the afterlife where my loved ones await me. One day, but not today. I thank Father's Divine Force for that.

There's no time to revel in the majesty of the scene, however, as my new head quickly guides the rest of my elongated body out of the narrow opening. I slip onto the side of the pyramid, grateful the white limestone is not yet blinding, as the still rising sun has yet to spark it. I cling as best I can to the triangular slopes, but quickly feel myself sliding against the smooth surface.

An image of a snake plummeting, then crashing to the bottom of the pyramid, ending in a bruised and broken heap at its base flashes through my mind. It's both gut-churning and ludicrous. It would seem that every time I escape death, it finds one more way to taunt me with its overbearing closeness.

My morbid thoughts are cut through by the chilling

screech of a hawk.

Now I'm convinced the next few moments will only result in my death, just one more temporary reprieve before long-term surety. Trying to move any faster with this bulk in my middle will only ensure I slide to my death, and there's no way I can turn around and make it back to the airshaft in time to hide out of reach. Not that I would want to trap myself in a pyramid ever again, so my options are limited as to which sort of ending I don't want the least. And that doesn't either consider how much longer this sand will hold me in this shape. What had Rasidi told me when she hid me from the queen? *Hours* at best?

I barely manage a fierce hiss at the hawk before releasing my tenuous grip on the pyramid, figuring I'd rather take my chances on a death-slide than be eaten by a bird.

Little that helps. The hawk swoops straight and true as an expertly released arrow, snatching me behind the head with one sharp talon, then the tip of my tail in the other, in a neat catch which leaves me unable to attack. My bulging middle dangles in a useless curve as the hawk beats its wings against the air and lifts me away from the pyramid.

I resign myself to the ride as it takes to the sky and flies from the Valley of the Kings, wondering which rock it'll choose to bash me against, praying my father was right in believing that I don't need a heart's measure to reach the next life. I doubt there will be much of anything left by the time this hawk finishes with me. I can't help but notice the irony of a spirit girl dying trapped in the body of a snake.

Below, the Nile flows past the greenery and the life

pressing close as it weaves up the length of Egypt and out into a glittering bejeweled sea. I try to figure out where we're heading and just how much longer I have.

I fight back my rising frustration. Time and time again, I have done the best I can with the course my life has taken, and still it is not enough. There are no thoughts or words for that feeling of having given everything only to know that nothing has come of it, the futility and emptiness of it all. I skirted death, and death has still found me, the inevitability of my life being prolonged so I can be lost in a moment of ignominy. And should Bakari and Rasidi and Bakenranef finally break into the pyramid somehow, should they finally figure out a way to pry it open and search for what's been buried deep, my skeleton will not be there. Nor will the secrets I uncovered.

With such dark thoughts circling my mind, I freeze in surprise when the hawk slows and gently lowers me into a deep cover of reeds near the riverbank.

As soon as I'm released, I rise up in a hiss, but the hawk is already hovering overhead, an upturned pouch in its talons. Sand, obsidian sparkling sand, drifts over me. As I realize what it is, I hastily unhinge my jaw and spit out the pouch of evidence.

The hawk flutters away. Within minutes, the change comes over me again, that strange sensation which now feels like my *ka* is being set free. I shift again…my smell and view and height restored.

Hands, legs, torso, head, all come back to me, and I return to myself tired and hungry and as beaten as in that last moment in the passage. I shift in the reeds, only to notice I've been placed on a plain white dress. I quickly slip into it, not caring that the material is slightly itchy.

Only then do I struggle to stand, and I've barely poked my head above the tall papyrus when a sudden blur of white and torso almost topples me over again.

"Zizizizizizizizizizizizi!"

I laugh weakly. "You sound like a swarm of bees."

Bakari holds me at arm's length, but doesn't release me as he takes me in. A broad smile illuminates his face. "You stopped my heart dead!" he accuses.

"Yet somehow you're here."

"Fine, well, almost stopped."

"And what of mine?"

He doesn't answer, only peers closer at my face with a swirl of emotions on his and grips tighter the arms he's still holding in his paint-stained, rein-calloused hands.

"You look terrible," he blurts, then quickly amends, "and yet somehow the most beautiful desert flower I've ever seen."

"Please," I struggle to force words past the lump in my throat. "No poetry."

Before he can respond, I sway, and his grip tightens to keep me upright. Concern quickly replaces his relief. I force a reassuring smile.

"The snacks were all I had."

That spurs him to action. In the next moment, I'm off my feet and carried toward a small skiff. He carefully settles me inside and dives for a small nest of supplies. Next, Bakari's raising a *shaduf* of clear water to my lips and admonishing me to drink slowly, watching my every breath so I can't do anything but obey. I take several slow swallows, enjoying the cool water even more than that peach in the acacia tree, a mere moment of indulgence compared to this actual return to life.

Bakari runs a hand over his scalp as he watches me

regain myself. He shakes his head at me, smiles, then shakes his head again, wavering between joy, relief, and perhaps even fear.

"Why must you always be so difficult?" he asks in a shaky breath. He tries to smile again but his tone betrays him. That alone is enough to reveal how terrified he's been. "Good thing I always shaved my head," he mutters.

"Is that your way of apologizing?"

Bakari draws a breath. "I sincerely apologize, Zizi. I can't believe you were trapped inside a pyramid. I can't believe—I just—" He shakes his head, unable to continue. "And you *survived*."

"It won't be so easy to return me to death once you stole me from it," I warn, half in jest.

Bakari's grin returns with those words. "I sincerely hope so."

"How did you find me? And why were you a hawk?"

Bakari gives an uneven laugh. "Well," he begins, "after you went into the pyramid, I didn't stay at the entrance long, because I'd been spotted and called away to the banquet. By the time I could get myself away again, hours had passed and the entrance was well sealed. I looked everywhere but couldn't find you. Everyone began to leave and you were still nowhere to be seen. It took Bakenranef and two of his guards to hold me back from breaking through the door." Bakari pauses, his voice shaking as he relives those terrifying moments of the unknown. "They finally bound me, rowed me to the palace, and locked me in a room to 'simmer off.' "

"Didn't anyone look for you?"

Bakari nods. "They told them I'd had too much to drink and needed a few days to reset. I suppose it was

over me, praying for me in that other world I'm not yet fated to reach.

Bakari breaks the sudden quiet with a gentle nudge. "What was in the pouch, Zizi? What did you find in that pyramid?"

"Answers and buried secrets," I say, then tell him everything that happened from the moment I stepped inside.

His brow furrows and his eyes narrow as I speak. When I'm done, he dips the oars into the water and immediately rows us across the Nile.

"You know where to next."

Chapter Forty-Seven

Day 70

I sleep like the dead, but not with the dead. Not only because I'm far away and safe from the confines of the pyramid, but also because I don't sleep in the subterranean room with the bright and burning memory of Thonis encircling me.

By the time Bakari and I finished speaking and rowed across the Nile, I was exhausted and barely strong enough to present a full report of what I'd learned to the others. Bakari sent word to Bakenranef that I was alive and resting, then went to get me something to eat and maybe even some of Rasidi's restoring herbal tea.

Before that, however, I bathed, then asked him to help me to the roof.

"The roof?" he repeated blankly.

"I want to see the map of stars. I want to sleep under an endless sky."

Bakari nodded, understanding enough to drop any further questions. He helped me up and found a place where I could tuck in away from the sentries' torches. I only managed to eat a little, though I did finish the tea he'd brought from Rasidi. I was already struggling to keep my eyes open by the time the stars came out to dance, so I only just saw them before I drifted into a deep, surprisingly restful sleep.

I awake in the early morning to find Bakari sleeping soundly beside me. After what I'd put him through, little wonder he isn't letting me out of his sight just yet. I grin to myself as I stand on less shaky legs, thinking of what sort of words he would spin for his fellow soldiers in the barracks to explain why he didn't sleep in his own bed last night.

I inch toward the edge of the roof and look past it toward the Nile and the first glint of the Valley of the Kings beyond. I can't shake the lingering scent and feel and darkness from being trapped in the pyramid, and yet, somehow, having some real answers helps to keep the terror of it at bay. Even with all that still needs piecing together, there's a peace to knowing we've been on the right track all along, that the choice not to drink the poison just a few short months ago was the right one.

A shape near the shore of the Nile soon draws my attention. I squint toward the royal docks at the figure silhouetted upon them, standing as regal and commanding as the first time I set eyes on him mere weeks ago. This time, his back is turned toward the palace as if he too is looking toward the Valley of the Kings, divining the secrets it holds deep.

I quietly slip away from the roof and make my way toward him. I still don't know that I fully trust him, still feel a shiver at the ambiguous words he's told me more than once, but an instinct deep down dictates that I should stand before him now so he can see me alive and with the knowledge of the fourth crate in my eyes.

I don't know how soon Kemnebi hears my approach, but he doesn't turn to look at me until I'm standing beside him on the gently rocking dock.

"Kyky," he says. Then, after a heavy pause,

"Though not your real name."

"A nickname," I admit.

He nods but doesn't press further. I don't know if that means he knows my real name or if he doesn't care to know it, if knowing the deeper truth about me is enough for him and whatever sort of precarious balance teeters between us.

"An assumed dead girl to investigate the murder of a dead girl," he muses aloud.

"It seemed the most discreet way."

He nods again. "You haven't been in your tree of late."

"I've been in the pyramid."

And now he turns to look at me fully, the understanding dawning with the unfurling light from the rising sun.

"I saw you there," I say further, "when you left."

I see as each piece clicks together, when the words I've said and the ones I deliberately haven't finish forming the picture in his mind. He looks me over more carefully now, perhaps noticing I'm a little worse for the wear. The shock of what he's understanding is so deep he can't even revert to his commander's face, that look that can draw secrets and instill fear in almost anyone.

"Until now?" he asks, voice suddenly hoarse.

I nod in reply, and from the expression he doesn't hide I can tell I've surprised him, maybe even impressed him. Good. A long silence passes between us, a long silence during which the sun rises higher to light a new day and swift papyrus boats embrace the steady current of the Nile. Behind us, the palace gradually awakens. Far off, the first clangs and clashes of soldiers at training drift from the practice fields. Bread bakes in the kitchen.

Lambs are chosen for supper. Slaves stoke fires and maidservants shake their ladies awake and prepare dresses and jewelry and scented *kyphi.*

Life continues uninterrupted, and I feel it once more as a life removed, not just because I'm no longer a part of it, but also because it finally feels past. Thonis and Meryt will be avenged, but I am no longer bound by the weight of memory once dragging me down. My past is a sturdy limb upon which to stand, to climb higher and reach for the next limb and then the one above that.

"Did you find what you were looking for?" Kemnebi's careful question breaks through my musings.

I meet his gaze squarely. "I found a secret buried deep."

He nods. Having shared the story, then hidden the shabti in my sarcophagus himself, he knows I've learned of what he's done. Although I'm fairly certain he stands on the side of Egypt, that his Nubian half doesn't command his allegiance, I also don't know what information he should be trusted with. Still, there are things he must be told because, as a man of discretion and rank and connections, he must understand that there are those he should no longer trust. I tug out the pouch containing the pieces of pottery and the shattered name of my city.

"I brought this secret with me," I explain, handing him the pieces.

He looks curiously at the parts I place in his hand, deliberately lining them up across his palm so he sees the side with the name of Thonis. Once the writing is complete, he furrows his brow only a moment.

"Someone tried to execrate Thonis," he whispers in horror.

"Someone succeeded," I correct.

He nods and bows his head, a sudden heaviness weighs his shoulders and there's little wonder why. He stood in the empty echo of a once proud and glittering city. He knows what the city was and he knows what the city has become, the blessing and the curse, the fullness and the void.

"Turn them over," I say quietly.

He lifts his head enough to cast me a puzzled expression but does as I suggest. Not even half the pieces are flipped over before a deep exhale leaves him. He knows right away what the other side reveals.

He shakes his head at his palm. "It doesn't make sense," he barely manages to sound out.

"The queen may be a leader or she may just be part of a more powerful whole," I say. "Either way, she found a poisoner very quickly."

"He confessed," Kemnebi says immediately.

"And truthfully," I assure him. "Still, he was found rather quickly."

Kemnebi looks up at me, an unfamiliar veneer of confusion warring across his strong, confident features.

"What now, Kyky?" he asks, and there are so many notes to the tone of his question, I can barely identify them all.

Before I can respond, the quiet slap of bare feet on wood alerts us to the presence of a new visitor. I know even before I look to confirm that it's Bakari.

"Feeling better?" he asks me, then stops when he notices what I've placed in Kemnebi's hand. "You sure?" he questions, not bothering to shield his words from the commander.

"He needs to know," I reply, my eyes fixed on

Kemnebi. "Besides, this is about Egypt. And there's no doubt which country the commander serves."

Kemnebi nods but doesn't speak. He returns the shards to me with a sad smile, then bestows a similar smile upon Bakari before leaving us. We watch him walk away, head raised with confidence, the return of the slight limp from his healed wound the only indication that he must be troubled. I watch distantly as he greets the guards near the entry to the palace, how coolly he resumes his outward charm and charisma. Kemnebi is certainly a man who stands apart.

"I believe what I said about him," I tell Bakari, who may be temporarily appeased but certainly isn't pleased.

"We can argue about that later," he replies. "If you're up to it, let's go find Bakenranef."

We go straight to our nomarch's rooms. He isn't too thrilled at first by his abrupt early morning wakeup, though his demeanor instantly changes when he sees me.

"Azizi?" he breathes, squinting at me through his disbelief.

"Ready to hear what she has to say?" Bakari asks.

Bakenranef answers by moving aside and motioning for me to hurry in.

I'm seated at his main work table, the same one with the maps of the pyramid. I stab a finger at the hidden chamber that's supposed to be off the grand gallery, then trace it across and above the King's Chamber.

"This is here."

"What else is there?" Bakenranef asks, urging me to spill all.

I take out the pouch and lay out the sections of broken vase on the table.

"This was once in Queen Sekhmet's rooms," I say,

at the same time Rasidi is ushered in. I flip the pieces over, showing the script that spells out the name of our lost city.

"This doesn't prove she's connected," Bakenranef rushes to say, ever the careful politician, though he runs his hand over his scalp as he says it.

"Maybe," I agree, "but I don't see how not."

I look at Rasidi, who's now offering me a cup of something hot and herbal. I take it gratefully and without comment, nodding my thanks. A few sips reinvigorate my *ka* so it's almost as if I was never starving and locked away. Almost.

"I saw Thonis," I tell her directly, "exactly modeled and sparkling black as the sand that saved us. When I reached out to touch it, I felt a pressure build and then a sudden release, which flung me back. What dark arts was it?"

Rasidi listens with a drawn expression as I continue to describe what I found. It's evident she's worried by what she's hearing.

"Start from the beginning," she urges gently, and so I do.

When I'm done, I look toward her again. We all do, awaiting an explanation.

"What you saw," she begins in a heavy voice, "the city, those pieces, was all to destroy Thonis. It's very, very powerful dark arts, beyond a regular execration because it didn't destroy one name but the unwritten names of the thousands who were destroyed with Thonis. It's something well beyond my abilities. Beyond most abilities."

"Tsillah," I say.

Rasidi doesn't look as certain. "Perhaps," she

allows, "and those toads certainly attest to her being there, but I don't think even she could have done all that on her own."

"Someone else is involved," Bakari asserts.

Rasidi nods. "Someone else, or even more than one. Most likely an entire web of very powerful individuals with great reach and resources, all considered."

"Destroying a prosperous port city, murdering a beloved wife," Bakenranef lists, "what other horror can they be planning that we don't even have hint of?"

"Something to do with the shabti Kemnebi hid away?" I suggest. "The fall of Egypt itself?"

"We would know for certain if we knew who we're facing," Bakari says.

"The Nubian connection!" I exclaim.

Bakari immediately opens his mouth to counter me, then stops. He glances to Bakenranef, whose brow has furrowed, drawing down his forehead, and some of his scalp too.

"Could it be?" Bakari questions.

"Crippling trade, striking at the heart of the king, plus this whole business with the shabti statuettes," Bakenranef murmurs.

"The queen and Tsillah have Nubian blood," I add. "Nkuku was Nubian too."

"Kemnebi is half Nubian," Bakari reminds me.

"Kemnebi chose his side," I counter.

"It does look like there's something there," Bakenranef agrees, cutting into our short, heated exchange. "Of course, with our two countries at peace, we'd have to look deeper before we start making accusations such as these."

"Deep as a secret is buried?" Rasidi asks.

Bakari's eyes immediately whip to mine and there's no mistaking the mischief beginning to spark in his eyes.

"Don't say it!" I warn.

"You're being difficult?" he teases.

I shake my head at him, then spare a glance at Bakenranef, then Rasidi, their expressions clear. Bakari's not even hiding his gleeful smile now.

A sudden, warm understanding settles over me, something beyond the mystery and the secrets we grapple with. My family, my cousin, my city, all are gone from this world, but sitting with this mismatched group, I don't quite feel alone. I will always remember Thonis and keep my loved ones close to my heart, for in that remembrance and the deeds it inspires is their true measure. My gaze sweeps the room before landing again on Bakari.

"We're going to Nubia, aren't we?"

"Well," Bakari says slowly, "you've always wanted to travel."

"How do we get Bakari to Nubia?" Rasidi asks.

The answer is evident. "We may have to write some poetry to a black panther after all."

"You wouldn't!" Bakari cackles.

"I *would*!" I rejoin.

"Then we *have* gotten somewhere!" Bakari declares, beaming at me.

And it doesn't matter what I'm about to say, because my own face betrays me. His words break through the once drowning grief of the past and offer a glimpse of a smiling future. I am not lost without a lady to serve. I am not lost without a tree to climb. I finally know what he's been trying to show me since the day he asked me not to drink the poison, since the day he admitted that humor and smiles and laughter weren't a defiance of what had been but the only way he could still live.

When he encouraged me to climb, when he teased and worried and encouraged me to win at *senet*, it wasn't just to remind me of fun and living but also to point me toward the way I knew how to live. To tell me that the horizon isn't only a distance that joins a sea and sky, a distance I see from the height of a tree branch or when watching dancing stars, but something I can find each time I fix a point within myself to reach and strive toward, every day I live.

I am no longer a servant. I am no longer a spirit.

I am what my living will speak of.

I'm going to Nubia, not because my past or my service requires it but because I want to go and find the truth, not in despair and darkness but to face it with strength and confidence in what will not be forgotten.

My city is not a curse. My past is not a weight. I match Bakari's grin with one free and joyous and ready.

For the first time since Thonis, I too believe that when we choose to live, we are truly of the Blessed.

A word about the author...

E. L. Tenenbaum is an author, writer, and educator. When not distracted building new worlds or puttering around her Substack, she enjoys presenting about writing, and has been a visiting author at schools around the world.

Come for a visit and take a book off the shelf at: www.ELTenenbaum.com.